THE NULL-FREQUENCY IMPULSER

JAMES NELSON COLEMAN

A BERKLEY MEDALLION BOOK
PUBLISHED BY
BERKLEY PUBLISHING CORPORATION

Dedicated to Rene and Rick and Mother,
who made everything possible

BERKLEY MEDALLION EDITION, MARCH, 1969

BERKLEY MEDALLION BOOKS *are published by*
Berkley Publishing Corporation
200 Madison Avenue
New York, N.Y. 10016

BERKLEY MEDALLION BOOKS ® TM 757,375

Printed in the United States of America

Chapter One

CATHERINE ROGERS had just come from a meeting with a noted space scientist. It had been fruitless; and thinking back on it and other similar meetings, she was angry and more than a little discouraged. There were just too many scientists around who were willing to waste her time with excuses as to why progress in space research was not being made. They all had a lot of high ideals about free enterprise in space for Earthmen; but in spite of their high ideals, little or no progress was being made against the steel-jawed, Five Company monopoly in all branches of space technology. The growth of man in space appeared to have been stunted, and she was honestly confused as to the cause.

She rejected the easy explanation that there was too much scientific research to be done and too few trained and qualified scientists to do it. This explanation did not jive with the facts.

Certainly, she argued with herself, science had a long way to go before Earthmen would achieve a genuine and expert independence in space, an independence free of Five Company monopoly. A whole new technology in spacecraft design, engineering and manufacturing know-how would have to be developed; and it would have to be a technology which did not infringe upon the patent monopoly already held by the Five Companies. This, she knew, was the difficult part of it; but as difficult as it was, it did not explain science's failure to progress in this area.

In spite of the tremendous job which had to be done, there were enough fully qualified scientists around the world for science to do it. Yet, science was not doing it.

Virtually no scientific progress was being made in the field of astronautics or in any field allied to it. It was almost, she told herself, as if all of the space scientists had gone on a holiday.

Then, casually looking toward the automatic news vendor, she chanced to see a headline. . .

"LEADING SPACE SCIENTIST KILLED IN LABORATORY ACCIDENT," it screamed, but suddenly she had no time to read further. She was waiting for a tube car, and it had just pulled into the terminal and was taking on passengers. She had time only to insert the proper coins into the machine and snatch her paper from the slot. Then the tube car was closing its doors and she had to make an unladylike dash across the loading platform to catch it.

She made it just in time and squeezed through the narrow opening between the closing doors a moment before they snapped shut. As the tube car accelerated along one of a complex of tunnels beneath the city, she took a seat, settled back and opened the paper to scan the article beneath the headline:

> "Angel City (API)—Dr. Lenord Kingsley, famous space researcher, was killed at 5 P.M. today by a mysterious explosion as he worked in his private laboratory at the rear of his home at 715 West Johnson Place, this city.
>
> Police and fire department investigators are at a loss to determine the cause of the mysterious explosion which decapitated Dr. Kingsley, completely demolished his laboratory, and was felt by all the residents in the immediate area.
>
> While Dr. Kingsley's specialty was rocketry, his wife states that he never worked with explosive chemicals in his home laboratory. Investigators discount this, however, and speculate that Dr. Kingsley must have been working on some secret project which involved the use of several highly volatile chemicals. . . ."

Something clicked in Catherine's mind, a sudden suspicion formed, and she had no need to read any further. She suddenly realized that this was the twelfth case of a mysterious and accidental death befalling a noted space scientist in as many months.

Why hadn't she seen it before? she asked herself, and raising her hand, she ticked off their names on her fingers. Immediately she was surprised to realize how many of them she had known personally, and suddenly she was trying to recall the details and particulars of each "accident." Taken separately, none of the circumstances surrounding any of the "accidents" were such that they would cause more than a passing doubt or suspicion. But, when they were viewed together, the "accident" theory became just a little too pat and convenient.

Yet the implications of a plot to kill off all Earth's leading space scientists under cover of what appeared to be a series of unfortunate and unrelated accidents was staggering. As the tube car began to decelerate near its terminal, her mind struggled with the idea.

There was no question as to who was responsible. She had been fighting the Five Company secret police for too long not to recognize their work. The old, familiar pattern of their gestapolike terrorism was there. However well disguised, this was obviously a sinister plot by them to prevent space scientists from giving their fellow Earthmen the new space technology which they needed to open up space to free enterprise and travel. Yet she had never imagined them capable of anything so monstrous as the premeditated murder of space scientists on a large scale.

It was the uselessness of such a pogrom which upset her most. She believed that the Five Companies were fighting a losing battle because history had taught her that no society, no matter how totalitarian, had ever existed which had been able to suppress completely scientific research and its resultant technological progress. And, since she knew that the men in the hierarchy of the Five Companies were at least as intelligent as she, she wondered why their knowledge of history had not taught them the same lesson.

As the tube car slowed and came to a rest at the station, this question weighed heavily upon her mind. Then the doors were opening and the people around her rising, and she had to put it aside for another time. Quickly she left the car with the other passengers and

7

made her way up out of the tunnel complex beneath the city. She emerged from the main entrance into a street crowded with late afternoon shoppers who jammed the sidewalks in front of the stores. Adjacent to the sidewalks, a colorful assortment of jetmobiles whizzed along a jet thoroughfare.

It was a bright, sunny day; and in contrast to her dark thoughts about murder and the Five Company secret police, there was a pleasant buoyancy in the air, a lightness and a sparkle that was refreshing.

As she walked, the sun beamed down and warmed her spirit as well as her body; and soon this warmth was reflected outward as it seemed to light up her beautiful face. Before long, she was walking with a vigor in her step which bespoke of the good health of her beautiful body and her basic keen relish for life.

Minutes later, however, as she approached her destination, she was overtaken by a painful nostalgia. . . . The private rocket field where she was headed and which served as the headquarters for the Rogers Group was just ahead. Suddenly she was assailed by memories of the old days when it had been only a large tract of waste land such as one might find in any large city. She had been just a young girl when it was bought by the Rogers Group, reinforced, filled in, a fence put up, and a private rocket field constructed. Then had followed the few truly happy years of her life. It was a time in which all operators of spacecraft could operate their ships on a competitive basis. And the Rogers Group under her father, Captain Rogers, had engaged in hauling food, machinery and dry goods out to the small colonies on the moons of Saturn and Jupiter.

She smiled to herself, recalling that period in her life. Those long trips had given her an opportunity to acquire an incredible fund of knowledge and experience in the operation and navigation of interplanetary spaceships. Under her father's strict guidance and instruction, she had qualified for command of such ships, becoming the youngest person and the first woman in the history of Earth to earn a space captain's ticket.

Then had come a period of struggle. Years in which, in spite of the devouring Five Company monopoly in space, the Rogers Group managed to hang on and stay in business, continuing to operate their spaceship, an old atomic freighter, when all the other independent spacecraft operators had gone bankrupt or sold out. Suddenly, one day the Five Company secret police had struck, knocking them to their knees with the murder of her father and half the Rogers Group, and the destruction of their spaceship, the last spaceship left in the hands of a private owner.

The memory of it brought pain to her heart as she walked across the private rocket field, now lonely and deserted, for the most part left to run down. Only the solitary administration building in one corner had been kept up and remained in use. This building was the headquarters of a new and younger Rogers Group, a Rogers Group of her generation, the sons and daughters of the men and women who had fallen victim to the Five Company secret police and who had helped pioneer man's efforts in space. Here, under her leadership, they worked diligently on their scientific projects and held daily meetings to discuss their endeavors and progress toward getting back into space.

In a few minutes, she was scheduled to attend just such a meeting. When she reached the administration building, she saw a trail of blood leading up the front steps. It looked as if someone who had had a bad accident had approached the building from a direction other than her own and had gone inside. Wondering who, she quickly sidestepped the splashes of blood and ran up the steps to the main hall.

Jackie, the Rogers Group's pretty business manager, met her at the door. She was out of breath and very relieved to see Catherine. Immediately she exclaimed, "I'm so glad you're here! There's trouble!"

"Well, what is it?"

Before answering, Jackie looked nervously over Catherine's shoulder. She was looking out at the deserted rocket field and acted as if at any moment she expected something horrible to come charging over the tarmac. When she did speak, it was desperately. "Dr. Paul Griskell is here!"

"The space scientist?"

"Yes—h-h-he's been shot, and he's badly hurt." Jackie supplied this information brokenly. Then she broke down and cried, "Oh, Catherine, it's horrible!"

"How—?" asked Catherine in confusion. "Why did he come here?"

"He won't say. He refuses to talk to anyone but you. Phil is doing what he can for him, but you'd better come quick. He's dying!"

With that, Jackie turned and fled down the hall, and Catherine followed in her footsteps. With a feeling of dread, she noted the trail of blood which preceded them. It led to the end of the main hallway, and then down some steps where it ended at a door on the landing below. When they reached it, Jackie quickly rapped on the door. A voice immediately answered, "Who is it?"

"Jackie! I've got Catherine here."

"Get in here quick!" Phil returned. "The Five Company secret police are after Dr. Griskell!"

Catherine did not need any further warning. She quickly stepped into the room and Jackie followed.

Once they were inside with the door closed firmly behind them, Phil forestalled a further outburst by putting his finger to his lips. He was the group's doctor and expert on internal space medicine. With dreadful implication, he cautioned them with his eyes and nodded toward a table in the corner of the room on which the famous space scientist lay sprawled.

When she looked, Catherine gasped. There was a gaping hole in his chest, and the whole front of his tunic was soaked in blood. "He's bleeding to death!" she exclaimed. "Can't you do anything for him?"

Phil shook his head. "He's finished! Beam from a laser cannon hit him squarely in the chest. It was all I could do to keep him alive until you got here."

"How long has he got?"

"He may go any time. You'd better speak to him immediately."

Quickly Catherine turned and walked over to the famous scientist. As she approached and saw the extent of the internal damage which had been inflicted by the laser beam, her complexion turned a deathly white. Above the table a strong light beat down upon his body, illuminating his face in stark detail. Suffering and pain were etched there. His breath came in labored gurgles as if the source of his air was coming from a deep well of liquid. And his

10

eyes, drawn to slits in the harsh light, stared off into space, as if at some unknown and unseen horror.

Slowly Catherine leaned over the table and looked down at him. His contorted features had an almost inhuman appearance. Yet, in spite of this, she recognized the distinctive profile of the great man, a man she had never known personally, but a man to whom she and all Earthmen owed a great deal for his contributions to the advancement of Earthmen in space. For over forty-five years his brain had produced and engineered most of the greatest scientific inventions and discoveries of the modern Space Age period.

Softly she whispered, "Dr. Griskell, can you hear me? Dr. Griskell——"

"C-C-Catherine Rogers?" came the weak response. Then Dr. Griskell's eyes shifted and came to rest upon her. They questioned, and in answer Catherine nodded.

"Yes, I'm Catherine Rogers."

A barely audible sigh escaped the great man's lips, and he tried to smile.

"I've been waiting for you," his lips intoned.

Catherine could barely hear him, and she anxiously leaned forward. "I'm here," she whispered. "What can I do to help you?"

"P-P-Pocket——" he wheezed. "M-M-My pocket——" Then his voice trailed off as he experienced difficulty in breathing. When he recovered, he looked at her pleadingly, and raising his hand weakly motioned for her to move closer. "Pocket!" he gasped.

Catherine reached for the pocket of his tunic, hesitated, then felt inside. When she withdrew her hand, she held a small, red booklet. "Is this what you wanted me to get?" she asked, holding it above his eyes where he could see it without turning his head.

He nodded weakly. "Key inside," he wheezed. "A key to the future! You must take it—protect it with your life—use it to save us!"

Catherine frowned in confusion at his broken appeal. "I don't understand, Dr. Griskell," she said. "Can you tell me exactly what you want me to do?"

In response Dr. Griskell seemed to gather himself together for a major effort. The fingers of his hand motioned for her to lean still closer, and as she did so, putting her ear almost to his lips, he began.

From time to time, as she listened, she gasped in disbelief, and her face under the harsh light reflected her growing incredulousness at what she was hearing. Suddenly, after speaking for several minutes, he grasped her hand in a spasm of pain. "Promise me!" he cried in a heavy wheeze, a short expiration of breath.

Catherine had barely enough time to whisper, "I promise!" before she realized that there was no following intake of air. Then she cried, "Phil! Come quickly! He's stopped breathing!"

Instantly, Phil was at her side. He grabbed Dr. Griskell's wrist in the fingers of one hand, felt his pulse and raised one of his eyelids. Then he stepped back, took a deep breath and shook his head at Catherine. "He's gone," he said softly.

Under the circumstances, Catherine took only a moment to feel sorrow and inwardly to pay her last respects to a very great scientist. Then she went into action. "Jackie!" she called, and there was a mixture of authority and fear in her voice. "Get some help and clean up the trail of blood leading to this room. Also, clean it up on the rocket field for as far back from this building as you can. Move fast and try not to be seen. We may get a visit from the Five Company secret police, and they mustn't find any evidence that Dr. Griskell has been here."

"He said that he was running from them when he came here," Phil said quickly. "What did he tell you?"

"He told me that he was shot with a laser cannon while trying to escape from three of their agents."

"But why?" asked Jackie, her face creased in lines of horror.

In answer Catherine raised the small, red booklet which she held in her hand. "They're after this," she declared with a strange awe in her voice as if she feared the thing which she held. "And I promised Dr. Griskell that we'll do everything in our power to prevent them from getting their hands on it."

Suddenly there came a furious knocking at the door. "Phil—Jackie!" someone shouted on the other side. "The Five Company secret police are out on the rocket field. They're coming this way!"

Instantly Catherine ran to the door and threw it open. Steve, one of the group's rocket structural design engineers, stood there in a state of near panic. "How soon will they be here?" asked Catherine, ignoring the fear which seemed to radiate from every bone in his body.

"A minute—two, at most!"

"The trail of blood!" gasped Jackie. "It leads right to this room, and there's no time to clean it up!"

They looked at each other in sudden hopelessness.

"Just how important," asked Phil suddenly, "is this little booklet which Dr. Griskell gave you?"

"There's no time to explain now," replied Catherine. "But if what he told me is true, this little booklet and the key it contains—in the right hands—can defeat the Five Companies and free space for all Earthmen!"

"If it's that important," said Steve from the doorway, "we'd better do something quickly. They'll be here in a minute!"

In spite of the urgency in his voice, no one moved. They just stood there in painful silence, staring at each other and trying to overcome the dreadful fear of the Five Company secret police which each of them felt. No one could think while experiencing such fear; everyone in the room was imagining the interrogation to which they would be subjected.

If they were not involved in some way, why had Dr. Griskell fled to them? Why had they not called the city police? Why had they not called a hospital to ask for medical assistance? . . . indicated in some way that they were not involved? . . . that they did not desire to become involved?

Considering that they had done none of these things, there was no excuse they could give which would stand up under such an interrogation. Their conduct would have branded them guilty, and anything they said in an attempt to convince the Five Company secret police of their innocence would serve only to involve them further in the mystery which surrounded Dr. Griskell's death.

The inability to establish their innocence would provide just the excuse for which the secret police had been waiting to brutalize them. It would provide the justification they needed to use brute force and violence to crush the

13

Rogers Group and end the long history of their opposition to the monopolistic policies of the Five Companies in space.

This realization took only an instant to pass through their minds. Then Phil broke free of the fear which shackled his mind. He reached into his medical bag and took out a gleaming, razor-sharp scalpel. As he did so, he shouted, "Catherine—you and Steve take Dr. Griskell's body down through the basement—out the back door—and hide it somewhere away from the building! Jackie, you run upstairs—get Elizabeth and bring her down here quickly! I'm going to need medical attention!"

"Medical attention?" repeated Jackie, her eyes growing large at the sight of the scalpel in her fiancé's hand. "Phil, what are you planning to do?"

"This!"

Before any of them could move to object, he made a deep, slashing gash across the front of his chest down into his lower rib cage. His white doctor's tunic suddenly exploded into bright red, the cloth parted, and his chest opened up diagonally across the front of his body like a volcanic split in the Earth.

At this instant Jackie screamed and ran to him, crying: "No, Phil darling, please!"

"D-D-Don't argue!" cried Phil, doubling up in pain. "G-G-Get Elizabeth—quick!"

"Oh God, no!" gasped Jackie as his blood gushed out on the floor in front of her and mixed with that of Dr. Griskell. Her knees gave way, and she staggered.

"For Space sake, don't faint!" shouted Catherine. You've got to get hold of yourself and get Elizabeth quickly—before he bleeds to death!"

They had to get Elizabeth, the only other member of the Rogers Group with a medical degree, to help Phil. There was no time for fainting or hysterics. There was no time for vacillation; and after a moment, when Jackie still did not realize this, Catherine steeled herself and slapped her hard across the face. Then she turned her around and firmly pushed her out of the door, yelling instructions: "Be sure to tell Elizabeth to tell the secret police that it is Phil's blood they have been following—that he got hit by a jetcar!"

"No!" cried Steve. "They can check that!" For a moment his mind struggled furiously to think. Then he shouted to Jackie: "Tell them that he was attacked and cut by a man who tried to rob him—that we haven't had time to notify the police!"

Jackie let them know that she had heard by nodding weakly as she stumbled up the steps. Then Steve turned to Catherine. "Come on," he said, "let's find some place to hide this body!"

As he spoke, he was already lifting Dr. Griskell's body to his shoulders, and immediately Catherine helped Phil onto the table where it had lain. Then she ran to catch up with Steve, who was heading down the stairs to the basement.

At that moment, Phil called after them. Through gritted teeth and lips which were contorted in pain, he managed to warn, "Be careful! Be sure that you don't make a new trail of blood on your way down to the basement. . ."

Chapter Two

IN a laboratory on the second floor, several members of the Rogers Group were involved in an argument while waiting to be called to attend their daily executive meeting. Unaware of events elsewhere in the building, they were casually sitting or standing among several of the more comfortable workbenches in one corner of the laboratory. Surrounding them were windowless walls, covered with astronautical charts, blueprints of an odd assortment of the space vehicles of the day, and blackboards crammed with schematics of everything from simple spacecraft electronic circuitry to complicated quantum mechanics in light pulsation. The laboratory itself, one of many in the building, looked like a vast and gleaming junk yard with the innards of every imaginable sort of electronic and mechanical spacecraft device scattered over its numerous workbenches.

At the moment, Dr. Ted Fields, the group's physicist, was saying, "You can't really believe, Patricia, that fear of the Five Company secret police is the single factor which has stopped all scientific progress in space."

"Certainly I do!" replied Patricia, the group's electronics expert. "Just look at our own example." Pausing, her eyes took them all in. "In our present state of mind," she continued, "no one in this group can honestly say that he's been able to do his best work."

"I think that you're being a bit unfair," retorted Dr. Fields, and there was a slightly injured tone in his deep voice. "We've tried——"

"Tried how?" interrupted Patricia, and she struck the work bench in front of her with a small, trembling, white fist. "We live in constant fear that we might do the very thing that we keep telling ourselves that we are trying to do. We fear that we might discover something—that we might make some scientific contribution to the cause of man in space which the Five Companies will consider a threat to their monopoly!"

"Okay! Certainly we're afraid of retaliation from the Five Company secret police," Dr. Fields admitted, harshly. "But that's only because we're a small, independent group with no power to protect ourselves. Still, our position in the scientific world is not typical."

"How in Space can you say that?" exploded Patricia. "Just look at the thousands of independent space scientists who are working in university laboratories all over the world! They are every bit as frightened of the Five Company secret police as we are."

"What about the scientists in the Space Patrol, who work for the World Government?"

"What about them?"

"Well," said Dr. Fields as if it ought to be obvious, "they aren't making any significant scientific progress in space, either." He pointed his black finger at Patricia. "And that's where your fear hypothesis breaks down— because scientists in the Space Patrol don't have to live in fear of the secret police as we do."

"Not on the surface, no." Phyllis, the group's space vehicle design engineer, spoke up in aid of Patricia. "But they have other problems to worry about which are just as inhibiting to scientific progress as fear!"

"Regardless of that, the fact is that they can conduct space research without fear of retaliation by the secret police."

"Yes, Dr. Fields," Phyllis agreed patiently, "but you are missing your orbit if you think for a minute that the Space Combine Political Party, which is backed by the Five Companies, will ever allow the World Congress to vote the Patrol a big enough budget for them to be able to conduct any real space research."

"She's right, you know, Ted," interposed Sid, who was the group's public relations man. He wrote a daily human interest column on space and was extremely familiar with the political side of the problem. "The Freedom-in-Space Party simply hasn't enough support in the World Congress to appropriate the money for any meaningful space research programs for the Patrol. So you really can't expect them to make any progress."

"In spite of that," Dr. Fields observed dryly, "the Space Patrol seems to have managed to put research outposts——" He ticked the places off on his black fingers —"on the moon—on Mars and Venus—one in the asteroids—and one each on the moons of Saturn and Jupiter!"

"Doesn't mean a thing," declared Patricia, shaking her lovely red head. "The biggest of those space research outposts accommodates only four space scientists and the most necessary of routine equipment."

"And don't forget," broke in Phyllis, again supporting Patricia, "everywhere that the Patrol has a research outpost, the Five Companies have one of their own there too—usually close by so that they can look right over the Patrol's shoulder. If the Patrol ever did discover anything, the Five Companies would be the first to know about it."

"That supports my point," exclaimed Patricia, excitedly. "What you just said means that the secret police don't have to engage in a fear campaign against government space scientists. They can afford to let the Space Patrol alone and just sit back and take full advantage of any meaningful research they may manage to do."

"On the other hand," added Phyllis bitterly, "they don't give anyone but themselves the benefit of any space research done by their own scientists."

"What we need——" Eleanor spoke up for the first

time. She was the group's biophysicist and part-time architect of Earth satellite vehicles, a leading authority in her field; and she received the group's close attention. "What we need," she repeated, "is a place, a sanctuary where independent space scientists can go and be free to do space research without fear of secret-police retaliation."

Both Claudia, the group's security director, and Jerry, who was an astronavigator and one of the best dead-reckoning space pilots in the solar system, started to answer at the same time. Then Claudia gave way and let Jerry have the floor.

"There is no place on Earth where you can go that the Five Companies or their secret police don't have a solid sphere of influence," he pointed out. "And, because they own and control all of Earth's space enterprises, they virtually have a life and death grip on the Earth colonies. Things are as bad there as they are here."

"Oh, I know all that," said Eleanor, annoyed. "I wasn't thinking of anyplace on Earth or of the Earth colonies."

"Have you thought of something which we haven't?" asked Sid, leaning forward. "If you have, tell us!"

"I was thinking of a space platform," answered Eleanor. "Oh——!" she exclaimed, momentarily raising her hand to forestall comment. "Not like the space platform that we have now which was put up by the World Government. It's too small. How many scientific personnel does it accommodate?"

"Six!" Sid answered her question. "Two Space Patrol scientists, three Five Company space scientists, and one Space Patrol technician."

"Well, suppose——" said Eleanor with a dreamy look in her eyes as if she could see her vision right there in the lab with them. "Just suppose, we were able to build a fantastically large space platform—one which would accommodate hundreds of space scientists and their families too. A city in space—a satellite city!"

"Whoa there! Not so fast," said Sid hastily. "The cost of putting into orbit the materials to build such a satellite is prohibitive. The World Government simply wouldn't undertake such a project. Too expensive! The average taxpayer just isn't that interested."

"Even if the taxpayer would stand still for it," Claudia spoke up, "the World Government still wouldn't consider it. As you pointed out, Sid, the Freedom-in-Space Party hasn't enough power in the World Congress.

Sid nodded, but made no comment. Eleanor said, "I was thinking that a satellite city could be privately financed."

"As a privately financed project," said Jerry, shaking his fiery-red head, "and forgetting for a moment the prohibitive cost of the orbital insertion of materials—materials handling and storage in space—and the actual building of the satellite, you still have the Five Company obstacle. They might conceivably lease the necessary shuttle rockets to the World Government. They certainly wouldn't to a private concern—one which was in competition with them—and certainly not for your purpose: to build a sanctuary in space for independent space scientists."

"The whole idea is nothing but a daydream!" blasted Dr. Fields, cruelly. "And, I think——"

Suddenly his voice faltered and stopped. An expression of surprise, then of fear came over his dark-skinned features. The others caught it and immediately looked up, swiveling their heads to see the cause.

Framed in the doorway stood a man dressed in a plain, black, civilian tunic. His appearance was perfectly nondescript, yet they instantly knew who he was and what he represented. Something about him seemed to convey an aura of cruelty. It was not in his face. That was expressionless. It was in his eyes. They were too cold, too quick and too alert. They surveyed the laboratory, shifting back and forth, missing nothing. Finally they came to rest upon the people in it, glaring starkly coldly, seeing their fear and contributing to it by giving no hint of human warmth.

After several moments his hand flashed from his tunic, briefly revealed an identification card and then flashed back again. "Five Company secret police," he said in a hard, matter-of-fact voice.

Sid was the first to respond, half rising from his seat in the center of the group. His eyes were transfixed on the secret policeman; his mouth hung open, and he looked like someone who had been caught red-handed at some

19

illegal task. "W-W-What——" he stuttered, "have we done?"

The question hung in the air. No one moved. Like statues, the members of the Rogers Group sat frozen in their seats, holding their breaths, waiting for an answer.

During the interval of silence that followed, the secret policeman stared at them, his eyes utterly without kindness. A chill settled over the group, a premonition that, whatever their crime, it was great.

Finally, without a single change of expression, the secret policeman said, "You are wanted downstairs for questioning! You will come with me immediately!"

"Are the city police waiting downstairs to question us?" asked Claudia, who stood up to face him.

"No, this is strictly a secret police matter."

"Well, maybe it's useless to point this out," returned Claudia with a courage which she did not feel, "but, secret police or not, you don't have any authority to come in here like this and demand that we go anywhere with you to answer questions!"

"Your first observation is correct," answered the secret policeman, his eyes flashing menacingly. "It is quite useless for you to point out that we don't have lawful authority. We are here for what we consider good reason." His voice hardened perceptively. "And to prevent interference with our purpose, the area around this building has been sealed off and all vidphones have been secured. There is no one to whom you can appeal for help! And, therefore, it will be useless for you to resist!"

"This is private property, and you are trespassing!" shouted Jerry in the hot-headed manner he usually displayed when he was faced with trouble. Angrily he jumped from his seat and shook his fist in the secret policeman's face. "We're not criminals, and we won't be treated like this!"

For an instant the secret policeman was startled. Then his face changed; the stiff edge of his hand flashed out in a vicious arc, ending with a dull thud at a point above Jerry's left ear. Jerry's head snapped sideways, an incredulous expression passed over his face, and then his body crashed to the floor, his arms and legs sprawling, his senses reeling.

Instantly the secret policeman jumped to a defensive

stance, poised over him, ready to strike him again if it should become necessary.

In an attempt to prevent further violence, Dr. Fields stepped forward and gripped Jerry's arm in one of his strong black hands. Dazed, Jerry looked up and met his eyes; immediately Dr. Fields shook his head warningly. Then he and Phyllis helped him to his feet.

Eleanor stepped forward, and in a manner which emphasized her calm dignity, she asked, "Will you strike me, too—if I ask you a question?"

"You may ask me anything you like," answered the secret policeman, taking some of the tension out of the air. "Just don't tell me what you aren't going to put up with—because I have my orders and I intend to carry them out!"

"That's perfectly clear," said Eleanor. "Now, would you please tell us what it is you want to question us about."

"You'll find that out immediately when you get downstairs," the secret policeman assured her. Then he addressed them all: "Now, shall we go—without further conversation!"

The tone of his voice precluded argument, made his words a command. They had no choice but to obey. Yet, feeling humiliated, they hesitated, looking to Eleanor for guidance. Unruffled and serenely composed, she made their yielding to the secret policeman as palatable as possible by gracefully shrugging her shoulders and marching past him with quiet dignity.

Finally they reached the top of the stairs and began to descend in tense silence. As they neared the bottom, they saw the trail of dark, dry blood on the marble floor of the main corridor and, simultaneously, a large number of secret policemen running about in orderly confusion, apparently searching for something in the office off the main corridor.

Instantly, apprehensive glances passed between them. They could not imagine what was being searched for, and the sight of the blood in company with so many secret policemen together at one time unnerved them completely.

"This way," the secret policeman nodded curtly, directing them along the trail of blood which led down another flight of steps to a room off the main landing. When

21

they reached it, he ordered them to enter and herded them inside.

As they crowded into the room, they became conscious of several things at once. Phil lay unconscious stretched out on a table in one corner, with the upper half of his torso wrapped in bandages. Around his table, the floor was heavily smeared with blood. Against the far wall, Jackie and Elizabeth sat in two straight-backed chairs, weeping and exclaiming strong denials as they were questioned by a secret policeman with a markedly cultured voice, who stood ramrod straight in a military stance and seemed to be in charge of things.

As they entered, he turned to face them. They saw a face that was classic. Old English aristocratic. His crewcut was sharply lined—not a hair out of place—bone military and Dutch blond. He was the perfect picture of the old-school, military disciplinarian. Strangely, this gave them a sense of security.

"Where did you find these people?"

"They were having some kind of discussion upstairs in one of the laboratories."

"What else did you find?"

"I found nothing else."

Nodding, he turned his eyes upon the newcomers, scanning each of their faces and missing no detail. As he did so, they immediately realized that their first estimation of him had been mistaken, and the sense of security which they had felt evaporated. His eyes were frigid with a glittering, inhuman quality. There was an alienness about him, an impression which made them feel that he had never known the meaning of mercy.

"My name is Inspector Becket," he said without preamble. "I'm going to ask you some questions, and I expect your answers to be absolutely truthful." He paused and glanced at each of them sharply. "I warn you," he continued solemnly, "if I get even the slightest suspicion that you are lying, I shall order a brain probe to be used on you."

"But that's illegal!" exclaimed Sid. "A person is no more than a vegetable after the brain probe has been used."

"I'm glad that you understand the implications of such a course of action. It will save us a good deal of time."

Eleanor tried, saying with her calm dignity: "We would not lie. We have nothing to lie about!"

This had no effect. "Where," Inspector Becket shouted suddenly, "are you hiding Dr. Paul Griskell?"

"Dr. Paul Griskell——?"

"The famous space scientist——?"

"Hiding him——?"

These exclamations came simultaneously as the members of the Rogers Group who were facing Inspector Becket exchanged puzzled glances. From their straight-backed chairs against the wall, Jackie and Elizabeth, their eyes red from weeping, tried frantically to attract their attention. By means of their facial expressions alone, they tried to convey a message across the room without their efforts being detected by any of the secret policemen who were standing nearby.

They were successful as far as the secret policemen were concerned, but their efforts were detected by an unseen observer. And he stirred . . .

The members of the Rogers Group who were standing before Inspector Becket were bewildered because they did not understand what Jackie and Elizabeth were trying to tell them. As a result, they were uncertain of their position. They did not know how to answer Inspector Becket. They hesitated, and he took this hesitation as a reluctance on their part to talk.

When several moments passed and they still did not speak up, he suddenly pointed at Eleanor and shouted, "Take her! Prop her leg on a chair and break it!"

Promptly two secret policemen stepped forward, grabbed Eleanor by her arms and began dragging her toward a chair. A pandemonium of shocked protest and pleading broke loose. The men, Sid, Jerry and Dr. Fields, tried to interfere, and other secret policemen moved forward to shove them violently back.

"No! No!" Elizabeth rose screaming from her chair. Rushing forward, she grasped Inspector Becket by the lapels of his tunic. "None of them know anything about Dr. Griskell! Don't you see—even if he did come here as you seem to think, they wouldn't know anything about it because they were upstairs at the time you claim he must have arrived."

"But you were not upstairs!" snapped Inspector Becket,

flinging her violently aside. "If you wish to save her, then tell me the truth! Where are you hiding Dr. Paul Griskell?"

"That's not his blood," screamed Jackie from her chair against the wall. "Oh, please, believe me!" she pleaded, "that's not Dr. Griskell's blood!"

"It's my blood you've been following," Phil moaned weakly from the table. "I tell you I was attacked by some hoodlums while I was coming toward the building."

They are lying!

Immediately Inspector Becket's eyes blinked, and his attention turned inward. *I suspect as much,* was his answering thought. *But why can't you scan the surface of their minds and get the information we want?*

Because they are radiating fear, and it is too intense for me to penetrate without their becoming aware of my presence. I've told you before that fear in you human beings is a very effective mind shield. I cannot read through it without using force. Therefore, since you keep insisting that my presence in your mind remain a secret, you must make them talk all by yourself!

Just give me time, Trabzon, and I'll make them talk!

You've got time. But do not fail!

Trabzon drew back to wait and watch, and Inspector Becket became conscious of Dr. Fields shouting: "Take me instead of her!" He had violently broken away from the secret policeman who had been holding him and placed himself before the two who were dragging Eleanor to a chair. "Break my leg instead of hers!" he demanded. "Break both of them! Then you'll see that we're telling the truth! We're not hiding Dr. Griskell!"

"If you do this——" cried Jerry, and although he could not break the restraint imposed on him by the two secret policemen who were holding his arms, he did manage to drag them and himself forward. "If you do this," he repeated desperately, "you're going to have to kill me first!" Tears of frustration suddenly filled his eyes. "I don't know what this is all about, but I won't stand by and let you do a thing like this to a defenseless woman!"

The secret policemen paused not an instant and Jerry's legs were kicked from under him, and he was thrown to the floor. Dr. Fields' arms were locked behind his back, and he was pulled aside. The secret policemen who held Eleanor continued to drag her toward the chair which was being readied as a prop to break her leg.

Suddenly another secret policeman appeared, escorting two young girls with blond pigtails. They were Valerie and Linda, Catherine Rogers' younger sisters. As soon as they entered the room and saw Eleanor being dragged toward a chair by two secret policeman, they joined in the cries of protest and ran to help her.

Valerie, being fifteen and older than her little sister by two years, pounded on the chest of one of the secret policemen who was dragging Eleanor. And, as she pounded, she cried in a frenzy of emotion: "Let her alone! Let her alone!"

At the same time, Linda, her little sister, threw her arms around Eleanor's waist, bringing the whole procession to a halt and wept, "Oh, aunt Eleanor!"

The secret policemen dragging Eleanor fell back, surprised and momentarily frustrated.

"Where on Earth did these two come from?" asked Inspector Becket, shouting above the desperate commotion throughout the room.

"I found them playing on the bank of the river at the rear of the building," answered the secret policeman who had brought them in. "The rear door leading from the basement was open—so, I figured, they had been in the basement. Thought I'd better bring them up for questioning!"

"Did you find anything else?"

"No, the basement is clean. Nothing down there but a lot of old scientific equipment!"

As this answer was given, Valerie and Linda were in the process of being subdued by the secret police; but from their effort to restrain the two struggling, biting, kicking and scratching young girls, a major battle had developed.

The secret police were handicapped. They had never been required to fight young girls before, and they were not prepared for it. Inspector Becket immediately realized that the only way that he could save his men from receiving an assortment of small, painful injuries at the hands of Valerie and Linda was to call a halt to the breaking of Eleanor's leg, and at once he ordered her released. When

25

things were finally back under manageable control, he confronted them.

"Who are you?"

"I'm Valerie Rogers, and this is my sister, Linda," answered Valerie as, with rosy-cheeked faces and shiny noses, they stared up at him in defiance. Neither of them had suffered more than disheveled hair and clothing during the scuffle with the secret police, and consequently, they did not feel the same physical fear of them as the adults in the Rogers Group.

Trabzon detected this, and instantly he stirred. Swiftly he moved forward within Inspector Becket's mind. A sudden glitter, an unhuman quality came into Inspector Becket's eyes.

I want these two! came Trabzon's thought as Valerie, startled by the sudden gleam, the sudden loss of human warmth in Inspector Becket's eyes, grasped her little sister's hand in an instinctive, protective manner and took a step backward.

No, Trabzon! Inspector Becket's thought was tinged with a sudden fear. *You promised that, if I helped you, you would not feast upon human beings!* . .

At the moment, I was not thinking of feasting. I have detected that these two do not fear you as the others do. Their young minds are not shielded by an intense screen of fear. If you take them to some place where we will not be interrupted, I will enter their minds without their knowing it and secure the information which we want.

No, I cannot trust you to do that! You've broken your promise to me too many times! You would feed on their life force just as you did on the life forces of all of the others whom we have questioned. Only this time we would be in trouble because there is no way I could make the deaths of these two young girls look like an accident. It was difficult enough with the twelve space scientists . . .

I am growing weak! I need a little——

I cannot permit it, I tell you! We human beings are not the fools that you seem to think we are! Let anything unnatural happen to these young girls, and there would be an investigation unlike any of the others we've had to put up with. I would be brain-probed, and your presence in my mind would be exposed!

One of the adults, perhaps?

No!

Suppose I give you no choice?

If you take over my mind, you will defeat your own purpose. My men will notice the alienness about me. They will know that I am possessed by something not of this world. Trabzon gave the equivalent of a sigh, and Inspector Becket drove home his sole bargaining point. *As long as you need me, I am not totally at your mercy. I have some say-so, and I say, "No!" If you let me handle things, we'll both get what we want!*

Okay, conceded Trabzon, *I will be patient a little longer.*

Good! I will take the girls to another room and question them in such a way that you can scan the truth when it comes to the surface of their minds. There will be no need for you to penetrate!

For the moment, I have agreed to spare them. Proceed!

Promptly Inspector Becket directed his attention back to Valerie and Linda. Only moments had passed since they had seen the alienness in his eyes and recoiled, and before their minds could dwell on it, he ordered sternly: "Come into the next room with me!" Stepping forward quickly, he took them by the shoulders, spun them around and shoved them ahead of him toward the door.

Chapter Three

IN the late afternoon sunlight, a sleek, yellow jetmobile blowtorched along one of the main jetways leading out of Angel City. At top speed it sped to the south toward the grassy, green hills of the soil-bank countryside which framed that sector of the city. Steve sat behind the steering console, nervous and with beads of sweat breaking out on his forehead. Beside him sat Catherine Rogers, partly turned in her seat, watching the jetway through the rear window. Behind her, covered by a blanket on the back seat floor, lay the body of Dr. Paul Griskell.

As they sped along, Catherine was saying to Steve: "I don't think anyone saw us putting Dr. Griskell's body in the back."

"Probably not, but it was touch and go there for a while. I still don't see why you weren't satisfied with hiding his body in the basement—or with just leaving it somewhere along the river bank."

"I was trying to look ahead," replied Catherine, keeping her eyes on the jetway behind. "If we had hidden it in the basement, then we'd have been unable to remove it later, in the event the Five Company secret police were suspicious and had the building watched. If we had left it somewhere along the river bank, they would have been sure to find it. Then they would know definitely that Dr. Griskell is dead. Given that knowledge, they might also figure that, before he died, he gave us the thing they are seeking."

"What are they seeking, anyway? That key and the little booklet which Dr. Griskell gave you?"

"Yes! To begin with, Dr. Graskell told me that he was the headman of a worldwide, secret group of independent space scientists who call themselves 'The Inventors.' "

"That's a strange name." Steve frowned, but kept his eyes on the jetway, his hands on the steering console. "The Inventors!"

Catherine nodded. "Yes, can you imagine it? For the past several years, they have been withholding from mankind every significant new invention relating to space."

"But why on Earth would they do that?"

"It's a negative reprisal against the Five Companies. Not knowing how to break the Five Company monopoly in space, Dr. Griskell said that The Inventors decided not to contribute to it. The way they went about it was to deny the Five Companies knowledge of any new inventions that had been developed by independent space scientists anywhere in the world. When somebody invented something, no patent was applied for. The invention and all the research data pertaining to it were taken away and hidden. I understand they have accumulated quite a few marvelous inventions. And that is what the Five Company secret police are after."

28

"I suppose all these marvelous inventions are hidden in one place?"

"Yes," nodded Catherine, and she held up the key which Dr. Griskell had given her. "And this is the key to that place. And this little booklet——" she showed him the small, red booklet, "—tells where it is. In fact, we're going there now!"

"Then it's at the address you gave me?"

"Yes. Dr. Griskell said that it is a secret cavern, concealed under the barn on an abandoned farm."

"Okay, so that explains why the secret police were after Dr. Griskell. They wanted the key and the little booklet which he gave you. But how did they know he had it? How did they know that he was the headman of this secret group of space scientists?"

"Dr. Griskell believed that one of the space scientists who was murdered in the past several months talked before he was killed—that he told the secret police that Dr. Griskell was headman."

"You say, 'murdered?' I wasn't aware that any space scientists had been murdered."

"Sorry," apologized Catherine. "It's just a theory of mine—and apparently Dr. Griskell had the same idea. If you've been keeping up with the news, you know that quite a number of distinguished space scientists have had fatal accidents in recent months—and all these accidents occurred under very mysterious circumstances. All the space scientists who met with these mysterious accidents were members of The Inventors."

Steve did not comment immediately, and the only indication that he had heard and was thinking was the slight frown on his sweaty forehead. The jetmobile took a curve; leaning over the steering console, his fingers moved easily over a row of buttons. Then the jetmobile roared into a straightaway, and he asked, "Any sign of anyone following us?"

"None."

"Then, I think, we got away without anyone seeing us put Dr. Griskell's body in the back." He relaxed a little, then said, "What I don't understand is: Why would the Five Company secret police want to murder all those space scientists? What can they hope to gain?"

"That's a question I haven't been able to figure out

myself," replied Catherine thoughtfully. "Early this afternoon, I thought they might be systematically killing off all the best and most noted space scientists to prevent them from making any significant contribution to Earth's space technology." Steve nodded, and Catherine continued, "Later, when I talked to Dr. Griskell, I began to believe that the explanation was that the secret police had questioned each of the space scientists who was killed in an attempt to find out the location of the secret hiding place of The Inventors. I thought perhaps they had killed them while trying to make them talk."

"No," Steve shook his head. "If all they wanted was information, they wouldn't have to kill anyone to get it. They could always use the brain probe."

"Right," agreed Catherine. "So we must conclude that something more than information was wanted ... Turn here!"

Instantly Steve punched the "turnoff" manual, and the jetmobile swerved into a country lane. Then it straightened and sped on.

"If the address you have in that little booklet is correct," he said, "then the abandoned farm where The Inventors have their secret hiding place should be about five miles down this road."

Catherine nodded but made no comment. Instead, she tried to relax her mind and derive some appreciation from the beautiful countryside.

Rich farmland skirted both sides of the road, yet little of it was under cultivation. For the first time in history, there was food in enough abundance to feed the world's population. The world's vast deserts were fully irrigated and under cultivation; and because of the worldwide use of advanced agricultural techniques, Earthmen were able to keep a good three-fifths of the world's farmland under soil-bank conservation, supporting only rich, green carpets of grass to prevent soil erosion. Under these circumstances, it was not at all unusual for many farms in any area to be in an abandoned or semi-abandoned condition.

The abandoned farmhouse in front of which the jetmobile finally slowed was, therefore, in no way more or less remarkable than any of the others in the area; and this fact made it a perfect hideout.

"The house looks kind of creepy to me," commented Steve as the jetmobile pulled past the dilapidated front porch and into what normally would have been the barnyard. "It looks like the place hasn't been worked for a good ten years."

"Most of the farms in this area were put into the soil bank about ten years ago," agreed Catherine. Then she pointed. "There's the barn. Drive up to the door, and I'll get out and look around."

"Good thing we can't be seen from the road," said Steve as he complied. "Somebody might wonder what we are doing here. What's the chance of some other member of this secret group of space scientists showing up?"

"None," answered Catherine as she stepped out of the jetmobile. "Dr. Griskell said that, for reasons of security, he was the only member of The Inventors who knew the location of this place. That's why he gave up his life trying to escape from the secret police. Had he allowed them to question him, they probably would have been able to force the information out of him, and everything would have been lost!"

Steve nodded, and Catherine walked around to the front of the jetmobile, opened the crookedly hanging barn doors, and disappeared inside. A moment later she reappeared and forced the doors open. Then she motioned for him to drive the jetmobile inside. When he did so, she closed the doors. He climbed out and looked around.

Inside, the barn looked as if it might collapse at any moment. The walls looked rickety and weak. The floor boards, under a light scattering of hay, appeared warped and decaying. The rear was filled with several rows of empty, dirty cow stalls, and overhead there was a rotted and bare hayloft.

Daylight spilled through small cracks in the walls and ceiling, giving the place an eerie quality. Feeling uneasy, Steve kicked nervously at the hay underfoot. The toe of his shoe struck a floorboard, and to his surprise, he discovered that it was solid and had a ring to it as if it was made of metal.

Instantly he knelt and swept aside the hay. The appearance of the whole structure was deceptive, he realized, and quickly he looked up at Catherine to make a comment.

31

He saw her kneeling in a corner, running her fingers into a little mound of straw.

Suddenly she called, "Here it is—just as it says in the little booklet!"

Quickly she brushed aside the straw, revealing a small, square control box. She inserted the key Dr. Griskell had given her and turned it. Instantly there was a high-pitched whine, ending in a soft, steady hum. Then the floor began to vibrate ever so slightly—and descend.

They were shocked, and in silence they stared at each other as the floor sank down. Soon their heads were well below the original level of the barn floor. A false floor slid silently from both sides of the wall, providing a ceiling for the shaft into which they were sinking.

"I don't know what I was expecting——" Catherine gave a big sigh, "—sliding doors—a secret stairway!"

Apparently they were riding a huge elevator, and to soothe his tense nerves, Steve muttered, "I wonder how they ventilate this place?" Before Catherine could answer, he noticed the close tolerances between the moving parts of the elevator and the shaft and commented: "The workmanship is superb."

"Whoever built it was a fine craftsman," agreed Catherine. "Hold it——!"

She held up her hand for silence as the floor of the barn suddenly stopped its descent and a section of the elevator shaft slid silently back to reveal a large, well lighted cavern.

Their first impression was that they were looking into the future. The most amazing and incredible-looking machines confronted them. Strange instruments and handsomely shaped weapons lay gleaming on a raised dais. Row upon row of servomechanisms of the most futuristic design formed neat aisles, leading into the dim recesses of the cavern.

They were overwhelmed.

"I wonder where the light is coming from?" was the only comment Steve could make.

Catherine's expression was one of awe. "It looks like we're a hundred years in the future."

"I don't think we should enter," said Steve cautiously. His voice was almost a whisper. "Those things—those servomechanisms—I've got a strange feeling that they're alive, that they're watching us."

"I feel it, too," whispered Catherine. "But we can't just stand here this way. Dr. Griskell wanted us to understand how to use these wonderful machines. He wanted us to use them for the benefit of mankind——"

"You didn't tell me that part of it!" exclaimed Steve. "That's a pretty tall order to give anyone. I mean, just to say, 'Here—take this and use it for the benefit of mankind.'"

"I realize that," said Catherine. "And I'm certainly against touching anything which we don't understand—or can't learn to use constructively."

"I'm not sure that we have the right to touch any of this stuff," persisted Steve as his eyes continued to travel over the marvelous machines. "What about all the other scientists in this secret group? It seems to me that, since they were responsible for inventing this stuff, they would be more qualified than we to judge just what should be used—and how."

"But who are these other scientists?" asked Catherine, pleadingly. "We know that they exist, but we don't know who they are. How in Space would we go about contacting them to turn over the responsibility for this?" She waved generally at the fantastic contents of the cavern.

"Doesn't the little red booklet give any clue who some of those space scientists are?"

"No, it only gives instructions about some of these inventions. For instance——" Catherine eagerly opened the little booklet—"it gives detailed instructions on how to activate and direct these servomechanisms. It says that they can perform any job that can be done by a human being. There's a master brain with control consoles somewhere in the cavern——" She rapidly flipped pages and started speaking again before Steve could think of a retort. "The cavern also contains a formula for an alloy that has one thousand times the tensile strength of the strongest steel yet developed by Earthmen. The booklet describes it as a combination of metal and plastic, Plasti-Metal, and says that it can be produced very cheaply and by a process so simple that it can be manufactured in the kitchen of the average home." Still not giving Steve time to react, she flipped more pages and went on: "And here, it

33

gives detailed instructions on the operation of a matter and psychic teleportation machine——"

"A teleportation machine!" exclaimed Steve. He whistled. "That I'll have to see to believe!"

"Then let's go," Catherine urged him. "We can't accomplish anything standing here."

"Shall I bring Dr. Griskell's body?"

"Yes, it should be safe to hide his body here in the cavern."

Steve went back to the jetmobile and lifted Dr. Griskell's body from the rear floor. Then he followed Catherine into the cavern.

"Put it there for now," she instructed him, indicating a bare corner of the dais which ran along one wall. "We'll see if we can't find something to preserve it with before we leave."

"Some form of refrigeration ought to do it," said Steve as he laid Dr. Griskell's body face up on the dais. "Anything in your little booklet that can be used for the job?"

"I don't know. I haven't had a chance to read it through completely. We'll have to wait and see if we run across anything."

"Inventorying the contents of this cavern is going to be a pretty big job——"

"We don't have to do it all right now," Catherine interrupted him. "I only want to get a look at the more fantastic inventions."

"They all seem pretty fantastic to me," snorted Steve, turning his head to look at the amazing machines surrounding them. "Doesn't all of this seem kind of alien to you?"

"I don't understand what you mean by alien," replied Catherine absently as she went over to a movie-projectorlike machine, read the card attached to it and began looking for references to it in her little booklet.

Steve followed her. "Well," he began, "this is pretty advanced stuff——"

"Look here!" Catherine interrupted and held up the booklet. "This here——" she indicated the projectorlike machine, "—is a pressor beam generator." For a moment Steve looked blank. "You know," Catherine explained, "the opposite of a traction beam generator. This machine

34

generates a beam of energy which repels matter—solid objects!"

Steve nodded pensively. "Wait a minute," he said. "Slow down, Catherine. You're acting like a little girl in a candy store!" He took her arm firmly and made her look at him. "Now think for a minute," he said, looking down into her beautiful face. "Doesn't this machine—this pressor beam generator prove my point?"

Catherine pouted. "What point?"

"Why, that there is an alienness about the inventions in this place."

"I don't see anything alien about them," disagreed Catherine. "I think these inventions are marvelous—and wonderful!"

"That's because you're still looking at the candy store aspect of it," scolded Steve, "instead of asking yourself: How were these inventions made? Where did the scientific know-how come from?"

"What does it matter?" asked Catherine, perplexed. "We know who invented them—The Inventors."

"So Dr. Griskell told you," said Steve. "But think, Catherine! As brilliant as Dr. Griskell was—and granted that the other space scientists who belong to The Inventors are also among Earth's most brilliant scientists—still, does it seem reasonable to you that they could have invented a machine like this in the time since they formed their secret organization? Why this pressor beam generator is at least two hundred years ahead of Earth's present level of technology in the field!"

Suddenly Catherine was looking at Steve with a wide-eyed, shocked expression. "I see your point," she admitted as if all the joy had gone out of the wonder of the secret cavern. "You're saying that The Inventors could not have made such a fantastic jump over Earth's present level of scientific technology all by themselves. It's impossible!"

"Of course, it is," nodded Steve. He turned from her and began to wander down one of the gleaming aisles of servomechanisms. His hands were in his pockets, and there was a deep frown on his face.

Catherine followed. "Sorry," she said apologetically. "I should have thought of that myself—especially when I read in this little booklet about the matter and psychic teleportation machine." Suddenly she stopped dead in her tracks, gasped and grabbed Steve by the arm. "Steve," she cried, "the matter and psychic teleportation machine—there it is!"

Steve saw it and did a double take, his mouth agape.

Before them, at the end of the aisle was a brilliant sheet of raw, vibrant energy. Square in form, it extended from the floor to the roof of the cavern. Colorless, it neither reflected nor absorbed light. Coruscating sparks of its own energy, it was like a thing in space and, at the same time, apart from space.

Around its perimeter was a thin lattice of electronic webbing, providing a frame, giving it boundary, implying definition. Before it, and to one side, sat its control console, studded with knobs, switches, relays and gages of all shapes and sizes

Taking this all in, it took Steve a moment to find his tongue. "Space!" he exclaimed finally. "It's alive! I thought you said that nothing was activated?"

"I never said that, but I guessed from what Dr. Griskell said that none of these inventions had ever been used! Maybe he just forgot and left it on?"

"Or maybe someone else has been here? Maybe he's still here?"

Immediately they both glanced around nervously. Then they saw it. A tiny, shining sphere of bright yellow luminescence. It was behind them, back the way they had come, and it was floating suspended, motionless above Dr. Griskell's body.

"What is it?" gasped Catherine.

"Whatever it is," Steve's answer was almost a whisper, "we'd better get out of here before it sees us!"

"But we don't even know if it can see us, or even if it's alive. Maybe it's just one of these machines?"

"Did you read about any machine like that in your little booklet?"

"No!"

"Then we'd better assume that it's not a machine and get out of here."

"No, it would be cowardly to run. Even if it is alive, we don't know that it's hostile."

"No—but we do know that it's alien! Oh, oh, I think it sees us!"

They froze and watched—tensely, ready to run as the

tiny, luminescent globe suddenly changed from a bright to a pale yellow. And then small, golden drops of liquid slowly began to form on its spherical surface and slid down to fall on the body of Dr. Griskell.

"Why, it's crying," exclaimed Catherine, without knowing why she was so certain of it.

"Why would an alien mourn over the body of a human being?"

"That's exactly what I intend to find out," answered Catherine as she started forward.

Before she could take two steps, Steve caught her arm and halted her. "If you're wrong," he warned, "it could be dangerous. We're dealing with a total unknown here."

"I'm sure Dr. Griskell would have warned us of any danger."

"Perhaps, but there are obviously many things that he didn't tell you. For one thing, maybe these fantastic inventions belong to that alien. If not, remember—this teleportation machine was already activated when we got here. Who knows from where that alien may have been teleported?"

"There's really only one way to find out," replied Catherine, and she firmly disengaged her arm from his restraint.

Steve shrugged. "I wish I had stayed in bed this morning," he groaned. Nevertheless, he followed her down the aisle.

As they approached Dr. Griskell's body, the tiny sphere of luminescence stopped its excretion of golden liquid and began to change back to its original color of bright yellow. As they got nearer, it began to revolve. Then in a flash of motion, it suddenly darted toward the opposite side of the cavern.

Immediately Catherine shouted, "We won't hurt you. We're friends!" Then she turned to Steve, exclaiming, "Oh, it's frightened!"

"That doesn't make it any less dangerous," said Steve dryly. Then suddenly, a new thought struck him, and instantly he acted. "Quick!" he shouted. "Back to the teleportation machine. I think it's trying to escape."

Simultaneously he grabbed Catherine's hand and rushed with her back down the aisle. They came to a skidding halt before the complicated control console of the teleportation machine. "Turn it off!" he shouted, as he frantically looked around for a sign of the tiny, luminescent sphere.

Catherine stared in desperate confusion at the maze of switches and dials on the teleportation machine's console and blurted in exasperation: "How in Space do you expect me to turn it off?"

"Look in your little book! You said that it gave detailed instructions on the operation of these machines."

"Yes, but this still might be pretty complicated," she protested. Hurriedly she thumbed through the little booklet and after several seconds, she exclaimed, "Here it is!"

"And here it comes," shouted Steve. He pointed as a bright yellow streak of luminescence shot toward the energy screen of the teleportation machine.

Catherine leaned over the machine's console and frantically fumbled with the unfamiliar switches. She exclaimed suddenly, "I've got it!" An instant later she clicked one of the switches. Promptly there was loud crack as the machine's energy screen snapped from existence, and an instant later the tiny sphere of luminescence shot between the lattices of electronic webbing where the screen had been. Then it veered sharply before colliding with the rear wall of the cavern.

"We've got it," shouted Steve. "Now, unless it can work the elevator, it's trapped!"

"We're not trying to trap it," scolded Catherine. "We only want to find out what it is!" Suddenly her expression changed, and she pointed. "Look at the poor thing! See how it's acting? I told you it was frightened!"

For several moments they watched it as it flashed erratically back and forth near the top of the cavern. Then Steve turned to Catherine and asked, "Now, just how do you plan to get it down to find out what it is? If it's actually frightened, it's not just coming down to hold a conversation."

"No, but perhaps I can communicate with it and make it realize that we don't intend to hurt it. You stay here, and I'll go and try to coax it down."

"Oh, I'll be glad to stay here," Steve assured her. "But I warn you, be careful!"

"I will."

Slowly Catherine moved away from Steve to a position where she stood almost directly in the center of the frantic gyrations of the strange luminescence. It was acting like a bird that had entered a building by mistake and was trying to find its way out. This brought a question to Catherine's mind. Was it some sort of alien pet belonging to Dr. Griskell? If it was a pet, then it could not be considered to be intelligent and its fear was probably instinctive—a mere reaction to the strange presence of herself and Steve, to the unknown—by fear.

Trying to calm it down, she employed the most basic means that she knew. She extended her hand into the air and intoned soothingly, coaxingly: "Come here—I won't hurt you!" And all the time she pivoted slowly as it erratically flashed around and around the ceiling of the cavern. After a time, when this did not seem to have any effect, she gave up and went back to Steve. "I'm going to turn on the teleportation machine," she said. "If it wants out of here that badly, we have no right to hold it."

Steve, who had been leaning against the console of the teleportation machine, patiently watching her, smiled. "How do you know that it won't be teleported back to some alien planet where it will promptly get in touch with its friends, who will then come charging back here in force and eat us alive?"

Catherine shrugged her beautiful shoulders. "I suppose," she said, "before we turn it back on, we should check to find out where the machine is set to teleport."

Steve nodded his agreement, and Catherine began to study the detailed instructions regarding the operation of the machine in the little booklet Dr. Griskell had given her. While she was comparing the notes in the booklet with the actual readings on the console's instruments, Steve became absorbed in reading over her shoulder. Neither noticed the tiny sphere of luminescence when it ceased its erratic darting about and dived for the servomechanism control consoles on the other side of the cavern.

There, it went into a weird, gyrating dance. Almost at once, without its ever touching anything, switches flipped, activation lights flashed on, and dials turned as if a score of invisible hands were manipulating the board.

Suddenly all of the servomechanisms in the cavern came to life. As if in one accord, row upon row, they swung, turned, pivoted, crawled, stepped or rolled around to face Catherine and Steve. Slowly, they began to advance.

They were of all descriptions. Some were ugly and seemingly awkward; others were of the most modern design imaginable. They were of all sizes. Some of them were humanoid; others moved on wheels or caterpillar treads and had futuristic-looking lenses or antennas for eyes. Still others were completely smooth-surfaced and featureless, their purpose incomprehensible. All of them, however, advanced upon Catherine and Steve and—with hand, vice, claw, clamp, mouth or tentacle—reached for them.

Catherine was the first to become aware of the movement around them. Looking up, she saw the servomechanisms coming and screamed in terror. Her scream alerted Steve, and he whirled just in time to avoid a tentacle which was reaching out to encircle his neck. Then he ducked a viselike claw and sidestepped a giant clamp which sought his wrist.

Simultaneously two Plasti-Metal hands tried to close around Catherine's throat, but she managed to escape with a violent jerk of her head. Then she threw herself backward against the console of the teleportation machine, narrowly avoiding a mouth with needle-sharp teeth which snapped shut just were her waist had been an instant before.

Seconds later, both she and Steve were backing away, dodging and ducking as they moved, from a solid line of advancing servomechanisms. Simultaneously, before the consoles of the servomechanisms' master brain, the tiny sphere of luminescence continued its weird dance, manipulating switches, dials and levers as if by the power of its will alone.

In response, the line of servomechanisms began to encircle them in an inescapable ring of sleek and gleaming Plasti-Metal. Instantly both Catherine and Steve realized what was happening; turning, they attempted to dash through the narrow opening between the two closing halves of the circle.

Steve was the first to try to squeeze through, but he was not fast enough. Like a flash of lightning, a tentacle lashed

40

out and encircled his waist, lifting his struggling body from the floor as if he weighed no more than a feather.

Seeing Steve's capture, Catherine came to a panic-stricken halt and screamed. Barely had the first shrill sound escaped her throat when her body was seized by two crablike pincers. She was lifted high into the air, her arms flailing and her beautiful legs kicking frantically in a vain effort to free herself. Then, as she and Steve continued to struggle, they were conveyed to the center of the cavern and held suspended in the air, some twenty feet above the floor, while two giant, whirling drill bits, as long as swords, came to rest just inches from their stomachs.

Chapter Four

A MOMENT after Catherine and Steve were conveyed to the center of the cavern and held there suspended in mid-air while the two sword-long drill bits whirled before their stomachs, the tiny sphere of bright yellow luminescence ceased its weird dance before the control console of the servomechanisms' master brain and sped to a position directly in front of their faces. There it floated motionlessly, suspended in the air before their eyes. Suddenly a cold thought pierced both their minds: *Why did you kill Dr. Griskell?*

Hearing this question with his mind instead of with his ears caused Steve's face to contort in sudden shock. He could not believe that he was experiencing mental telepathy. He was an engineer, the type of person who could not accept anything which could not be scientifically measured and explained. As a result, his mind froze.

Catherine experienced a different reaction. She was suddenly calm. Instantly the fear she was experiencing at being seized by the servomechanisms was forgotten, and her mind began to analyze the situation.

The use of mental telepathy by the tiny sphere of

41

luminescence did not startle her because she had observed that it had no opening on its smooth, golden surface that could serve as a speech organ. She figured that it was natural, therefore, that it would use a means of communication other than speech. What struck her most was the mental tone of the question the tiny sphere of luminescence had asked. Somehow it did not sound like the cold, sharp query of an executioner. Keeping this in mind, she was able to disregard the threatening, whirling menace of the sword-long drill bit before her stomach and use all her mental facilities to think an answer back at the alien luminescence.

We did not kill Dr. Griskell, she thought. *And would you please tell these servomechanisms to release us? We bear you no ill will.*

The luminescence ignored her plea. *If you did not kill Dr. Griskell,* the thought stabbed at her mind, *then how did you come into possession of his body?*

These servomechanisms are hurting us, Catherine formed the thought. *I beg of you, please release us before we are injured.*

Answer my question and I may release you. But, remember, I will know if you are lying.

Since you are obviously telepathic, Catherine formed the thought as she grimaced in pain from the pressure of the two crablike pincers holding her, *why don't you save us a lot of time and pain by reading my mind.*

I can't "read" your mind without your permission. Will you give permission?

Yes, only please hurry.

A moment later she felt it in her mind. It was as if a gentle breeze was passing through her brain, but no sooner she was aware of it than it was gone. And the tiny sphere of luminescence was flashing back to the control console of the servomechanisms' master brain. There, it went into its weird gyrations again, obviously using some strange power to give the brain a new set of instructions.

The result was immediately apparent. The whirling drill bits withdrew from positions before their stomachs. Then the servomechanisms which held them captive lowered their bodies gently to the floor and released them. After that, the servomechanisms alll began to roll, crawl or step

42

back to their former positions. And there, among the other machines of the cavern, they formed neat rows with aisles in between.

Simultaneously the tiny sphere of luminescence floated back to Catherine and Steve, coming to a position level with their eyes. Again its stabbing thought entered Catherine's mind. *I found the manner of Dr. Griskell's death very clear in your memory.*

Then you know that we are innocent? Catherine thought back while she rubbed the sore spots on her body. *And that we mean you no harm?*

Yes, your intentions were clear in your mind.

"I gather that you're in telepathic communication with this alien thing," said Steve suddenly, glancing curiously from Catherine to the sphere of luminescence and back again. When Catherine nodded, he exclaimed, "I thought so! I can't hear what you're thinking, but I am catching its projections!"

"I noticed your first reaction to its use of telepathy," said Catherine sympathetically. "It seemed to hit you pretty hard."

"That's right, I panicked when I first heard this thing speaking to us in my mind. I couldn't believe it. I tell you—it was the strangest thing I've ever experienced!"

"It doesn't mean us any harm. It just wanted to know how Dr. Griskell had died."

"I gathered from its initial treatment of us—and from its questions—that it thought we had killed him."

"Yes," replied Catherine, and then, turning from Steve, she directed a thought at the tiny sphere: *What was Dr. Griskell to you?*

Dr. Griskell, came the answering thought, *rescued me from Trabzon, the traitor to my—his—race, after the spaceship in which he was holding me a prisoner crashed here on Earth.*

You mean, thought Catherine, repeating the flow of thoughts which she had received, *that you were being held prisoner aboard a spaceship by someone—by this Trabzon —and the spaceship crashed here on Earth—and Dr. Griskell rescued you?*

The tiny sphere of luminescence radiated a bright yellow. *Yes,* the thought came. *You see, within my race I am the Tisza! In your language that means I am the princess*

43

*or the queen, or more precisely, I am the Monoleader of
my race.*

As the tiny sphere of luminescence projected these
thoughts, Catherine received the vague image of a young
girl with a shining crown of stars on her head.

You are a young child among your "people?" she inter-
preted the picture, and the tiny luminescence shone
brighter. *A female child—?* Again she got a positive
reaction. *You are a princess.* . . . *You are from the ruling,*
she struggled with the concept, *family, class, monocracy—
—?*

At this point, Tisza, the Monoleader, seemed to become
very excited. She glowed brightly, projecting a steady
stream of thoughts: *Soon, when I become of age,* the
thoughts came, *I will rule as queen of our planet, Triskellia. I will be the sole ruler of my race, of all my people.
All our young will spring from me, and all my people will
replenish their lights from mine.*

For a moment both Steve and Catherine experienced
confusion as they struggled with the alien concepts coming
into their minds. Catherine thought of the word, "mono-
phyletic," development from a common parent; but she
found it extremely difficult to imagine the tiny sphere of
luminescence possessing the ability to propagate an entire
race, to populate an entire planet. Even more difficult to
grasp was the concept of her sustaining such a race,
feeding it, nourishing it or doing whatever else was meant
by "all my people will replenish their lights from mine."

After a moment the Tisza projected again: *How can I
make you understand? Dr. Griskell said that I am to my
race what a queen bee is to her hive here on Earth.*

Catherine nodded, but before she could form an answering thought, Steve said, "Ask her where the spaceship
she was in crashed. Maybe we can learn something about
her race and where she's from by analyzing the wreck-
age."

"You ask her," said Catherine wearily. "My brain is
tired."

Steve made a face at her; then seriously, he turned to
the tiny sphere of luminescence and tried to concentrate,
thinking: *Should I call you Tisza, the Monoleader?* The
response was positive. *Okay, Tisza, you said that the*

spaceship you were in crashed. Do you know where it crashed in relation to our present location?"

Yes, the Tisza projected her answer, *but after Dr. Griskell rescued me from Trabzon, the traitor to my—his race, it was completely destroyed.*

Oh! Steve projected a concept of disappointment. *How was it destroyed?*

Since it was damaged beyond repair, Trabzon, the traitor, caused it to disintegrate by disrupting the atomic nucleus of its space drive.

This Trabzon, Catherine formed the thought, *who is he?*

He is a criminal deviate. The people of my race regard him as you would regard a civilized member of the human race who had suddenly became a cannibal.

You mean that this Trabzon eats members of his own race?

No, from the viewpoint of our people, he does something far worse. He has developed an insane craving to feed upon the life force of other life forms.

Are you saying that he eats people's souls? Steve thought the question.

The answer is no, if by "soul" you mean the fundamental essence within all human beings, answered the Tisza. *Nothing in the universe, that I know of, can act upon the fundamental essence or "soul" as you call it—except, perhaps, the power of the Christian God of whom Dr. Griskell spoke to me. What Trabzon does is feed upon the aura or life force that is excreted or radiated by the fundamental essence or "soul" of his victim. As a result, the victim dies a physical death, but the fundamental essence or "soul" itself remains unaffected.*

How could your people have allowed a creature like Trabzon to run loose? asked Catherine, feeling a sense of horror.

No! No! exclaimed the Tisza, affected by the emotion behind the question. *We did not allow Trabzon to run loose. When we discovered that he had become criminally deviant, he was committed to a place similar to your insane asylums, a place where he could be watched and, at the same time, receive treatment for his condition.*

But you said that he was holding you prisoner aboard a spaceship?

45

Yes, somehow, he escaped from the asylum where he was incarcerated. He remained in hiding for a time, and then he very cleverly slipped into my royal residence, disabled my royal guards and chaperons, and kidnaped me. Then, holding me as a hostage, he went to the nearest spaceport, forced his way aboard a spaceship and fled our planet. He was trying to reach a star system beyond this one when the hyperspace drive of the spaceship went out of phase and forced him to crash-land on this planet. We crashed in the mountains, and I escaped. Dr. Griskell, who happened to be on a camping trip in the mountains at that time, helped prevent him from recapturing me.

He doesn't need you as a hostage any more, why should he want to recapture you?

To know that, you must have an understanding of our race. Nine-tenths of the Triskellion people are female; but they have no power to reproduce. If I may use the analogy of the queen bee again, like her I am the only member of my race with the power to propagate it. When I become of age and the old queen retires, the young males of my race will flock to me for the purpose of mating. . . . Trabzon is a young male of my race. He was to be one of my future consorts. That is still his desire. It is the only way he can replenish his light. Unless a male of my race performs his mating duties, his light grows dim and he expires—he dies!

Then all you have to do, thought Catherine matter of factly, *is refuse to mate with him, and he will expire, he will die.*

I told you that I was very young. I am not fully developed. Trabzon is older and stronger than I am. If he recaptures me, he will force me to mate with him.

Catherine nodded. *Then we must see that he does not recapture you!*

That's what Dr. Griskell was trying to do, but now he's dead!

Just a minute, thought Steve, suddenly interrupting. *If Trabzon did mate with you, what would be the result?*

If Trabzon and I were to mate, projected the Tisza, *over a period of time, I would populate this entire planet with Triskellions. From each union with Trabzon, I would have a hundred million offspring!*

That's the answer I feared, thought Steve. Then apolo-

46

getically: *Please don't misunderstand me, Tisza. I do not dread the possibility of such a thing because I fear Earthmen would have prejudice or intolerance for your race. If we had to, I'm sure that we could get along on the same planet. It's just that——*

I quite understand! projected the Tisza. *And I know that it must not happen! Should Trabzon be able to make the offspring of a union between him and myself criminally deviant in the same way that he is, the entire human race would be wiped out. Like the young of any life form, without proper upbringing, my offspring could revert to savagery. Under Trabzon's influence, they could take to feeding on the life forces of the members of your race!*

Then you think, asked Steve, surprised at himself that he could discuss such a horrifying prospect so calmly, *that your offspring could become like Trabzon, that they could begin to crave feeding on the life forces of human beings?*

I don't know, came the Tisza's worried thought. *I cannot be positive because I have no knowledge of how Trabzon became the way he is. You see, before it becomes time for a male of my race to perform his mating duties, he is allowed to pursue any career which he desires. Trabzon chose that of an interstellar explorer. He went to the stars; and somewhere during his explorations, he encountered something which influenced him evilly. He became alien to his people. . . . And I cannot stress too strongly how abhorrent this is to all Triskellions.*

Isn't there some way, asked Steve, frowning in concentration, *that Earthmen could kill Trabzon before he does any harm?*

No, there is within each of my people psi power beyond Earthmen's wildest dreams of the concept. Given time and the will, Trabzon could annihilate the entire human population of Earth single-handedly! Steve gulped and Catherine turned deathly pale. *Or much worse,* the Tisza continued, *he could use your race as a food supply for his evil craving.*

There must be something we can do! exclaimed Catherine. She was imagining a tiny sphere of luminescence like the Tisza, moving throughout the world, feeding on the life forces of human beings. Then she imagined them by the millions, having no regard for human life except as

47

food. It was a frightening thought, and she had to fight to keep from trembling.

There is something you can do, projected the Tisza, knowing exactly how Catherine felt. *You can help me contact the other members of my race as Dr. Griskell and the other Earth scientists have been doing. It is my only hope! It is the only hope for your race!*

You say that Dr. Griskell and The Inventors were helping you to contact your people! How?

It was our plan to build a space platform in orbit around this planet. On the platform we were going to build a space beacon——

What is a space beacon? asked Steve, his engineer's curiosity aroused.

Imagine a giant spotlight sweeping the heavens—back and forth—reaching scores of light-years into space. Only instead of a beam of light, it will project a beam of energy for which there is no name in your language. This beam of energy will be detected by my people, by one of the numerous search parties which are undoubtedly combing space at this moment in search of me. . . . Once they have detected it, they will know where I am and come in force to rescue me. When they arrive, Trabzon will be taken prisoner and then taken back to Triskellia where he will be dealt with properly.

As the Tisza finished, Steve shook his head slowly. *Someone of Dr. Griskell's brilliance,* he thought, *might have been able to help you build such a space platform and beacon, but I'm afraid the same isn't true of us. We just don't have the knowledge or education to follow through on a plan like that!*

As I told you, projected the Tisza fiercely, *I possess the light of my people. In me is stored all the scientific knowledge and racial experience of all the countless ages of the existence of my race. . . . Look around you! With all due respect to Dr. Griskell and the other brilliant Earth scientists who helped him build the instruments, tools and machines in this cavern, the scientific knowledge which enabled them to do so was supplied by me.*

"I told you that there was an alienness about these machines!" exclaimed Steve, turning to Catherine. She nodded.

The preliminary work has already been done, the Tisza

48

projected, ignoring Steve's remark. *All the instruments, tools and machines necessary to do the job were built elsewhere on Earth by your most brilliant scientists following my instructions. Then they were brought here secretly by Dr. Griskell and assembled under my direction.* The Tisza seemed to grow brighter as if taking pride in her accomplishment. *If you will carefully study the little booklet which Dr. Griskell gave you,* she projected the thought at Catherine particularly, *you will see that most of the equipment in this cavern has been designed to operate in a deep space environment, as well as on and within the space platform once construction is completed. Nothing has been overlooked. We can start work immediately!*

What about labor? asked Steve. *A platform of any size would require hundreds of skilled men.*

The actual work will be done by the servomechanisms you see around you. They have been designed to perform every task which can be performed by a human being.

How were you planning to accomplish orbital insertion of materials and machines?

We intended to teleport these machines and the necessary materials into orbit.

Of course! exclaimed Steve, snapping his fingers. *Why didn't I see it!*

When we came in, Catherine formed the thought, *the matter and psychic teleportation machine was on. Later, you tried to escape through its teleport screen. Where is the machine set to teleport?*

To a woods near here. Dr. Griskell left it on so that if Trabzon discovered this place while he was gone, I would have an escape route.

Do you have any idea where Trabzon is right now?

I don't know where he is, the Tisza answered and fairly coruscated in bright hues of yellow. *But I know that he is nearby, and looking for me!*

I shouldn't think he'd have any trouble finding you if his psi abilities are as great as you've indicated.

This cavern is insulated in such a way as to prevent his using psi to locate me, answered the Tisza. *That was one of the first things I had Dr. Griskell attend to.*

Then, if you stay within this cavern, you should be safe, thought Catherine with relief. *After all, being an*

49

alien, Trabzon cannot move around too freely to search for you. Even at night, he would attract attention. There would be reports in the newspapers of people sighting a strange phenomenon, a strange yellow light, a sphere of luminescence. . . .

Moving about would be no problem for Trabzon, disagreed the Tisza. *He would merely conceal himself within the mind of a human being.*

Possession? exclaimed Steve, frowning.

It would not be possession as, I see in your mind, you mean the term. While it is possible for one of us to take over the mind of a human being, it is also possible for us to exist within the mind of a human being and yet remain apart from that mind. . . . And, of course, I must stress that no Triskellion would do such a thing without the permission of the host intelligence—that is, except Trabzon.

Then there are two possibilities, thought Cathèrine, trying to analyze the situation calmly. *Trabzon could conduct his search for you by concealing himself within the mind of a human being and taking possession of it. Or he may do so by securing the host's cooperation.*

If he took over the mind of a human being, then that human's friends would probably be able to detect a certain alienness about him and become suspicious. So, most likely, he will secure the human's cooperation.

What could Trabzon possibly promise a human being to secure his cooperation? asked Catherine, thinking that anyone who would cooperate with Trabzon must either be ignorant of the facts or a traitor to mankind.

Look around you. The Tisza indicated the contents of the cavern by revolving slowly. *Would you tell me there are no Earthmen who would betray their race for possession of the advanced scientific instruments and machines which you see.*

"I'm ashamed to admit it," said Steve to Catherine, "but the Tisza is right. There are such people."

From the circumstances surrounding the death of Dr. Griskell and some of the other space scientists who have aided me, it is obvious Trabzon realizes that I am making an effort to contact our people and that he is desperately trying to stop me. If he fails, he knows he is doomed.

Therefore, you must realize that he will go to any lengths —stop at nothing—promise anything——

Yes, I can see that, Catherine interrupted. Her head was spinning from the effort of mental communication, but she forced herself to form the thought: *Tisza, when you scanned my memory to get details of Dr. Griskell's death, did you see that he had put the contents of this cavern into our care?*

Yes!

And do you have any objection?

No, answered the Tisza. *Dr. Griskell had faith in you that you would carry on his work. Not knowing you personally beforehand, he took a desperate gamble, but from reading your mind, I see that it paid off. Still,* the Tisza hesitated, *I noted from your memory that he died before he could tell you the whole story.*

That's true, admitted Catherine, *but knowing the whole story now, I have no choice but to do everything I can to help. After this is over, however, can some of these inventions be used for the benefit of mankind?*

Yes, that was the agreement I had with Dr. Griskell and the other Earth scientists who have aided me. My people will owe your people that much!

The first thing we'd better do then, thought Catherine, *is find you a better place to hide than this cavern.* Suddenly she got an idea. *Tisza,* she thought excitedly before she could lose her nerve and change her mind, *you intimated that you have the ability to occupy the mind of a human being without harming that human being?*

Yes, replied the Tisza, *and I know what you're thinking.*

Well, then, why don't you conceal yourself in my mind?

Only with your permission, answered the Tisza; and when Catherine gave it, she glowed a bright yellow, then gold. Slowly she moved forward and gently touched Catherine's forehead. Then, even before Catherine could tense, she disappeared inside.

Chapter Five

WHEN Inspector Becket got Valerie and Linda alone in the next room, a complete change came over his character. He was no longer bone military. Smiling, he stood rather relaxed before a table upon which Valerie and Linda sat with their legs dangling comfortably over the edge. He told them a funny story about a space suit that had come out of hyperspace wearing the spaceman. He had them laughing and in a good mood. Then, just at the right moment, he leaned forward and said:

"I have two little girls about your ages; and the two most important things that I've always tried to teach them are: first, to have a proper respect for authority—and second, to always tell the truth!"

"That's exactly what our older sister, Catherine, has always tried to teach us," said Linda, and when she smiled up at him, the dimples in her pretty cheeks deepened. "Our teacher in school says the same thing!"

Inspector Becket returned her smile. "I can see then," he said, "that your moral education has not been neglected."

"It hasn't," Valerie spoke up. "Catherine has always taught us never to tell lies—even if it means that we'll be punished for telling the truth!"

"Do you really believe," Inspector Becket's face reflected complete surprise, "that you should always tell the truth, regardless of the consequences?"

"Yes!"

"Certainly!"

Inspector Becket scrutinized both their innocent faces with perceptive and experienced eyes. Suddenly he abandoned his former tack and asked directly: "Where are they hiding Dr. Paul Griskell?"

During the instant that followed, there was a knowing

smile on Inspector Becket's face which seemed to dare her to lie to him. It was as if she could feel him waiting to pounce on any untruth which passed her lips, and she was forced to hesitate, to search for an answer, to review past events in her mind.

She and Linda had been on the way home from school when they had paused by the bank of the river which ran behind the Rogers Group administration building. They were playing a game when the door leading from the basement of the building had opened and Catherine and Steve had emerged. They were supporting between them a man who had blood all over his tunic and a gaping hole in his chest.

Valerie had immediately recognized the man as Dr. Paul Griskell, the famous space scientist. Nevertheless, the implications of who he was did not register immediately. What did register in her mind and that of her younger sister was the horror of seeing a man dead in such a fashion.

As Catherine passed, she told them to look away and forget what they had seen. She told them that she would explain later, and then she and Steve had continued to carry Dr. Griskell's body down the path which ran along the river bank until they had passed out of sight around a bend.

A few minutes later, a secret policeman had come out of the door leading from the basement and corralled them as they stood there trying to adjust their young minds to the shock of what they had seen. He had made a brief investigation of the river bank, and then he had ordered them to accompany him into the building where he had taken them to Inspector Becket. And subsequent events had conspired to place them in their present predicament.

These thoughts flashed through Valerie's mind in the space of an instant. She collected herself to deliver, in just the right tone of voice, a statement that was absolutely true as far as it went. Before she could speak, however, Inspector Becket's attention seemed to suddenly turn inward.

I have been scanning the surface of her mind, came Trabzon's thought. *In the last several instants, she has relived the whole story.*

53

Is it what we suspect? asked Inspector Becket. Promptly Trabzon began relaying impressions of what Valerie had been thinking.

When he had finished, Inspector Becket thought, *We still don't know where they've taken Dr. Griskell, and we can't take any overt action until we do.*

I disagree! returned Trabzon. *The girl's memory indicates that he was dead. Therefore, they must have taken him to the secret hiding place of The Inventors. It is the only safe place where they could hide his body.*

You're concluding that Dr. Griskell turned over all his secrets to them before he died. I can't go along with that. He didn't know any of the Rogers Group!

He knew them by reputation! He was dying! He had to trust someone!

All right! Suppose that he did trust the Rogers Group with his secrets. Suppose that he told them everything— right down to the location of The Inventors' secret hiding place. We must still proceed cautiously!

I disagree, replied Trabzon. *There is no longer any need for extreme caution. We know that the people who took Dr. Griskell's body away from here now have his secrets. All we have to do is capture them, and I am not particular how we go about it!*

We'll set a trap for them, thought Inspector Becket suddenly, nervously. *Yes, a trap. I'll get on it right away.*

No! Trabzon's thought was like a whiplash across his mind. *I will take over from here! I will give the orders!*

Inspector Becket shivered mentally. He had always known that the moment would come when Trabzon would feel that he was so close to his goal that he no longer needed him as a "cover." Yet now that it was here, he found himself unprepared for it. The thought of Trabzon doing things his way was terrifying, and Becket felt that it was his duty to delay such an event for as long as possible.

Carefully he formed the thought: *I see no reason to change the way we've been operating. I understand human beings better than you do. If you'll just let me continue to handle things, we'll both get what we want.*

You fear that I will be too heavy-handed, too merciless with your race. Trabzon's thought was almost a laugh.

Don't bother to deny it. You keep forgetting that I can read your mind as easily as I read the minds of others!

I have as much desire for success in this matter as you do.

Yes, of course you do! With what I have promised you, you would be a fool not to. The trouble is you are trying to play both sides of the street at once. You see yourself as protecting mankind from me and at the same time, you seek to justify your betrayal of mankind on the pretext of providing it with such protection.

I don't believe in the useless destruction of human life, that's all, insisted Inspector Becket. *And you promised me, when I first agreed to cooperate with you, that you would refrain from gratifying your monstrous desires on human beings.*

That promise is cancelled, returned Trabzon. *From now on, I will treat human beings as I please. And furthermore, if I get any more argument from you, yours will be the first life force I feed upon.*

You still need me!

Not anymore!

Just then a knock sounded at the door, and Inspector Becket whirled, grateful for the interruption. Leaving Valerie and Linda sitting on the edge of the table, staring at him in wonder at his silent preoccupation with something they could not see or understand, he quickly strode to the door and threw it open. A secret policeman stood on the other side.

"We're getting a call on the vidphone," he said immediately. "We haven't answered it, so we don't know who is calling. But we figured it might have something to do with the matter at hand!"

"Have you run a tracer on it?"

"Can't, sir, until somebody answers it."

"That's right!" Inspector Becket ran his hand wearily over his face. "Not thinking straight——"

Tell him to let it ring until we get somebody to answer it.

"Let it ring," said Inspector Becket. "We'll get someone to answer it in a moment."

"Better hurry, sir. If it's someone who is involved in this Griskell affair, he might become suspicious at the delay."

55

"I'll get right on it," said Inspector Becket. He closed the door in the secret policeman's face.

As it swung shut, Trabzon formed the thought: *Let the young girl, Valerie, answer it!*

No! I say let it ring! If we let her or any of the others answer it, they may manage to warn the caller. We can't take that chance!

There will be no chances taken, replied Trabzon. *Observe the young girl.*

Inspector Becket turned and glanced at Valerie. He was just in time to see her mouth pop open in sudden shock. Then the muscles of her face slackened, and the spark of life seemed to go out of her eyes. She gave a quick gasp as if surprised at something which had occurred within herself, and then her body stiffened. Slowly she slid off the table where she was sitting, and then she walked toward them, stiffly.

What have you done to her? exclaimed Inspector Becket, observing the cold, unnatural quality of her face, the deathlike stare of her eyes. *She's not natural!*

She is mind-controlled, came Trabzon's thought.

You devil! The thought, couched in horror, slipped from Inspector Becket's mind before he could stop it.

Don't waste your time calling me names, replied Trabzon unperturbed. *This is the easiest way to solve the problem. Now she will answer the vidphone for us without betraying the presence of you or your secret police to the caller.*

I won't stand by and allow you to degrade human beings in this manner! Inspector Becket's thought was firm, but he began to sweat in fear, and being aware of it, Trabzon was not impressed.

You have no choice, he pointed out. *Now, don't argue! Move—before it's too late!* Inspector Becket flinched from the force of Trabzon's thought, and he suddenly experienced a vile and coldly loathsome impression of Trabzon of which he had never before been aware. It was suddenly as if a hideous creature occupied a corner of his mind, spreading an aura of evil outward. He shuddered, but the terror of his new realization caused him to turn and obey immediately. *Take her by the arm,* ordered Trabzon, *and walk close to her so that your men will not notice the strangeness about her.*

Obeying, Inspector Becket turned to Linda as he opened the door. She was staring at her older sister with a stunned look. "You remain here," he ordered her. "If you keep quiet and cause no trouble, your sister will be returned to you safely. Otherwise———!"

He left the sentence unfinished as he closed the door, locked it and then escorted Valerie down the hall to an office where one of his secret policemen stood waiting.

"In here, sir!"

Nodding, he quickly led Valerie inside, closed the door and pushed her toward the vidphone and telescreen on a table against one wall. It gave a loud, steady purr at five-second intervals. Valerie walked stiffly forward and flipped the answering switch.

How will she know what to say? asked Inspector Becket, moving out of pickup range of the vidphone's telescanners.

I told you, she is mind-controlled!

I don't understand exactly what that means. Are you going to tell her what to say?

Yes, I am directly influencing her mind. She can think no thought, speak no word, make no movement, except by telepathic stimulus from me.

"Hello———" The telescreen lit up but stayed blank, and Valerie spoke into the vidphone. "Rogers Group administration building—Valerie Rogers here! Who's calling please?"

"Val! This is Catherine. What took you so long to answer?"

"I-I-I was downstairs. But where are you?"

"I can't tell you that now. Are the others around?"

"No, they're all downstairs. Turn on your telescanner so that I can see you."

"No, your screen will have to remain blank. There's too much danger of a trace. Listen, hon—are the secret police still there?"

"No, they left some time ago!"

"Did they have any suspicions?"

"None," answered Valerie, her voice an even monotone, her face remaining unchanged. "They believed the story that we gave them."

"You're sure?"

"Y-Y-Yes! Were you able to dispose of the———?"

57

"Don't say it over the phone," snapped Catherine. "We may be monitored."

"I told you, they don't suspect a thing!"

"Well, you never know!"

"When can we expect you back?"

"Steve and I will return very shortly." Catherine's voice from the speaker suddenly sounded troubled. "Val—are you sick or—— Nothing!"

"What were you going to ask?"

"Noth——" Catherine's voice trailed away as Valerie's face suddenly fell, the muscles going completely slack and her expression disintegrating. For an instant her face seemed to become a battleground, a mirror of the silent struggle between two opposing forces within her mind. Her shoulders sagged as if under the addition of some unbearable weight. A moment later, her body stiffened and her face reassembled itself into its former dead expression.

She fought me, came Trabzon's thought in Inspector Becket's mind. *Tried to warn her sister!*

You should have left the telescanners off. If Catherine Rogers saw her sister's face fall like that——

It's all right. It lasted only for an instant. For someone so young, she put up a terrific fight; but I fixed her— good!

"Val," Catherine's voice came from the speaker, "I'm going to switch off now. You hang on there, and I'll return soon."

"We'll be waiting for you," answered Valerie as the connection on the other end was cut. Then, flipping the switch on her end, she turned.

Instantly Inspector Becket gasped: *She's like—like a zombie!*

She made me use more force than would normally be required. I had to force her id back upon itself, down into the depths of her mind. Now she has no will of her own.

Well, bring her back! exclaimed Inspector Becket, watching Valerie as she stood before him, her face devoid of life, her eyes staring into a point in space before her nose. *If anyone sees her like this, they'll know something's wrong.*

At the moment, I have no time to nursemaid her back!

58

came Trabzon's cold thought. *We must prepare a trap for Catherine Rogers and the man Steve who is with her.*

But——

Don't argue, lashed Trabzon's thought. *See if your men were able to trace that call!*

Turning, Inspector Becket opened the door and immediately got a report from his man in the hallway. "No, sir," the secret policeman reported. "She left the telescanner off on her end, and we didn't have enough time to run a trace on the audio alone."

Ask him where he is holding the other members of the Rogers Group!

Inspector Becket obeyed, and the secret policeman answered, "We moved them to a laboratory at the rear of the building."

Good, came Trabzon's thought. *Now have him remove his men from that laboratory. I want them to be alone together.*

As Inspector Becket obeyed, Trabzon caused Valerie to walk across the office and sit down. Then, as the secret policeman turned and hurried down the hall with his instructions, Inspector Becket asked, *What are you going to do with her?* He indicated Valerie, who sat hunched over in her chair, slack-faced and staring vacantly into space.

Leave her where she is, answered Trabzon. *She is no more than a mindless hulk, a vegetable. She cannot give us any trouble. You don't even have to bother to lock the office door. We can just forget about her!*

What about her younger sister, Linda?

I think the warning you gave her is sufficient. She will do nothing to jeopardize her older sister's safety. She will remain quiet and out of the way.

And now?

And now we go to the laboratory where the rest of the Rogers Group is gathered.

"They are all inside," said the secret policeman who was guarding the door of the laboratory when they came up. "All our men have been withdrawn and are stationed out of sight."

Tell him to hide himself then, came Trabzon's thought, *and we will remain here.*

You mean, you just want me to stand here outside the

door, asked Inspector Becket when his man had retired, *and do nothing?*

Keep quiet! I'm concentrating!

Gulping, Inspector Becket tried to blank his mind and stare thoughtlessly at the closed door before his face. In the laboratory on the other side of the door, the members of the Rogers Group were holding a hushed and worried conversation. Some of them were standing and others were sitting, while in the center of the group, Phil, his chest wrapped in bandages, was lying on a table.

"And that's the story," he was saying. "Under the circumstances, it was the only thing we could do. We only had a few minutes to get Dr. Griskell's body out of here and think of a story to cover the trail of blood which he had left."

The others nodded.

"Better not talk anymore," cautioned Elizabeth, examining the bandages which covered his torso. "You should be resting."

"The question now," spoke up Jerry, "is whether they believe the story you told them."

"We can't be sure yet," answered Dr. Fields. "They seem to be checking it from every possible angle."

"I've been worried about Valerie and Linda," said Eleanor quietly. "What do you suppose the secret police have done with them?"

As she spoke, she looked anxiously at the closed laboratory door. And on the other side, Trabzon told Inspector Becket: *You can go in now!*

Nodding, Inspector Becket opened the door and stepped into the laboratory, but no member of the Rogers Group took notice of him.

Phil was saying, "And that's the story. Under the circumstances, it was the only thing we could do. We only had a few minutes to get Dr. Griskell's body out of here and think of a story to cover the trail of blood which he had left."

The others nodded.

"Better not talk anymore," cautioned Elizabeth, examining the bandages which covered his torso. "You should be resting."

"The question now is whether they believe the story you told them."

It was Jerry who spoke and as he did so, Inspector Becket walked forward and stepped into their midst. They still did not notice him, and he was struck by the lifeless, unaware quality in their eyes. It was as if his presence was invisible to them. They went right on with their conversation as if he did not exist.

"They won't talk," Sid assured her. "Just look at the way they stood up for Eleanor when the secret police were going to break her leg."

Suddenly Inspector Becket snapped his fingers before Sid's face, but he still got no response. Puzzled, he examined the others.

"And that's the story," Phil was saying. "Under the circumstances, it was the only thing we could do. We only had a few minutes. . . ."

What have you done to them, Trabzon? asked Inspector Becket, bewildered. *Their conversation is going around in circles.*

For them, I have altered the awareness of time and circumstances, came Trabzon's cold thought. *They will relive this moment in time ad infinitum. Their thoughts and body movements are locked in a closed cycle. Their conversation will go around and around——*

What, interrupted Inspector Becket, *is your purpose in making them like this?*

I'm setting the stage, laughed Trabzon. *When Catherine Rogers returns, she will find things appearing normal, and by the time she realizes that they are not, we will have her. The trap will be sprung!*

But all this is not necessary! exclaimed Inspector Becket, feeling a sudden loathing for the thing in his mind. *We could have captured her and her companion without all this window dressing! No, Trabzon, I think you have done this horrible thing merely because you enjoy committing atrocities upon the minds of human beings!*

Trabzon laughed. *What you have seen is just a glimpse of the power I will someday exercise over all human beings.*

Chapter Six

"DID you see that?" asked Catherine, turning to Steve. They were standing in one of the tiny alcoves of the secret cavern. Before them was a vidphone, and she had just broken the connection after speaking to Valerie. The conversation with her younger sister had been a shocking experience, and there was a deep frown on her beautiful face which told how thoroughly shaken she was.

On Steve's face was a puzzled expression, and his eyes lingered on the telescreen, now blank, where only a moment before Valerie's face had been pictured.

"Her face fell!" he exclaimed, struggling to keep the shock out of his voice. "It was as if all of the life had suddenly gone out of her expression."

There was no life in her expression to begin with, came the Tisza's thought in both their minds. *Her vacant stare! Her deathlike expression! I recognized these details the moment her face came on the telescreen. She was mind-controlled! That's why I stopped you when you started to ask her if she was sick. I didn't want you to tip off Trabzon.*

"Trabzon!" Catherine exclaimed, her mind whirling with a confusion of half-formed fears. "I don't see what he would have to do with my sister!"

He's the only one who could make her like that, pointed out the Tisza. *The minute I saw her I knew that he must be nearby, somewhere out of range of the vidphone's telescanners, controlling her mind. I didn't want you to tip him off that you suspected that something was wrong.*

Catherine sighed, reluctantly accepting the Tisza's argument and the horror that went with it. "If Trabzon has my sister under his control——" She spoke out loud so that Steve could hear her end of the conversation. "——he must also have the other members of the Rogers Group under his control. They were all at the administration building when we left."

"How about the Five Company secret police?" asked Steve. "Since they must have arrived within minutes after we left, they have to figure in this somewhere."

The answer is obvious, projected the Tisza. *Just as I am concealed within Catherine's mind, Trabzon must be concealed within the mind of a secret policeman.*

"Probably one who is in command," said Catherine. "Otherwise, his actions would be restricted."

"Then all we have to do is find out who is in command," said Steve, "and we'll know where Trabzon's hiding."

"How would you suggest we go about finding out?" asked Catherine. "We can't go back and ask. From what Valerie said, I'd say that they were just waiting for us to show up."

"Well, we've got to do something," said Steve in sudden agitation. "We can't just stand by and leave our friends, the people we love, in the hands of someone like Trabzon!"

"We can't just walk into a trap either! That won't help them!"

"Hold it!" Steve held up his hand in a defensive gesture. "We're both scared and upset. Let's not bite off each other's head! What we need is a plan of action!"

Would you be willing to let me lead you against Trabzon? asked the Tisza. *I am young and inexperienced, but I have knowledge and abilities of which you would never dream.*

Catherine glanced at Steve. After a second, he nodded: "We'll follow you, Tisza," he said. "Just tell us what to do."

The first thing I suggest is that we pay a secret visit to the Rogers Group administration building.

"How can we possibly do that?" asked Steve. "They'll have every approach to the building watched."

We use the teleportation machine and teleport ourselves there, replied the Tisza. *I'll show you how to set the teleport screen and viewer.*

"The only trouble with that is," said Catherine, "once we get there we'll be stuck."

No we won't. The teleport screen works two ways.

63

"You don't need equipment at the other end?"

Not for any jump less than interstellar distances. The teleport screen, in effect, opens a doorway between two places in time and space—and that door remains open as long as the screen is activated.

"Then let's get started," said Catherine, and she and Steve walked over to the control console of the teleportation machine.

Now take a deep breath, thought the Tisza when she stood before it. *Let me take charge of your hands and fingers.*

Catherine did so, and suddenly her hands seemed to take on life of their own. She watched fascinated as, expertly, her hands began to manipulate the large control console, flipping switches, pressing buttons and adjusting dials. Involuntarily her eyes scanned the gages and returned to the small viewer inset into the center of the console's face. It came to life, lighting up. Steve gave a sudden gasp as, in detail, it pictured the activity taking place on a main street of their city.

"Why, that's Capital Avenue!" he exclaimed. "And it's as if you have a remote-controlled television camera right there on the scene above the street."

You don't have the necessary scientific backgrounds to enable you to understand just how this works, the Tisza projected apologetically, *so it would be useless for me to explain. I had to spend two weeks teaching Dr. Griskell a new system of mathematics before he could grasp the scientific concepts involved—and you know how brilliant he was.*

"You don't have to apologize, Tisza," said Catherine. "The knowledge that these machines can be understood by some human beings, if not others, keeps us from feeling inferior."

"I would say," said Steve, "that the purpose of this viewer is to enable the operator to see exactly where he is setting the teleport screen to teleport."

That's right. Otherwise the machine would be useless, unless you had exact coordinates worked out for each teleport. Without exact coordinates or without being able to see in advance just where you wish to teleport, you might end up anywhere: in space, under water, within the Earth or two miles above the surface.

64

"I suppose," said Steve, "that you just keep changing the settings on the control console until you see in the viewer that you are at the place where you wish to teleport?"

Right, answered the Tisza, and Catherine's hands moved competently over the control console. As she turned a set of dials, the scene on the viewer shifted down Capital Avenue, across a whole section of the city in seconds, through a vast suburb and finally came to rest on a bird's-eye view of the private rocket field of the Rogers Group. The administration building, the size of a doll house, filled one corner. *I did not have to ask you any questions,* the Tisza said to Catherine, *because I could simply read your memory and get the location of the administration building in relation to the rest of the city.*

"I understand," replied Catherine. "Do you want any help in selecting the exact spot within the ad building where it would be best to teleport?"

Yes, that's going to be a matter of judgment. From your memory, I have made myself intimately familiar with the interior of the building, but I think that we should use the viewer first and see where everyone is located inside.

"Good idea," agreed Catherine. She leaned over the control console again, her fingers adjusting an altitude position dial.

Promptly the scene on the viewer shifted, the private rocket field and the administration building growing larger as if the viewer were closing in on them with the zoom lens of a television camera. Abruptly they were inside the building, traveling along the main hallway. Again the scene shifted. It passed through a wall, and suddenly they were looking into one of the offices where a secret policeman was standing, peering through the crack of a slightly opened door into the vacant hallway.

"They're waiting for us all right!" exclaimed Steve. "I wonder where our friends are located?"

We'll see, replied the Tisza, and she caused Catherine's fingers to turn the horizontal position dial.

On the viewer the scene shifted again as room after room passed in view. They found Linda locked in one of the offices and watched her for a moment as she used a letter opener on the doorlock in an attempt to free herself.

Then they came to the office where Valerie was sitting, her body hunched forward, staring zombielike into space.

Seeing her younger sister like this, Catherine suddenly broke into tears and covered her face.

I think I can correct what Trabzon has done to her, consoled the Tisza, *but you must learn to expect things like this when dealing with Trabzon. If we're to have any hope of defeating him, you've got to keep an iron-willed control on your emotions.*

"I'm sorry that I broke down," said Catherine, dabbing her eyes with a handkerchief. "It's just so unthinkable that anyone would do that to a young girl."

"You know, the viewer feature of this teleportation machine could be used as a spy device," Steve pointed out in an attempt to get Catherine's mind off Valerie. "And as such, it could destroy civilization as we know it. No one would have any privacy. You could look right into people's houses, into their bedrooms and bathrooms. You could look into bank vaults and safe deposit boxes—into secret government laboratories and even see and photograph secret papers on the desks of highly placed government officials."

Dr. Griskell and I discussed that aspect of it, said the Tisza as she made Catherine's fingers send the viewer on through the administration building. *A device of this nature would definitely not be an advantage to human beings. It would undoubtedly be misused. Therefore, Dr. Griskell and I decided to destroy this particular feature of the machine after we had accomplished our purpose, and we designed in a destruct circuit. There is a destruct button on the control console which will destroy the viewer unit without harming the rest of the machine, and I intend to see that it is activated before I leave Earth. When I am gone, human beings can work out a standard set of teleport coordinates for this and any duplicate machines they may put into use.*

Steve nodded, but before he could answer, Catherine held up her hand for attention. "We've got our friends on the viewer," she said and pointed toward the viewscreen. The members of the Rogers Group were pictured in one of the rear laboratories, sitting or standing around Phil, who was lying on a table, his torso wrapped in bandages.

They seemed to be holding a conversation, and after several moments of observation, Steve said:

"I wish there was audio on this viewer. I can't put my finger on it, but there's something unnatural about them."

"We'll find out what it is when we get there," said Catherine. "Meanwhile let's have a look at the other laboratories. Then we can decide into what room we'll teleport."

Silently they studied the viewer. Minutes later, Steve said, "Well, now that we know where all the secret policemen are stationed, where do we go in?"

Why not enter at the office where Linda is locked? She may be able to give us information as to who is in charge of the secret police.

"The door of that office has been locked from the outside," Steve pointed out. "How do we get out of there into the hall without breaking it down?"

Locks are no problem for my psi abilities, replied the Tisza.

Steve nodded. "Good enough," he said. "Let's go!"

Just a moment, projected the Tisza. *Before I activate the teleport screen, there is a device over on the dais which we must get. I want to take it with us.*

"Which one is it?" asked Catherine as she and Steve turned and walked over to the dais which was covered with gleaming instruments and tools.

There, replied the Tisza, and she caused Catherine's hand to point out a gleaming oblong box with wires and clamps dangling from it.

"What is it?" asked Steve, picking it up and staring at it curiously.

It's a null-frequency impulser. Dr. Griskell and I designed it to meet the present contingency, and I'm going to base our plan of action on it.

As the Tisza "spoke," Catherine turned and started back toward the teleportation machine. Steve cradled the null-frequency impulser in his arms and followed. His mind was full of questions. When they reached the machine, Catherine leaned intently over the control console and her fingers, controlled by the Tisza, rapidly began flipping switches and adjusting dials. Immediately the scene on the viewer returned to the office where Linda was still trying to free herself by jimmying the lock on the office door with a letter opener.

I'll position the screen near the rear of the office behind the desk, projected the Tisza. *There, no one will accidentally stumble into it on that end and end up here.*

A few more twists of a combination of dials and the Tisza had the screen where she desired it. Then Catherine's finger reached and flipped an activation switch. Immediately, within the frame of electronic webbing, the teleport screen, a raw, vibrant sheet of coruscating energy, sprang into existence.

"What do we do?" asked Catherine, staring at it in wonderment. "Just walk through it?"

Yes, projected the Tisza. *It looks awesome, but it won't hurt you.*

In spite of the Tisza's assurance, Catherine and Steve approached the teleport screen with caution. Reaching it first, Steve paused and experimentally poked it with his finger. Except for a slight tingling sensation, nothing happened. Reassured, he withdrew his finger and saw that it was unharmed. Then, as Catherine came up beside him, he took a deep breath, stepped into the screen and disappeared. Catherine followed.

Instantaneously they were standing in an office of the Rogers Group administration building. Behind them was the coruscating screen of vibrant energy, appearing like a large, colorless curtain draped across the rear of the room. In front of them, Linda knelt at the door, prying at the woodwork around the lock with a letter opener.

"Linda!" Catherine exclaimed. Linda whirled— startled. Then she recognized her sister, and as Catherine stepped forward, her arms open, Linda gave a shout of joy and rushed into her arms. "There—there," Catherine soothed as they embraced. "I'm here now. Everything is going to be all right."

"He did something horrible to Valerie," cried Linda. "Then he took her away and locked me in here."

"Who is the 'he' you're referring to?" asked Steve.

"Inspector Becket," answered Linda, looking up at him. "He's in charge of the secret policemen who came here after you left. He brought Valerie and me in here to question us, and then he——"

They listened carefully as Linda told the story of what

had happened. When she had finished, the Tisza projected: *This Inspector Becket—he's our man. Trabzon must be hiding within his mind.*

A sudden, incredulous look crossed Linda's face, and Catherine, knowing it was because she could hear the Tisza's thoughts in her mind, said: "Don't be frightened. The 'person' you hear speaking in your mind is a friend."

"But where is she?" asked Linda, looking around the office. "I don't see anyone here."

"Well, let's just say that she's hidden right now," replied Catherine. She squeezed Linda reassuringly. "You can't see her, but she's here, and she's a friend. Okay?"

Linda nodded uncertainly, and Steve, setting the null-frequency impulser on the desk, walked over and examined the locked door. Then he straightened and asked, "What do we do now?"

We must get Inspector Becket into this office, answered the Tisza. *And once we get him here, we must hit him with something and knock him out.*

"You get him in here," said Steve, raising his fist, "and I'll knock him out."

You must do it with one blow, came the Tisza's thought. *And you must do it instantly before he realizes what is happening. Otherwise it will be useless!*

"Why is that?" asked Catherine. "What difference can it make?"

If Trabzon is concealed within Inspector Becket's mind, explained the Tisza, *and if he has been concealed there for some time, he has probably made himself comfortable. That is, he has probably established total contact with all of Inspector Becket's senses. Therefore, any sudden stimulus or shock which is experienced by Inspector Becket will also be experienced by Trabzon.*

"I see what you're getting at," said Steve. "You're saying that, if I can knock out Inspector Becket, the shock of the impact will travel along his nerves, reach Trabzon and knock him out also."

Yes, but you must hit Inspector Becket while he is relaxed and unaware of any threat. That is the only way that shock from the impact of your blow will catch Trabzon before he can break his connection with Inspector Becket's senses.

"What happens," asked Catherine, "after we've rendered Inspector Becket and Trabzon unconscious?"

Before either of them can regain consciousness, we must tie up Inspector Becket and connect the null-frequency impulser to his major nerve centers. By running null-frequency impulses into his body, along his nerve trunks, we can paralyze Trabzon and immobilize him.

"What about the other secret policemen?"

I can handle them, answered the Tisza. *Immobilizing Trabzon is what we have to worry about.*

"All right," said Steve, "let's get Inspector Becket in here so I can knock him out."

"How?" asked Catherine. "We can't just go out into the hallway and call him."

Let Linda go and find a secret policeman, projected the Tisza. *My psi senses tell me that the nearest one is hidden across the hall, four offices down. Have Linda bring him here, and I will hypnotize him and have him do what we want.*

"Linda," asked Catherine, looking down at her little sister, "are you up to it? Do you think you can get a secret policeman to come back to this office with you?"

Linda nodded eagerly. "I'll tell him that there's another secret policeman in here, and he wants to speak to him."

"No," said Steve. "They all probably know where all the others are stationed. Tell him—let's see——" Steve rubbed his chin. "Tell him that there's a fire in here—in the waste basket—and you need help to put it out. If your manner is urgent enough, he probably won't stop to ask you any questions."

"Suppose he calls other secret policemen?"

We'll have to take that chance, replied the Tisza. *Anyway, I can deal with all who come as long as Trabzon is not among them.*

"It's settled then," said Steve. "Tisza, unlock the door and let Linda out."

Click! The Tisza reached out with her psi power, and the lock turned. Steve opened the door, and Linda started down the hall.

Minutes later she was back leading a worried-looking secret policeman by the hand. "Where's the fire?" he was asking as he stepped into the office. Then, as the Tisza's psi power struck him, he froze dead in his tracks, his mind instantly slipping into a deep hypnotic trance. For a moment his eyes closed, and he swayed on his feet. Then they opened, and he looked directly at Catherine. "I'm at your service," he said. "What do you wish me to do?"

You will go to Inspector Becket, the Tisza projected.

"I will go to Inspector Becket," the secret policeman repeated.

You will inform him that there was a fire in this office— that the young girl whom he locked in here was badly burned—that she needs medical attention—and that he must come at once to see to her.

"I will inform him," repeated the secret policeman, "that there was a fire in this office—that the young girl whom he locked in here was badly burned—that she needs medical attention—and that he must come at once to see to her."

That is correct. You may go now! commanded the Tisza. Obediently the secret policeman turned, left the office and started down the hallway. *Now let us get ready!* The Tisza "spoke" to Catherine and Steve. *Our timing must be split-second perfect!* Under the Tisza's direction, Catherine's eyes went involuntarily to Steve. *I cannot express too strongly,* the thought entered his mind, *that you must knock out Inspector Becket before he has any inkling of what is really happening. Trabzon must not be given even one instant to disconnect himself from Inspector Becket's neurochannels! Otherwise, you may knock out Inspector Becket, but Trabzon will remain untouched. And in that event, we will all be doomed!*

Steve nodded and placed himself at a strategic point beside the door. Catherine and Linda stepped back against the wall where they would be out of sight of anyone entering the office. Then they waited quietly.

Several minutes passed and then the Tisza whispered softly in Catherine's mind: *They're coming down the hall now. Tell Steve to get ready!*

In response Catherine touched Steve's arm and motioned. A moment later the door opened and Inspector Becket strode into the office. "Where——?" He had just opened his mouth when Steve's fist smashed into the side of his jaw, and his body went sailing across the office like a limp, rag doll. It careened off a table and hit the wall

71

and slid limply to the floor. Instantly Steve dived and was on him, showering his chin with a series of lightning blows.

"That's enough, Steve!" yelled Catherine. "You'll kill him!"

He's out! projected the Tisza, *and so is Trabzon! Now you must hurry! Tie him up and connect the null-frequency impulser to his body! Trabzon won't remain unconscious for very long!*

Steve nodded, and hurriedly tied Inspector Becket's hands and feet. Then Catherine knelt beside him with the null-frequency impulser, which she immediately attached with deft fingers controlled by the Tisza.

That should do it, the Tisza projected when she had finished. Catherine's hand, under the Tisza's direction, reached over and clicked a switch on the impulser. Instantly the room was filled with a soft, steady hum, and within Catherine's mind, the Tisza seemed to sigh mentally. It was as if a tension within her mind, unnoticed before, had suddenly dissolved. *Now,* the Tisza projected, *as long as the null-frequency impulser is on, Trabzon will remain immobilized, powerless to do anyone any harm!*

"What about him?" Catherine indicated the secret policeman who had brought Inspector Becket to the office. He was standing in the doorway, staring trancelike straight ahead of him.

We still have a use for his services, answered the Tisza. Then she commanded the secret policeman: *You will go and round up your fellow officers and bring them to this office immediately. Tell them you are acting on Inspector Becket's orders.*

"I will go and round up my fellow officers and bring them to this office immediately," repeated the secret policeman. "I will tell them that I am acting on Inspector Becket's orders."

"What are you planning to do?" asked Catherine as the policeman turned and left.

I am going to hypnotize them and send them away, adding a harmless posthypnotic suggestion that they are to remember the present matter as being resolved.

"Good," said Catherine. "When you have done that, I would like to get the members of my group together so

72

that we can start on the construction of the space platform."

"And what about Inspector Becket and Trabzon in the interim?" asked Steve. "Are we going to keep this null-frequency impulser on them until the space platform and beacon are built and the Tisza's people have rescued her?"

"I was wondering about that myself," said Catherine before the Tisza could answer Steve. "What's the maximum length of time we can keep Trabzon immobilized without causing irreparable harm to Inspector Becket's body?"

The null-frequency impulser will have no effect at all upon the human body, replied the Tisza. *That's why it was necessary to tie Inspector Becket before applying it.*

"Then there's no problem," said Catherine to Steve. "We can put Inspector Becket into a bed and keep him under heavy sedation. That should give us time——"

Just then a large group of secret policemen appeared at the office door, and the full force of the Tisza's psi power suddenly beamed out and enveloped their minds. Instantly the entire group slipped into a hypnotic trance, and for several minutes the Tisza gave them commands at the deepest subconscious level. Then she withdrew, and with one accord, they turned and filed out of the building.

Now, projected the Tisza with satisfaction, *we can concentrate on righting whatever wrong Trabzon has perpetrated upon your friends.*

Chapter Seven

CATHERINE, Steve and Linda had barely left the office when Trabzon regained consciousness. The first thing he became aware of was the null-frequency impulses coursing through Inspector Becket's neurochannels and into the matrix of his own being. He tried to withdraw

73

from total contact with Inspector Becket's senses, but immediately he found the task impossible. The null-frequency impulses held him fast. He could not move the matrices he had embedded in Inspector Becket's mind.

Next he found that the force of his psi power was inhibited. He could still reach out with his mind and touch things. He could still sense phenomena, but he could exert no force of will upon what he sensed. He could not influence atomic particles or cause the molecular interaction which had previously enabled him to manipulate his environment. He was helpless.

By the time that Inspector Becket regained consciousness, he had examined the extent of his helplessness and he was furious. *Wake up, you fool!* Trabzon projected as Inspector Becket stirred and groaned. *We have no time to waste!*

"Where—where am I?" groaned Inspector Becket aloud. Then mentally: *What happened, Trabzon?*

We were tricked! That's what happened!

My head aches! My hands and feet are tied, and there's a strange machine attached to my body. What is it?

How do I know what it is? lashed Trabzon. *I'm not a scientist! I only know what it does. It renders me powerless! It's as if I were paralyzed! I cannot seem to gather my faculties together! I cannot exert force with my will!*

You are powerless——? Inspector Becket turned the thought over in his mind, and it tantalized him.

Fool! Trabzon lashed. *I can still read your mind. And what you fail to realize is that, if I fail, you will fail too! And I don't need to tell you what the members of your race will do to you if the truth ever comes to light!*

You're right, Trabzon. Instantly Inspector Becket repented. *I wasn't thinking straight. We need each other.*

Can you free yourself from your bonds?

Inspector Becket tried, vigorously wiggling his hands and straining at the bonds which held his wrists and feet. Finally, however, he was forced to give up and admit defeat. *No, Trabzon,* he thought, *my wrists and ankles are too tightly bound!*

Then we must try something else.

How long have we got?

Not long! Catherine Rogers and her companion, the man named Steve, are presently in the laboratory at the

74

rear of the building with the other members of the Rogers Group. The object of our search, the Tisza, is with them. I sense that she is undoing my work, she is re-altering their awareness to conform with reality.

If she's like you, that won't take long.

She is not like me. She is young, and her psi powers are not fully developed. She is not nearly as strong as I am. This fact will give us a little more time, but not much.

What is that? Inspector Becket suddenly inquired, and Trabzon saw from his mind that he meant the teleport screen, which coruscated with vibrant energy at the rear of the office.

He explained: *That is how they got into the building without our being aware of their presence. It is a teleport screen, and on the other side of it probably lies all of the wealth I have been promising you.*

Inspector Becket relaxed, thinking of the wealth which would accrue to him just from possessing whatever machine made the teleport screen possible.

This is no time for dreaming, Trabzon pointed out roughly, giving him a mental kick. *If we don't free ourselves before they return, our cause will be lost!*

What about the young girl Valerie? Inspector Becket suddenly asked. *Did they bring her mind back?*

No, not yet. They looked in on her, but apparently decided to leave that job till last. She's still sitting where we left her.

I was thinking, thought Inspector Becket, *if they take the time to make her normal again before they come back here, it will give us more time. Perhaps I can work free of these bonds by then.*

That's it! exclaimed Trabzon, snapping his mental fingers. *Why didn't I think of it before?*

What——?

Shut up and let me concentrate!

Obeying, Inspector Becket tried to blank his thoughts. At the same time, Trabzon reached out with his mind to the office down the hall where Valerie was sitting. He touched her mind, and she stirred. There was no force behind the exertion of his will, but he cajoled, he implored, he beseeched and he nudged at her until the small bubble of awareness—all that was left of her mind—responded to him. The vegetablelike hulk that was her

75

body moved, and like a zombie, she slowly rose from her seat and left the office where she had been sitting.

A few moments later she entered the office where Inspector Becket was tied. Zombielike, she fixed him with her eyes, and then haltingly she stepped toward him.

What the devil! Inspector Becket exclaimed, watching her as she approached. *Trabzon——*

Quiet, you fool! It's taken all I've got to get her this far, and you're disturbing my concentration.

"Sorry," Inspector Becket murmured aloud. He watched, fascinated, as Valerie stiffly knelt by his side and began fumbling with the knots at his wrists. Her eyes were vacant; her face was void of expression, and she worked slowly as if each movement of her fingers required a separate mental effort. At last Inspector Becket felt the bonds on his wrist loosen, and with a quick jerk of his arms, he freed his hands.

At once he sat up and began working on the bonds which held his ankles. Out of the corner of his eye he saw Valerie stiffly reach for a switch on the oblong box of the null-frequency impulser. Instantly he slapped her hand away, then pushed her backward away from him.

What are you doing? exclaimed Trabzon. *She was going to turn the machine off and free me*

I am perfectly aware of what she was going to do, Trabzon, answered Inspector Becket, getting back to the task of releasing his ankles.

I don't like what I see in your mind, projected Trabzon in a turmoil of emotion. *Don't be a fool!*

Don't worry, I'm not, Inspector Becket assured him as his ankles came free and he quickly snatched up the oblong box and scrambled to his feet. *If this machine renders you helpless, I would be a fool to turn it off. For the first time, I'm not at your mercy.*

We still need each other——

Not anymore!

You can't wear that machine around all the time, you know. Sooner or later you'll have to take it off, and you know what I'll do to you when you do.

Inspector Becket laughed at this and gathered up the slack in the wires which ran from the oblong box to points of contact on his head. Slender rods protruded from his scalp at three points, held in place by a strong adhesive on

76

the bottom of three suction-cuplike devices. He looked like an electronic monster with the wires stemming from his head down to the oblong box he cradled under his arm.

When we first met, Trabzon, he thought as he approached Valerie, who still lay where he had pushed her, *you told me that your time was limited. That if you failed to capture your queen, the Tisza, and mate with her within a certain length of time, your light would grow dim and expire—that you would die.*

Trabzon did not answer, but within his mind, Inspector Becket could feel a sudden surge of terrible and loathsome hatred directed toward himself. Laughing, he took Valerie by the arm and pulled her to her feet. *Okay, Trabzon,* he sneered, *don't answer! But I remember what you said, and I intend to keep you helpless—to wear this machine until you die!*

With that he started to shove Valerie toward the teleport screen at the rear of the office, but just then someone shouted from the office door and he whirled to see Steve charging him from behind. Instantly he dodged, flinging Valerie into Steve's path and made a desperate dash for the teleport screen.

"No, you don't!" yelled Steve. He dived past Valerie as she stumbled toward him and caught Inspector Becket by one foot. Then he dragged him to a halting stop and tried to throw him by twisting his foot. Lying on his belly, however, he could not secure traction for the effort, and Inspector Becket was able to pivot on his free leg and yank his foot loose.

Immediately Steve scrambled to his hands and knees, but before he could rise to his feet, Inspector Becket stepped forward and kicked him full in the face. His head snapped backward and his body somersaulted into the side of a nearby desk where he sprawled to the floor on his back, unconscious.

For a moment Inspector Becket sneered down at him. Then, still holding the null-frequency impulser cradled tightly under one arm, he calmly stepped into the vibrant screen of coruscating energy and disappeared.

THERE, it is done, projected the Tisza. The members of the Rogers Group who had been standing or sitting around Phil, holding a merry-go-round conversation, suddenly snapped out of the private world of altered awareness in which they had been trapped.

Immediately there was a chorus of exclamations and greetings as, all at once, they suddenly became aware of Catherine standing in their midst. This was followed by a period of confusion in which Catherine had to bring them up to date on all that had happened since she and Steve had left the building with Dr. Griskell's body.

First, she explained about the Tisza; then about Trabzon and the threat to Earth which he posed, and then she answered their questions, filling in the loose ends. Finally she said, "If the situation is clear in everybody's mind, I'd like to get the Tisza to fix Phil's chest."

"I've already done everything possible for him," said Elizabeth. "I don't see what else the Tisza can do."

"With her psi powers," replied Catherine as she walked over to the table where Phil lay on his back, looking up at them, "the Tisza can heal his chest wound completely."

I can if you will allow me, the Tisza projected suddenly. *Will you give me your permission?*

They all looked at Phil, and he blinked as the heard the Tisza's words in his mind. "You have my permission," he asserted finally, recovering from the shock of hearing the Tisza with his mind for the first time. "Anything would be better than the way I feel now."

Just relax then, projected the Tisza. For several minutes, they all stood around the table, silently looking down at Phil as the Tisza worked on the wound which ran diagonally across his chest and down into his lower rib cage. With her psi powers, she reached through the bandages covering his torso, into his body. By manipulating his regenerative glands, she speeded up his healing processes a thousand times beyond their normal rate. Within minutes the cut had healed, becoming only a thin, threadlike scar. Even this disappeared when the Tisza manipulated the atomic structure of Phil's skin along its length and caused the tissues to flow together.

Finally, she projected: *He is healed. You can remove his bandages!*

In sudden excitement Elizabeth began peeling away his bandages. Phil sat up, feeling himself and grinning with joy. "I don't feel any pain at all!" he exclaimed. "I'm well!"

"Good," said Catherine. "I'd like to go now and see about Valerie. Steve and I looked in on her on our way here, and she was in a pretty bad way!"

"Is there anything we can do?"

"No, the Tisza is the only one who can bring back her mind."

I suggest, projected the Tisza to them all generally, *that you get yourselves ready to travel. As soon as I'm finished with Valerie, we're going to teleport all of you to the secret cavern where we will begin construction of the space platform and beacon immediately.*

Barely had the Tisza finished projecting this thought when Valerie came through the laboratory door, walking as if she was in a daze, her eyes staring straight ahead and unseeing.

"Valerie!" Catherine exclaimed and rushed to her side. A moment later, everyone was milling around her and exclaiming in horror at her zombielike appearance.

Give her room to breathe, came the Tisza's thought in all their minds, *and allow me to do what I can to help her.*

Almost at once everyone calmed down and backed off, forming a small circle around her. Only Catherine remained close, holding her younger sister in her arms and cradling her head on her shoulder.

Meanwhile the Tisza reached out and probed her mind. Then, after a moment, she projected: *In order to free her id, I will have to probe very deeply into her subconscious mind. It's a very delicate operation and since I am not very skilled, will everyone please remain absolutely quiet so that I can concentrate.*

Instantly a hush settled over the group. Faces tensed and all eyes focused on Catherine and Valerie at the center of the circle. Everyone waited, while inside Valerie's mind, the Tizsa was conducting an intense search. In nameless directions her psi powers were probing the infinite matrix of energy and emotion, swirling around a vortex of Val-

79

erie's psyche. Within this mental essence, folded back upon itself and trapped in a morass of primordial fears, the Tisza uncovered Valeri's id. She freed it and then allowed it to feed back to reality along the thin tentacles of her psi force which penetrated the fabric of Valerie's mind. Then she withdrew, leaving Valerie mentally exhausted but conscious.

There, it is done, she projected at last. Almost immediately a normal expression returned to Valerie's features. Her body straightened; she lifted her head from Catherine's shoulder, and then, as if she was just waking from a long sleep, she looked questioningly at her older sister and the others around her.

"Hi!" she said. "Why is everybody standing around looking at me?"

"Oh, you're all right!" Catherine exclaimed, wept for a moment, and hugged her tightly. "Oh, thank God!"

A moment later, the others also were pressing close and expressing their happiness when the Tisza's thought came urgently into Catherine's mind: *Trabzon and Inspector Becket have escaped!*

But how could they? exclaimed Catherine, suddenly releasing Valerie. *Inspector Becket was securely tied!*

While I was bringing Valerie back to normal, I read her memory, answered the Tisza. *She untied Inspector Becket before wandering here into this room. Apparently, because of her condition, Trabzon was able to coax her into releasing him.*

But . . . But . . . Catherine's thoughts faltered . . . *Steve went back to the office to make sure that Inspector Becket was securely tied. If anything were wrong, he'd have come back and told us.*

I probed the office, came the Tisza's thought, *and my psi senses tell me that Inspector Becket and Trabzon are gone and that Steve is lying unconscious before the teleport screen.*

We'd better go see if he's badly injured! replied Catherine. Leaving the others still swarming around Valerie, she took Elizabeth, who had medical training, and hurried to the office where Steve lay unconscious.

"He's not too badly hurt," Elizabeth offered the opinion after examining his sprawled body. "He'll be out for a while, though. He was kicked in the forehead pretty hard!"

Catherine, who was standing before the teleport screen, gazing at it in deep thought, nodded. "Do what you can for him," she said to Elizabeth. Then she asked the Tisza: *You say you don't think that either Trabzon or Inspector Becket know how to turn off the teleportation machine?*

It's obvious that they don't, answered the Tisza, *because the teleport screen is still on. If they knew how to turn it off, they would have done so immediately to prevent us from following them into the secret cavern.*

Maybe it's another trap. Maybe they want us to follow them.

Trabzon doesn't have to waste time playing games like that. The moment he was free he could have captured us right here in the building without any trouble. That's why I don't think that he is free.

You mean you think that Inspector Becket left the null-frequency impulser connected to his body after Valerie had untied him—that he has left it on and is imprisoning Trabzon within his mind?

That's the impression I received from Valerie's memory—although due to her condition at the time, her perception of events is vague and not too trustworthy.

The null-frequency impulser is gone——

Yes, and that tends to back up my theory that Inspector Becket has left the impulser connected and in full operation—that he's keeping Trabzon immobilized.

I just wish that I could be sure of that, Catherine frowned the thought.

Well, consider that Inspector Becket is probably as terrified of Trabzon as we are, answered the Tisza. *He might have jumped at the chance to keep Trabzon powerless and, at the same time, acquire the wealth of the secret cavern. On the other hand, Trabzon is not primarily interested in the contents of the cavern. He wants to capture me so that he can mate with me and reproduce his own kind. If he were free, I think that would be the first thing on his list. Most certainly he would have tried to capture us before going into the secret cavern.*

Perhaps you are right, admitted Catherine. *If Steve were conscious, he would be able to tell us for sure.*

But he is not conscious, returned the Tisza urgently.

81

*And we can't wait for him to regain consciousness. In-
spector Becket may be attempting to turn off the teleport
screen this very instant; and if he fools with the control
console long enough, he may succeed—or, at the very
least, he may distort the teleport screen, making it impossible for us to follow him. We might be spattered all over
another time-space continuum.*

What do you suggest that we do?

*I suggest that we return to the secret cavern immediate-
ly. Step through the teleport screen before it dissolves, and
if Trabzon is still immobilized, I'll handle Inspector Becket. Afterward we can teleport back here and get your
friends.*

Catherine nodded, but it took her several moments to
gather up her courage. Grim-faced, she turned and said to
Elizabeth, who was giving Steve first aid: "There's something that I have to do, but there's no time to explain
now. Will you tell everyone that I said to remain here
until I return?"

Elizabeth looked up and nodded, wonderingly. "Sure,"
she said simply, and immediately Catherine turned,
stepped into the teleport screen, and disappeared.

Chapter Eight

AS Inspector Becket stepped through the teleport
screen into the secret cavern, he froze, staring in stunned
disbelief at the amazing and fantastic array of gleaming
tools, instruments and machines which met his eyes.

Now you see, projected Trabzon drily, *what would
have been all yours if you had continued to play ball with
me.*

It is going to be mine anyway, Trabzon! exclaimed
Inspector Becket. His emotions soared with a sudden
sense of wealth and power. *In spite of you, it is going to
be mine.*

I know—I know, projected Trabzon hurriedly. *And I want to help you to make it yours.*

Inspector Becket laughed and continued on down the aisle. *As you said before, Trabzon,* he thought, *you're not a scientist, and you don't know any more about these machines than I do.*

I know that the Tisza's purpose in having these machines built is to contact the people of my race so that they can come and rescue her from me.

But you don't know the specific purpose of each machine?

No, but from the presence of so many servomechanisms, I would guess that these machines have been designed to build some other machine which will actually do the job of contacting my people.

I don't see why your Tisza didn't attempt construction of an interstellar spaceship and be done with it. She obviously has the knowledge.

For her to have tried to do so would have been a fatal mistake. The construction of an interstellar spaceship could not have been concealed, and we would have been able to discover her whereabouts long before now.

Look! Inspector Becket suddenly pointed. They had come to the end of the aisle at the front of the cavern, and there, on a dais against one wall, lay the body of Dr. Griskell. *It looks like you were right, Trabzon,* he thought walking over to it. *Catherine Rogers and her companion did bring him here.*

Now maybe you'll listen to me. . .

Forget it, Trabzon!

What are you going to do now?

Turn off the teleportation machine before anyone else comes through the teleport screen.

I'm afraid it's too late for that. Someone has already followed you through the screen.

Who? Inspector Becket suddenly stopped cold in his tracks and began to look about him uncertainly. *You're not trying to trick me, Trabzon?*

No, my psi senses tell me that Catherine Rogers and the Tisza have just entered the cavern.

Accepting Trabzon's statement as true for the moment, Inspector Becket instantly dropped to a crouched position, switched the null-frequency impulser from his right arm to his left, and drew a large, pistollike laser cannon from an armpit holster. Stealthily he advanced down one of the aisles toward the teleportation machine.

Turn off this infernal machine and release me, came Trabzon's thought. *Alone, you will be no match for the Tisza.*

No! thought Inspector Becket as he crept forward. *I'm still not sure that this isn't just another trick to get me to free you.*

If you don't release me now, protested Trabzon furiously, *I will give you no further help.*

"Suit yourself," muttered Inspector Becket. His eyes narrowed as he caught a flash of motion near the end of the aisle at the rear of the cavern. Instantly he froze; then slowly he raised the laser cannon and took careful aim. He waited, and moments of tense inactivity passed. Finally, when he saw no other movement, he lowered the pistollike cannon and cautiously moved forward again.

He had taken only two steps, however, when the inside of his brain seemed to explode in a blaze of fire and an invisible hand knocked him to the floor. For an instant he was dazed; he recovered to find himself still clutching the null-frequency impulser under one arm and the laser cannon in his right hand. Automatically his finger tightened on the trigger as he scrambled unsteadily to his feet. By pure reflex action he came up shooting at a blur of motion which he caught out of the corner of his eye.

It was Catherine Rogers. But as he fired at her, she disappeared and instantaneously reappeared in another spot.

Astonished, he whirled to fire again. Before he could pull the trigger, another blaze of fire exploded in his brain. Again an invisible hand slammed him to the floor.

Once more he recovered almost immediately, the white-hot pain in his brain receding an instant after it had struck him down. Then, still clutching the null-frequency impulser as if his very life depended upon it, he struggled to his feet and began firing his laser cannon at Catherine Rogers as fast as she could teleport from one spot to another.

What is happening, Trabzon? he yelled the question in

his mind as he whirled this way and that, firing at her phantomlike figure.

Before Trabzon could answer, however, Catherine suddenly reappeared behind him. Again he was struck inside of his brain by a thunderbolt of agonizing pain, followed by the blow of an invisible hand which knocked him to the floor.

You can't win, came Trabzon's cold thought as he recovered, struggled back to his feet and resumed firing. *She will strike you down with a mental thunderbolt every time you give her a moment to get set after she teleports to a new spot.*

Then why don't you help me, Trabzon! he exclaimed. He was tiring quickly. As he pivoted, firing uselessly at Catherine as she teleported about, his reflexes were measurably slower. *At least,* he thought desperately, *you can prevent her from attacking my mind.*

I could, but I won't, answered Trabzon. *As long as I am going to remain a prisoner, it doesn't matter to me who wins!*

As Trabzon finished this thought, another thunderbolt of mental energy struck Inspector Becket and he was thrown to the floor, knocked senseless.

Now, the Tisza's thought came in Catherine's mind, *move quickly! Kick the laser cannon from his hands!*

Instantly Catherine responded and started for Inspector Becket. Before she could reach him, he rolled over and fired at her. The next thing she knew she was standing in another spot, and the laser beam was ricocheting harmlessly off a servomechanism's housing beyond the spot where she had been. Before she could orient herself to her new position, Inspector Becket was turning to fire at her again. For an instant she was looking down the barrel of his laser cannon, and then instantaneously she was standing in a new spot.

I can't reach him, she thought at the Tisza desperately. *He recovers too quickly after you knock him down.*

I'm hitting him as hard as I can, exclaimed the Tisza, teleporting her to another spot. *But you know that my psi powers are not yet fully developed.*

Can't you at least wrench the laser cannon from his hand?

Not and be instantly ready to teleport you to another

85

spot when he fires at you. Your safety must be my first consideration——

Suddenly the Tisza's thoughts broke off as Inspector Becket again fired his laser cannon and she instantly teleported Catherine to another spot. Promptly Inspector Becket whirled, but he was too slow. Before he could fire again, the Tisza reached out with her psi power and struck his mind another stunning blow. Immediately he crashed to the floor, but this time he was standing too close to one of the machines. As he fell, one of the null-frequency impulser rods protruding from his scalp struck the base of a machine and broke off.

At once the null-frequency impulses coursing through the neurochannels in his brain were interrupted, and simultaneously Trabzon was free. *I told you what I would do to you when I got loose,* he exclaimed. At the same instant he attacked Inspector Becket's life force and, with relish, began to feed upon it.

Inspector Becket clutched at his head, and as his life force was eaten away he screamed in agony. As he died, his body twisted convulsively and his arms and legs contorted into unnatural angles. His eyes sank into his skull, and the skin on his face withered to a pale, wrinkled mask of horror.

"Oh, my God!" exclaimed Catherine in sudden terror as she watched his death struggle. "Trabzon is loose!"

Yes, Trabzon is loose, came Trabzon's taunting thought. Simultaneously a tiny sphere of luminescence materialized on Inspector Becket's forehead and instantly streaked toward her. Before she could move, it struck her between the eyes and, like a bullet, penetrated her brain.

The instant that Trabzon entered her mind, the Tisza screamed horribly. She tried to escape, but Trabzon was too fast and too powerful. She tried to fight back, but he ruthlessly beat down her efforts to resist him. Then he took her; he raped her and, against her will, replenished his light from hers. She screamed and writhed in agony under his brutal assault.

Involuntarily Catherine screamed too. Grabbing her head, she fell to the floor where she thrashed about, her fingers clawing at her forehead as her mind was ravished and torn apart by the force of the struggle. White-hot pain

86

lashed her brain, and finally her mind exploded in a burst of unbearable pain. Then she slipped into unconsciousness and lay still, her face and body grotesquely contorted.

Chapter Nine

WHEN Catherine awoke, she felt as if her mind had been fragmented, as if it had been shattered into a thousand tiny fragments of disoriented thought. The secret cavern . . . Steve lying unconscious on the office floor . . . Trabzon loose . . . Dr. Griskell's body . . . Valerie's zombielike appearance . . . the Tisza's being raped. These fragments were like jagged pieces of a jumbled picture puzzle, all lying on the surface of her consciousness. Individually they drifted into the focus of her attention, only to recede before she could grasp their meaning. And, once gone, she was unable to remember what they had been.

She had no awareness of how long she had lain in this state when suddenly she felt something stir within the depths of her mind. Her head felt suddenly as if it were swelling to twice its normal size, as if, momentarily, it would explode. And then there came an intense roar; and from her forehead, thousands upon thousands of tiny, glowing spheres of yellow luminescence gushed forth, bubbling upward toward the ceiling of the cavern.

The stream of tiny, yellow spheres seemed endless, and before long the vast ceiling of the secret cavern was flooded with millions and millions of tiny, baby Triskellions.

Instinctively Catherine was filled with revulsion, and without conscious thought she tried to bring up her hands to stop the horrid flow. The effort caused her fingers to twitch, but her hands would not move. Her muscles were rigid; they would not respond to stimulus from her brain. She could not even scream when suddenly from the front of the cavern there came a tremendous explosion and the cavern was filled with an intense light. Then a shock wave

87

lifted her body and slammed her against the base of a machine, knocking her unconscious.

Hours later, when she regained consciousness a second time, the first thing of which she was aware was the Tisza crying within her mind. It was as if the sound of her sobs was coming to her from the depths of a deep nimbus of pain and grief. Her distress was so poignant that Catherine found herself reaching out to her, trying to comfort her just as if she was a human child, a little girl.

Turning inward, she found the Tisza as shattered as the fragments of her own mind which were haphazardly whirling in and out of her consciousness, and she tried to imagine the reason for such devastation of spirit. It was the first effort that she had made to think of the past, and at first she could stimulate no memory of the events which had brought her to the present. Her memory was a complete blank.

Dizziness came as she concentrated. Then with a concerted effort the jagged fragments of disoriented thought in her mind seemed to go into a whirl of motion. They formed a kaleidoscope of partial images. After what seemed an endless time, the images slowed and came together, forming a coherent whole. And the first dim memories of the fight with Inspector Becket, his death and then Trabzon's escape returned to her mind.

Her recovery was rapid after that, though she had no valid concept of how long she lay in the secret cavern, her body sandwiched in a small gap between an overturned servomechanism and a huge pressor beam generator. When finally she felt strong enough to move, she wiggled out of the hole and struggled to her feet. She moved unsteadily down one of the aisles formed by the machines. The first thing she encountered was Inspector Becket's body, lying face upward, his limbs twisted, his face withered beyond recognition.

Her shock at seeing his corpse in this condition was so great that she almost fainted. Only sheer will power kept her on her feet. Looking down at him, her memory returned and, for a moment, she relived the horror of Trabzon's escape and the subsequent rape of the Tisza.

The memory was so vivid that the Tisza, aroused by the appalling nature of the emotions she was experiencing, was forced to speak: *I'm sorry that I let you down,* came her weak thought. *I did everything that I could to resist Trabzon, but he was too strong for me.*

I don't blame you, Tisza, replied Catherine gently as she swayed wearily over Inspector Becket's body. Her miniskirt and blouse were torn and tattered, her golden-blond hair was tangled and mussed, and her beautiful face was smudged with dirt, yet she gave no thought to herself. Her concern was for the Tisza and the barbaric treatment she had received from Trabzon. *We have a few brutes like that among human beings too,* she thought, trying to comfort her.

While you don't blame me now, when you see the death and destruction that Trabzon and my offspring will wreak upon the Earth, you will hate me!

As the Tisza spoke, Catherine had been staggering unsteadily down the aisle, but now she stopped and gave her attention to what she was saying.

You mean that there were offspring from your union with Trabzon? she exclaimed. Suddenly a memory of the flood of tiny baby Triskellions which had bubbled from her forehead assailed her mind.

I had at least a hundred million offspring, the Tisza wept. *And Trabzon has taken them away with him. They will be under his influence, and you know what that means. They will never have a chance to learn right from wrong. They may even take after Trabzon and develop a craving for feeding on the life forces of human beings.*

The Tisza was almost hysterical. Catching some of her hysteria, Catherine looked upward, uselessly, around the ceiling of the cavern. There was no trace of the baby Triskellions who had bubbled from her forehead, and in a panic, she thought: *How long has it been, Tisza? How long was I unconscious?*

I don't know. I'm not old enough for the mating experience, and it was such a shock that I have been in a daze since it happened. I've lost all track of time.

So have I, thought Catherine, noting that her watch was smashed. *I don't blame you for that. . . . But how long will it take Trabzon to start your baby Triskellions to feeding upon the life forces of human beings?*

Just long enough for them to get hungry, cried the Tisza. *They're like all babies everywhere. They're growing and they're always hungry. Under normal circumstances, they would be confined in a nursery, and I would remain there with them, replenishing their lights from my own until they had grown beyond infancy.*

Well, thought Catherine regretfully as she started down the aisle again, moving unsteadily, *it's out of our hands now. The proper authorities will have to be notified. The people of Earth will have to be warned. I just hope that too much time hasn't passed since Trabzon took your offspring out of the cavern.*

Several moments after she had finished this thought, she reached the end of the aisle and came upon the teleportation machine. It was a complete wreck. The teleport screen was shut off, and the teleportation machine itself was shattered. Fused parts of it were scattered all over the floor.

Trabzon destroyed it, wept the Tisza. *When he forced entry into your mind, he forced me to tell him how to use the contents of this cavern to contact my people.*

But why did he destroy only the teleportation machine? If he knew what we intended to do, why did he leave the other machines intact?

Because he realized that the other machines would be useless without the teleportation machine to teleport them into orbit around the Earth!

I see, thought Catherine wearily. *Well, we can't use the teleportation machine to get back to the administration building either.* She brushed her mussed hair from her forehead and tried to think. Finally, she had an idea. *Tisza, can't you teleport me back to the administration building without the aid of the teleportation machine? You did it repeatedly when Inspector Becket was firing his laser cannon at me.*

Yes, but only over distances of several feet, and I'm afraid that is about the limit of my ability. I can teleport you over short distances, but my psi powers are not yet developed enough to teleport you over the several miles which would be necessary to get you back to the administration building.

Wait! exclaimed Catherine. *I can use the jetmobile that Steve and I used to first get here. It should still be in the elevator at the front of the cavern.*

If you just want to warn the authorities, you can also use the vidphone in the cavern's alcove.

90

Catherine turned and began moving wearily back down the aisle, stumbling from machine to machine. Now she paused. *How do you feel about that, Tisza? After all, they are your offspring—and, you know, if they begin killing people, the authorities on Earth will have to take action against them.*

They're all my children, and I love them just as you would love your children, the Tisza cried. *But it is human beings for whom I grieve because I know that there is nothing which you can do to stop their destruction.*

But we must try, Tisza. Even if we know that we're going to fail, we must try!

I agree, wept the Tisza, *because I know that is the nature of human beings.*

Then I can still count on your help?

That is something which you do not have to ask.

Well, then . . . Catherine was slightly embarrassed. *I'd better use that vidphone. . . .*

When Catherine reached the alcove, the first call she put through was to her friends at the administration building. After several minutes of futile ringing, it became obvious that no one was going to answer. A worried frown crossed her face. *I can't understand why they don't answer,* she thought to the Tisza. *There are extensions to the main phone all over the building.*

I can't offer an explanation, replied the Tisza. *But isn't there someone else you could call?*

Catherine thought for a moment. *Yes,* she replied finally, *I'm going to call General Anderson of the Space Patrol. He was a very good friend of my father's, and he will listen with an open mind to what I have to say.*

Quickly she broke the connection and dialed again. The vidphone rang on the other end, and shortly the face of a pretty, young woman appeared on the telescreen.

"Space Patrol headquarters."

"Hello," answered Catherine, "may I speak to General Anderson?"

"Who's calling, please?"

"Catherine Rogers."

"One moment, please." The face of the young woman disappeared from the screen, revealing a large office in which men and women were working at their desks. Beyond them stretched a row of partially opened windows,

91

showing a magnificent panorama of the city. But it was not the view which attracted Catherine's attention. Just then a small cloud of tiny, luminescent spheres came swarming in through the windows. Like angry wasps, they swept toward the men and women sitting at the desks. It happened so fast that Catherine was petrified with shock. Before she could cry out a warning, the face of the young woman reappeared on the telescreen, blocking out her view. "General Anderson is not in at the moment," she said cheerfully. "Would you care to leave a——"

Suddenly her words broke off, and a startled expression crossed her face. Her attention seemed to turn inward, and for an instant it was as if she could not imagine what was happening to her. Then suddenly, as if realizing that she was being attacked within her mind by some invisible force, she brought up her hands and frantically began to claw at her forehead. She screamed, and before Catherine's eyes, the skin on her face turned a bloodless white and then instantly began to wither until it resembled the skin of a dried prune, wrinkled over a horrid mask of death.

Only the fact that Catherine had seen the same thing happen to Inspector Becket when Trabzon had attacked him enabled her to keep her sanity. Even so, as the young woman's body convulsively pitched forward and the office again came into view, the sight that met her eyes was too horrible to look at. With a short scream, she threw her arms across her face and tried to shut it out.

Attacked by the tiny spheres of luminescence, the other men and women had risen from their desks and staggered in all directions. Clutching their foreheads, they screamed in agony as their life forces were sucked from their bodies. And after a moment, they collapsed to the floor, thrashing about, their eyes sinking into their heads and their limbs contorting in contrary directions. Gradually the office became still as one by one they died. When Catherine looked again, she saw that the skin on their faces was an ashy white and as withered as if they had aged a hundred years in the span of an instant.

Trembling uncontrollably, she broke the connection, blanking the telescreen. Instantly she dialed the central police station. "Did you see what happened, Tisza?" she wept aloud. "They were all killed—all killed!"

92

Suddenly her body slumped weakly. Quickly she grasped the vidphone console, leaning forward over it as a wave of nausea struck her in the pit of the stomach. Her knees gave way, but before she could fall, the Tisza reacted and sent tentacles of energy coursing along her nerves, invigorating certain motor centers of her brain. Then the Tisza adjusted the secretions of the glands which controlled Catherine's emotional output, balancing her endocrine flow to force a calming effect on her body.

Forgive me for tampering with your body without your permission, but it was necessary, the Tisza projected. *You were about to faint.*

I understand, answered Catherine as the nausea passed. *Thank you, Tisza. I needed something to stiffen my spine.* She felt much better. Her body had stopped its trembling, and as she straightened, a new strength flowed into her muscles. Suddenly she remembered that she had dialed the central police station, and immediately she realized that, for several minutes, the vidphone had been giving a busy signal. *I don't understand why they don't answer,* she frowned the thought. *The police switchboard is supposed to be unlimited.*

Wouldn't the busy signal indicate they were flooded with calls? asked the Tisza. *That there was an emergency?*

Yes, replied Catherine thoughtfully. *That fits. If the killing we just witnessed at the Space Patrol headquarters is general, people must be in a panic.*

What do you plan to do?

I don't know—but for a starter, we'll take the jetmobile and get back to the city as fast as we can!

When Catherine reached the front of the cavern where the elevator shaft was located, she received another shock. The whole front of the cavern had been blown out as if by a tremendous explosion, and the elevator shaft where the jetmobile had been was no more. All that was left of it was a tangled mass of steel, buried under mounds of rock and dirt. Where the elevator shaft had been, high up above the rubble, was a jagged hole, and through it, Catherine could see daylight.

Trabzon must be responsible for this, came the Tisza's thought. *Rather than bother with the elevator or take the time to teach my offspring to teleport themselves out of the cavern or how to dematerialize themselves sufficiently to enable them to pass through several feet of solid rock, he evidently used his psi powers to blast a way out of the cavern.*

Well, replied Catherine, examining the damage, *to get out of here, I'm going to have to go through the same hole that they went through. Only I don't see how I can climb up to it.*

Hold still, commanded the Tisza. *I'll teleport you out of the cavern!*

Chapter Ten

AN instant later Catherine stood on the surface, blinking in the bright, warm sunshine which, from a cloudless sky, flooded the grassy countryside. It was a beautiful day, so beautiful that she found it difficult to believe that only minutes before she had witnessed the horrible death of at least a score of people. And that Trabzon and the horde of baby Triskellions who had escaped from the cavern with him were real. But she knew they were and that the threat they posed to human beings was deadly. Before too many people were killed, some way to combat them had to be found.

Before she could refresh herself, she had to draw a bucketful from an old well in the center of the barnyard and carry it into the abandoned farmhouse. The instant that she had finished washing herself and tidying her clothes, she left the farmhouse and started walking. Taking the cow path which ran past the front porch, she walked until she came to the country lane which ran by the abandoned farm. She followed the narrow, paved road for more than five miles until it intersected with the main jetway into the city.

She had walked for almost an hour when she saw a man dressed like a farmer approaching her in the distance. As he came nearer she noticed that he kept glancing around at the sky and that he held his gun as if he was ready to shoot instantly at anything which threatened him.

When they came abreast of each other, he stopped and looked at her strangely. Without lowering his gun, he tipped his broad-brimmed straw hat and said, "If you're going into the city, Miss—don't! If I were you, I would turn around and head right back to wherever you came from. And I'd do it fast!"

"I live in the city," said Catherine. "I have to go there."

"Even if it means that the Thingamajigs will get you?"

"The Thingamajigs?" Catherine frowned. "You mean, the Triskellions?"

"The Thingamajigs—the Triskellions—the Gismos—call them whatever you like. If you've heard the radio, you know what's been happening. To go into the city voluntarily now is to commit suicide!"

"I haven't heard the radio," Catherine shook her head. "I've been out of touch."

"Out of touch?" the man exclaimed in astonishment. "I don't see how it's possible for anyone to have been out of touch. These Triskellions, as you call them, have been spreading all over the countryside like locusts. There are millions of them, and they kill human beings on sight in the most horrible way that you've ever seen . . . I tell you, there's no stopping them. They come through solid walls and locked doors to get at you just like they do through open windows. You can't hide from them because they seem to have some sense which tells them where you are—and you can't kill them because nothing seems to have any effect on them. Everything has been tried—fire, explosives, chemicals, bullets——"

"Then why are you carrying that shotgun?" Catherine interrupted him. "If it won't protect you against the Triskellions, it's useless."

"I'm not carrying it to fight Triskellions," answered the man. "This shotgun is for human monsters."

"I don't understand."

"Whenever you have a catastrophe," he explained patiently, "there are always some people who react like monsters—looters, scavengers, rapists, self-styled dictators, setting up their own brand of law and order—you name it. In this situation, you got it."

"But surely things aren't that bad," exclaimed Catherine. "Not bad enough to have a breakdown of law and order?"

"I don't know where you've been!" The man shook his head. Early this morning, this whole district was declared a disaster area. The army was moved in. People in the cities were ordered to report to military checkpoints for evacuation."

"Evacuation?" exclaimed Catherine. "You mean, all the cities in this district have been evacuated?"

"Would you please let me finish!" The man was impatient. When Catherine nodded apologetically, he continued, "after the army was moved in and evacuation of civilians was ordered, it was immediately discovered that any large concentration of human beings in one place attracted the Triskellions. For some reason, they seem to prefer killing human beings in large groups, rather than singly or in pairs. So, the 'report for evacuation order' was rescinded within an hour after it was broadcast. The people in the cities were ordered to stay off the streets and to avoid congregating in large groups. Even the army was broken up into the smallest units possible and scattered—after the Triskellions wiped out almost half of them!"

"But you indicated that law and order had broken down."

"It has. The moment that it was discovered that, because of the Triskellions, people had to remain apart—that they could not band together for protection—it became every man for himself. The lawless element immediately took advantage of the situation, and so far they've had a field day. They've disrupted everything: communications, distribution of food and medicine, transportation. They've made things a dozen times worse than they would be if it was just a struggle between man and Triskellions. That's why I warn you not to go into the city. It's certain death because, if the Triskellions don't get you, some human monster will!"

"I can take care of myself," Catherine assured him. "But I want to thank you for your concern—and the information you've given me. I appreciate it."

The man shrugged, pulled his straw hat lower over his forehead, and clamped his jaw stubbornly. "Then you're still going into the city?"

"Yes, and from what you've told me, it's more urgent now than ever that I get there while the situation is still localized within this district—before it spreads!"

The man shook his head, unconvinced. "I don't see what you can do one way or the other—except get yourself raped or killed." He scratched his head and looked over her beautiful body with a significant glance. "You obviously have a lot of courage, though."

"Well, thank you for the compliment," said Catherine as she backed away from him. Then she turned and hurried on her way.

"Good luck," he called after her, and then he sighed, turned and hurried on his own way.

Catherine continued hiking. After another hour, she came across a flamed-out jetcoupe which had skidded sideways to a stop in the manual lane of the jetway. Both doors were open and two people, a man and a woman, were lying several feet from the vehicle, face downward on the tarmac. Their bodies were grotesque. Catherine did not have to turn them over or kneel beside them and look closely to know that the skin on their faces was an ashy white and withered.

They have been dead about twenty hours, the Tisza informed her suddenly. *I can tell by the degree of decomposition which has taken place.*

Catherine nodded, scowling as she went over and examined the jetcoupe. *I can pretty well reconstruct what happened here,* she thought, fingering the buckle of one of the safety belts. *The man obviously lost control of the vehicle when they were attacked. . . .* Suddenly she hesitated.

When they were attacked by my offspring, the Tisza finished for her. *You don't have to be afraid of hurting my feelings.*

Catherine nodded gravely, then changed the subject as she made a quick examination of the control console. *I think I can restart this vehicle,* she thought. *The ignition cutoff is automatic, and the batteries haven't run down. She's still got plenty of juice left.*

Turn on the ignition then, and try it!

Nodding, Catherine leaned over the control manual and

97

turned the ignition key. Then she slapped the "hold" button on the brakes and pushed the starter. Instantly the sleek jet above the roof of the streamlined vehicle roared into flame, and then, as she eased off on the power, it settled down to a steady purr.

The engine sounds pretty good.

Catherine fastened her safety belt and released the "hold" button on the brakes. Instantly the jetcoupe leaped forward. Leaning over the steering console, she turned the steering rods and brought the front end around, letting the jetcoupe pick up speed on the swing. As it straightened out, she edged it over into the high-speed lane, aimed it straight down the jetway and "revved' the jet to a high, piercing whine. A moment later it was streaking toward the city like a bullet.

Since it will be several minutes before we reach our destination, came the Tisza's thought, *why don't you turn on the radio and see if it can give us any addtional information?*

Good idea, Catherine nodded and kicked in the automatic steering control. Then she turned on the radio and leaned back in her seat to listen. The excited voice of a newscaster exploded from the speaker:

". . . AVOID LARGE CROWDS WHEN REPORTING TO FOOD DISTRIBUTION CENTERS . . . AT ALL OTHER TIMES STAY OFF THE STREETS . . . ALL ROADS ARE BLOCKED, AND ALL SURFACE TRANSPORTATION WITHIN THE AFFECTED AREAS IS AT A STANDSTILL. ONLY THE TUBE CARS BELOW THE SURFACE WHERE THE TINY SPHERES OF LUMINESCENCE HAVE NOT YET PENETRATED ARE STILL IN OPERATION. . . MODIFIED MARTIAL LAW HAS BEEN DECLARED IN SOME CITIES, AND ALL LOOTERS ARE BEING SHOT ON SIGHT. . . . THE MILITARY ADVISES ALL CITIZENS TO REMAIN CALM, STAY INDOORS, AND KEEP ALL DOORS AND WINDOWS LOCKED!"

There was a sudden pause; then the announcer exclaimed, "HOLD IT! HERE IS A BULLETIN WHICH WAS JUST HANDED TO ME! IT IS NOW BELIEVED THAT THE STRANGE SPHERES OF LUMINESCENCE ARE ALIEN CREATURES FROM

ANOTHER PLANET WHO ARE TRYING TO CONQUER EARTH . . . AN ALIEN SPACESHIP IS REPORTED TO HAVE LANDED NEAR ANGEL CITY, THE CITY WHERE THE SPHERES WERE FIRST SPOTTED. THIS REPORT HAS NOT·YET BEEN CONFIRMED, BUT AUTHORITIES STILL BELIEVE ANGEL CITY TO BE THE FOCAL POINT OF THE ALIEN INVASION FROM SPACE. JUST A FEW HOURS AGO, THE SPACE PATROL HEADQUARTERS THERE WAS ATTACKED BY A SWARM OF LUMINESCENT SPHERES; AND IT IS BELIEVED IN RESPONSIBLE QUARTERS THAT TOP-SECRET MILITARY PAPERS WERE TAKEN——"

"Hysteria!" Catherine exclaimed. Yet, as she punched the preselector again, her hand trembled.

"Click—z-z-zip!" the selector indicator shot across the tuning dial. ". . . FOR THOSE WHO HAVE JUST TUNED IN," came another excited voice, "I REPEAT: EARTH HAS BEEN INVADED BY ALIEN CREATURES FROM ANOTHER PLANET. THE ALIEN CREATURES, NUMBERING IN THE MILLIONS, HAVE ESTABLISHED A BEACHHEAD OVER SEVERAL THOUSAND SQUARE MILES AND ARE RAPIDLY MOVING THE BOUNDARIES OF THEIR STRIKE AND KILL TERRITORY OUTWARD IN ALL DIRECTIONS. THEY ARE KNOWN TO SHOW NO MERCY TOWARD HUMAN BEINGS. THEY TAKE NO PRISONERS. THEY KILL EVERYONE THEY COME ACROSS AND THEY USE A SECRET WEAPON WHICH HAS NEVER BEFORE BEEN ENCOUNTERED BY OUR MILITARY. THIS WEAPON LEAVES THE FACES OF THEIR VICTIMS HORRIBLY SHRIVELED——"

Grimacing, Catherine tuned the station off the air and let the preselector search for another.

Under the circumstances, came the Tisza's thought, *I don't think you'll be able to pick up anything but a lot of false reports and wild speculation.*

There's nothing else you can expect, nodded Catherine. *Without reliable background information, they're bound to be confused—to draw the wrong conclusions. That's why we're needed. Even if there is no other way we can help, at least, we can give the authorities a clear picture—*

"... MOMENTS AGO," the radio speaker suddenly erupted, "A REPORT WHICH WAS GIVEN EARLIER IN THE DAY OVER THIS STATION WAS CONFIRMED. AS WE REPORTED EARLIER, A NOTED SPACE SCIENTIST HAS ACCUSED A GROUP OF HIS DISTINGUISHED COLLEAGUES OF CONSPIRING WITH THE ALIEN CREATURES TO INVADE AND CONQUER OUR EARTH. DR. BORIS PAULMAN, AN OUTSTANDING EXPERIMENTAL PHYSICIST, SAYS THAT HE WAS RECENTLY A MEMBER OF A SUPERSECRET SCIENTIFIC ORGANIZATION CALLED, 'THE INVENTORS.' HE MAINTAINS THAT THIS ORGANIZATION HAS BEEN IN LEAGUE WITH THESE ALIEN CREATURES FOR SOME TIME.

"DR. PAULMAN TELLS AS WEIRD A STORY AS HAS EVER BEEN HEARD BY THIS REPORTER. HE MAINTAINS THAT A SPACESHIP CARRYING THESE ALIEN CREATURES CRASHED ON EARTH SOME TIME AGO, THAT THESE ALIENS THEN APPROACHED CERTAIN SPACE SCIENTISTS AND OFFERED THEM WEALTH AND POWER IF THEY WOULD AGREE TO BETRAY THEIR FELLOW HUMAN BEINGS AND HELP THEM TO CONQUER EARTH.

"DR. PAULMAN ALLEGES THAT HIS FAMOUS COLLEAGUE DR. PAUL GRISKELL ACTED AS SPOKESMAN FOR THE ALIEN CREATURES AND SPEARHEADED THE PLOT TO CONQUER EARTH —BUT HE WAS LATER REPORTED KILLED BY THE FIVE COMPANY SECRET POLICE WHEN THEY DISCOVERED THE PLOT.

"SINCE EARLY THIS MORNING WHEN NEWS OF THIS PLOT WAS FIRST RELEASED, PEOPLE HAVE BEEN ATTACKING AND LYNCHING SPACE SCIENTISTS——

"HOLD IT!" suddenly screamed the reporter. "HERE'S ONE HOT OFF THE WIRE! JUST HALF AN HOUR AGO, A LARGE CROWD OF ENRAGED CITIZENS, ANGERED BY REPORTS OF SPACE SCIENTISTS IN LEAGUE WITH ALIEN CREA-

100

TURES TO CONQUER EARTH, ATTACKED THE WORLD-RENOWNED MASSACHUSETTS INSTI-TUTE OF SPACE SCIENCE. BUILDINGS HAVE BEEN SACKED AND BURNED——

"BUT WAIT—THAT'S NOT ALL! THE MOB WAS IN THE ACT OF LYNCHING THREE SPACE SCIEN-TISTS WHOM THEY HAD FOUND INSIDE ONE OF THE INSTITUTE BUILDINGS WHEN IT WAS ATTACKED BY A SWARM OF LUMINESCENT SPHERES. EVERY MAN AND WOMAN IN THAT MOB IS REPORTED TO HAVE BEEN KILLED——

"AND NOW ... GET THIS! SOME PEOPLE ARE CHARGING THAT THIS INCIDENT PROVIDES DEFINITE PROOF THAT ALL SPACE SCIENTISTS ARE IN LEAGUE WITH THE ALIEN CREATURES TO CONQUER EARTH! THEIR ARGUMENT IS THAT THE ALIEN CREATURES ATTACKED AND KILLED THE PEOPLE IN THE MOB IN AN AT-TEMPT TO RESCUE THE THREE SPACE SCIEN-TISTS WHO WERE BEING LYNCHED."

"How irrational can you get?" Catherine interrupted aloud and angrily reached out and punched the preselec-tor. Immediately it sought another station, and as the tun-ing indicator ran down the dial, she snorted, "I'll bet it's been broadcast a thousand times that the so-called 'alien creatures' are more likely to attack human beings when they are concentrated together in a large group than when they are alone."

Apparently nobody in that mob took it seriously.

That's right! So now they're all dead, and we have a bunch of crackpots trying to blame it on space scien-tists.

Suddenly, for no apparent reason, the Tisza cried: *Watch out!* And the warning cracked like a whip across Catherine's mind. Startled, she instinctively glanced around.

The jetcoupe was just entering the city—still on auto-matic guidance—and as it zoomed into and then streaked out of a curve, she caught a fleeting glimpse of the jetway ahead. They were coming into an area where the other side of the jetway leading out of the city was totally blocked by a dense cluster of jetmobiles stalled at crazy angles along its length. Inside some of the vehicles were sprawled the bodies of people whose withered faces left no doubt as to how they had died. The doors of other vehicles hung open, and the contorted bodies of men and women who had tried to flee before they were killed dotted the roadway.

In one terrible instant, Catherine realized what must have happened. She could imagine the mass exodus from the city which must have occurred immediately after the baby Triskellions had first attacked. But, at the same time, she was puzzled. There was no danger here—now. Therefore, this could not be what the Tisza had warned her against.

What then? she thought the question. Before an answer was forthcoming, she suddenly found that she was no longer riding in the jetcoupe. She was standing a hundred feet away at the base of a ramp which led off the jetway, and the jetcoupe, now driverless except for the automatics, was speeding on into the city. Above and behind it, in hot pursuit, was a large swarm of baby Triskellions. Even as she watched in shocked surprise, they swooped down upon it, penetrating the roof and darting in and out of its open windows like a huge swarm of stinging wasps.

They have attacked the jetmobile because they thought we were inside, came the Tisza's urgent thought. *Now they've discovered that we're not. In another moment, Trabzon will have figured out that I teleported you out.*

Trabzon? How did he find us? How could he know that we were in that jetcoupe?

Locating us would not have been difficult, replied the Tisza quickly. *Trabzon would simply have let my offspring do it for him. In their infant stage of development, they have a homing instinct which is almost infallible. It would lead them to me. All Trabzon had to do was order some of them to find me, and then follow.*

But why would he show up at this time?

I don't know. I was unable to get a glimpse of his intentions because he was trying to sneak up on us. To keep from being detected, he had his mind shield up.

He probably intends to kill me, Catherine guessed, feeling a sudden panic. *He wants to get me out of the way——*

No, replied the Tisza, *it's more likely that he wants to mate with me again.*

Is that possible? asked Catherine in wonder. *I mean, you indicated that you were too young. . . . And also, it's so soon after the first time.*

I know, moaned the Tisza, *but Trabzon doesn't care about that. And if he forces me to unite with him sexually, what can I do to resist him?*

Suddenly she started to sob, and Catherine, not having a ready answer with which to console her, felt a sense of helpless frustration. She knew that she had to do something to protect herself and the Tisza, but there was no time for her to formulate a plan of action. Already Trabzon had realized that she and the Tisza had teleported out of the jetcoupe. In the distance, as the jetcoupe disappeared into the man-made canyons formed by the city's tall buildings, the huge swarm of baby Triskellions was heading back down the jetway toward her. It had deployed into a two-pronged search pattern, flying about fifty feet above the ground and crisscrossing low over the narrow strips of grassland bordering both sides of the jetway.

She calculated that it would be a few minutes before they reached the base of the ramp where she was standing. Knowing that it would be fatal for her to run, she did not move. She was in plain sight, and surely any motion on her part would instantly attract their attention.

"What are we to do? asked Catherine hopelessly. The swarm of baby Triskellions was getting closer, and she could see no possibility of escape. Also, since she was in full view of them, she could not see why they had not already noticed her and come swarming at her head. She kept thinking that, at any moment, they would do so.

I'm shielding you—making you invisible to them, came the Tisza's thought. *And so far Trabzon has not detected the fact.*

In another minute they'll be right on top of us!

Look—I'm trying to find a way out of this. If you'll just keep quiet!

Sorry, Catherine thought. Then after a moment: *Tisza— you said that it's probable that Trabzon wants to mate with you again. Why?*

He probably wants me to give him another hundred million baby Triskellions.

103

Are you capable of reproduction on that level so soon after your first mating?

Quite capable, replied the Tisza matter of factly. *In fact, during my lifetime, I will produce somewhere around thirty-two billion offspring.*

Incredulous, Catherine whistled mentally. *But you mustn't, Tisza*, she exclaimed suddenly. *You absolutely must not let Trabzon mate with you again. I shudder when I think of the consequences to mankind—another horde of baby Triskellions unleashed upon the Eearth!*

Yes, it's obvious by now that Trabzon intends to take over the world and use the life forces of human beings as a source of food. To do so with impunity, however, he knows that he must pull out all the stops—go all the way and completely conquer this whole world. And then he must go on to conquer mankind everywhere that it has established a foothold in space.

Somehow, we've got to stop him, Tisza!

I realize that as much as you do! Do you think that I want my offspring perverted to murder innocent people, even people of a different race?

I didn't mean to suggest that you did——

Hold it! An idea just occurred to me. Do you remember the null-frequency impulser?

Yes, its impulses nullified Trabzon's psi powers.

Right! Now suppose we were to build a sort of skullcap—a helmet made of wire screening or meshwork.

Yes! Catherine exclaimed eagerly. *I think that I understand what you're getting at. You want to attach a null-frequency impulser to a helmet made of wire meshwork——*

Yes—and have you wear it—and run null-frequency impulses through it——

I see! Then Trabzon would not be able to penetrate the null-frequency impulses in the screen. If I were wearing one, he wouldn't be able to get into my mind—at you. And that would mean, he couldn't mate with you.

Right!

Oh, Tisza—that's it! I think you've got it!

Don't be happy yet. We still have to build the helmet for you to wear—and another null-frequency impulser to attach it to. And before we can do that, we first have to escape!

Catherine's heart fell. The Tisza was right. They would first have to escape. At the moment, escape seemed impossible. They had been detected by Trabzon and the huge swarm of baby Triskellions. Above her head, they were closing ranks. They knew where she was. They darted about and spiraled and crisscrossed above her like a giant cloud of glowing electrons.

Individually each baby Triskellion was a small, glowing ball of luminescence, indistinguishable from every other. Yet, looking up at them as they swarmed above her head, their darting gyrations like some medieval dance of death, she was fascinated in spite of herself. Vaguely she found herself wondering which one was Trabzon, and instinctively she set herself against the agonizing pain she knew would come the moment that he invaded her mind and attacked the Tisza.

Just at the moment that the cloud of baby Triskellions started to descend and engulf her, the Tisza's thought came suddenly into her mind: *Here's what I've been waiting for!* Instantly the swirling cloud of baby Triskellions, the jetway, the city and the surrounding suburbs all disappeared from view to be simultaneously replaced by the interior of a tube car.

She was seated in a deserted tube car speeding through one of the tunnel complexes far beneath the city, but the transition was so sudden that for a moment she could not comprehend what had happened. Her mind was frozen, and though she did not realize it, her fear of Trabzon and the baby Triskellions had been so great that it took several moments of just sitting and watching the interior of the tunnel flash by through the tube-car window before she was able to recover her wits. A smile spread slowly over her beautiful face and joyously she exclaimed, *Tisza! Oh, Tisza, you did it! You saved us!*

Yes, the Tisza responded with a warm glow. *Right from the first my psi powers told me that there was a tube-car tunnel about a hundred feet below the spot where you were standing. Then I remembered that the radio in the jetcoupe had reported that the tube cars were still running—that they were the only form of transportation in operation. I prayed that this was still true; and before teleporting, I waited until a tube car came along. Unless one had, we would never have succeeded in escaping, you know. Trabzon could easily have followed us, except for the fact that, by the time he uses his psi powers to trace where we have teleported to, we'll no longer be there. We'll be halfway across the city.*

Chapter Eleven

"IS this what you want?" asked Patricia, the Rogers Group's electronic expert, as she rose from the sprawling electronic workbench in her laboratory on the second floor of the Rogers Group Administration Building. In one hand she held a wire-mesh skullcap which looked like a Trojan helmet, and in the other she held a small oblong box with a shoulder harness attached. Along the rear surface of the box sprouted a series of coils, and between the helmet and the box ran a complex of wires that made the whole affair look like a cross between an electrodynamometer and a miniature encephalograph.

That's it, projected the Tisza, and Catherine took the helmet from Patricia and quickly fitted it over her beautiful blond head. Then she turned her back and Patricia helped her slip into the harness that secured the small oblong box to her back.

"The switch to turn on the null-frequency impulser field is inside the helmet," said Patricia. "That way the Tisza can turn it on and off at will. Also, Trabzon will be unable to use his psi powers to turn it off—once it's on."

I'll say thank you now, projected the Tisza, *because after I turn on the null-frequency impulser and the wire mesh of the helmet is saturated with null-frequency impulses, I will be inside the impulser field and my only contact with the outside world will be through Catherine's senses. I will also have to speak through her since my telepathic powers will not penetrate the field.*

"I understand, perfectly," answered Patricia nodding. "The helmet's impulser field will prevent Trabzon from

106

reaching you or using his psi powers against you; but it will also prevent you from using your psi powers to communicate with or effect matter, energy or other phenomenon outside the field."

Right! replied the Tisza. Then she snapped on the impulser; and for a moment, as the null-frequency impulses surged into the helmet, Catherine felt a weird sensation inside her head. Then it went away and within her mind the Tisza said, *Now that I am fully protected against being forced to mate with Trabzon, you can breathe easier.*

Yes, answered Catherine, feeling truly relieved and thankful, *and the whole human race can breathe easier, too.*

"Catherine," Patricia motioned to attract her attention. Then, as she reseated herself at the spacious electronic workbench, she said, "You know, while I was building this null-frequency impulser and the wire-mesh helmet, I was thinking that the null-frequency helmet can be used for another purpose besides protecting the Tisza."

"What?"

Patricia pointed at her own head. "Do you remember when you got back to the administration building from the secret cavern?" she asked. "You found all of us hiding in the concrete storeroom in the basement."

"Yes." Catherine nodded. "You had been hiding down there since the baby Triskellions first attacked the city. That's why I wasn't able to get you when I called you on the vidphone from the secret cavern."

"Yes, we were hiding down there because we thought, with all that concrete surrounding us, it was the safest place to hide from the baby Triskellions. That was before we learned that they could dematerialize and pass through solid matter or teleport themselves into or out of any place they wanted to."

Catherine shook her head. "The psi powers of the baby Triskellions aren't sufficiently developed yet so that they can do those things with ease. So, all in all, I would say that your hiding in the basement storeroom was the wisest thing you could do. While it would not have protected you had Trabzon or any baby Triskellions come across you, its remoteness probably saved you from being discovered in the first place."

"Well," said Patricia, "the point is: now I've got a choice. I can either go back into hiding with the rest of our friends down in the basement—or I can build another null-frequency helmet like the one that you're wearing. Only this one will be for me to wear!"

"What good will your wearing a helmet do?"

"The answer to that question is as plain as the nose on your face," said Patricia impatiently. "If Trabzon is unable to penetrate the null-frequency impulses flowing through the helmet for the purpose of attacking the Tisza sexually and mating with her—then he will also be unable to penetrate it for the purpose of feeding upon the life force of the wearer. That means that anyone wearing a null-frequency helmet——"

"—will be safe from either Trabzon or the baby Triskellions!" Catherine finished for her and struck her forehead with the palm of her hand. "Why didn't I see that before?"

"Because you've been so distressed over the problem of preventing Trabzon from mating with the Tisza," replied Patricia, "that you didn't recognize the larger implications. In the state of mind you were in, it never occurred to you that the null-frequency helmet could be produced in quantity and distributed to all human beings to wear as protection against Trabzon and the baby Triskellions."

Catherine nodded agreement. "How long will it take you to build enough of them so that each of our friends has one to wear?"

"Hummm——" Patricia screwed up her pretty face in thought. "The rest of the day, anyway," she said after a moment. "Maybe less time if I can get some of the others to help. I'll go down into the basement and see——"

"I don't want anyone risking his life unnecessarily," Catherine interrupted. "Everyone who isn't absolutely needed to help you should stay in hiding until the helmets are ready."

"Are you still afraid that Trabzon and a swarm of baby Triskellions might show up, looking for the Tisza?"

"Yes, he won't have given up his idea of mating with her just because we escaped from him. He'll come looking for us. He knows the location of this building, and he probably will figure we headed this way. Chances are, he's on his way here now."

"Then I'd better get busy!" Patricia jumped from her chair before the electronic workbench and started for the door.

Catherine stopped her. "How about these schematics on the null-frequency helmet?" She pointed to a sheaf of papers Patricia had drawn under the Tisza's direction. "Do you still need them?"

"No!" Patricia pointed at her head. "I've memorized them."

"Then, if I take them with me, you can build a null-frequency helmet without them?"

"Yes, but where are you going?"

"To see if I can't get the authorities to begin mass-producing the helmet for distribution to the public. We can't keep this thing to ourselves, you know."

"I didn't figure we could. The problem is: How are you going to convince anyone in authority that the null-frequency helmet really is a protection against the Triskellions. The way they're being pressed by the mass murder of human beings, they're frantic. They won't be in any mood to listen to a proposal that they have to learn a new science to understand."

"I realize that, but I figure that, if I can contact General Anderson of the Space Patrol, he'll listen. He's scientifically oriented. He's broad-minded, and he knows that I'm not a crackpot. Besides that, he bucks a lot of weight in the upper echelons of the World Government. If I can convince him——"

"——Then he can convince the World Government." Patricia took the thought away from her. Then she frowned. "You still have the task of locating him, though," she said. "And, right now, he might be anywhere—even in space."

"I know. That's why I'm going to try to locate him on the vidphone first."

"Then why go out? You can use the one downstairs."

"No!" Catherine shook her head. "I want to get away from this building before Trabzon breaks in here looking for Tisza. As long as I'm here, there is that danger. But if I leave, there is a good chance I can decoy Trabzon away from here while you make enough null-frequency helmets for all our friends. After that, it won't matter."

Patricia nodded. "Well, if you're going outside," she

said, and turning, went back to the workbench, "you'd better take this with you."

"What——?" Catherine wondered. When Patricia reached the workbench, she pulled a laser cannon from a niche in the bench where it rested and handed it to Catherine. For a moment, Catherine turned it over in her hands, staring at it. Then she asked, "Where did you get this?"

"Someone left it here for me to fix, and it's been lying around collecting dust ever since." Patricia waved off the question as if it were unimportant. Turning back to the workbench, she rummaged in a drawer and came up with a power pack and a holster. "It's just a medium-caliber sports model," she said. "Deadly—but not as ugly as the heavy-duty variety."

Catherine nodded, jamming home the power pack. Then she slipped the laser cannon into the holster and buckled it to her side. "Well," she said, "I won't use it unless I have to. Now, I had better get started. Will you come to the door with me, and lock it after I leave?"

"Yes!" Patricia followed her downstairs to the glass-paneled doors at the entrance of the main hallway and let her out. Then she locked the doors, and turning, started back the way she had come.

Meantime, standing on the outside steps, Catherine formed a question in her mind for the Tisza: *Can you switch off the null-frequency helmet long enough for your offspring to get a fix on you?* she asked. *If they're nearby, I want them to sense that we're no longer in the ad building—that we're moving away from it.*

I can switch it off all right, came the Tisza's answer, *but doing so will be extremely dangerous.*

Just for a few minutes, Tisza!

All right, I'm switching it off now, replied the Tisza, *but while it's off, I'll have to keep a constant lookout for Trabzon. He'll sneak up on us again if he can. And you know what would happen if, in spite of all our precautions, he somehow managed to get to me—say by teleporting himself into your mind from a distance where we failed to detect him.*

As Catherine walked across the private rocket field away from the administration building, her lips formed a

110

surprised, "Oh!" and her mind formed the exclamation: *I never thought of that!*

Neither has Trabzon, replied the Tisza, *but he might. He certainly has to try and figure out some way to get inside of your mind before I can manage to teleport you away again as I did before.*

Catherine nodded. *Well,* she answered, *right now the only thing I'm going to worry about is contacting General Anderson.*

Ahead of her, just beyond the fence surrounding the perimeter of the private rocket field was a public vidphone. When she reached it, she immediately entered and dialed Space Patrol Headquarters. There was no answer; and after a minute, she cut the connection and dialed General Anderson's personal residence.

"General Anderson is not at home," the robot monitor answered her query; "you may leave a message!"

"This is urgent!" Catherine snapped impatiently. "Can you tell me where he can be reached?"

"General Anderson's whereabouts is classified information," answered the robot monitor. "You may leave a message, and he will contact you when he returns."

"Oh, never mind," snapped Catherine. "There isn't time for that!"

Peeved, she broke the connection, and the Tisza asked: *What are you going to do now?*

Try the spaceport! Angrily Catherine put the proper coins into the pay slot and dialed again. A few tense moments later, the telescreen lit up and a pretty young woman in military uniform stared out at her.

"Yes——?" she began. When she saw the Trojanlike helmet on Catherine's head, her face suddenly took on a startled expression.

"May I speak to General Anderson?" Catherine gave her no time to dwell on the oddity. "This is an emergency!"

The tone of her voice brought back the woman's attention, but she still looked startled as she asked for Catherine's name and, receiving it, disappeared from the telescreen.

She had been gone only a moment, however, when the Tisza suddenly switched Catherine's null-frequency helmet back on, and then exclaimed: *Trabzon's here!*

111

"Where——?" Catherine blurted, but before the Tisza could answer, she had whirled and was looking from the door of the booth. Instantly she saw the huge, swirling cloud of baby Triskellions directly above her. They were descending upon the vidphone booth like a swarm of angry wasps. Frantically she turned back to the vidphone. "Hello! Hello!" she called, jiggling the switch of the vid-sender.

"Yes——?" The military operator reappeared.

"What's the delay?" Catherine demanded. "Why hasn't my call to General Anderson gone through?"

The expression of the military operator remained incredulous at the sight of Catherine's helmet, but she answered calmly: "We are trying to locate General Anderson now. Would you please be patient?"

"My call must reach him immediately!" exclaimed Catherine. "It is gravely urgent that I reach him! General Anderson knows me personally, and he'll——"

Before she could finish her sentence, the swarm of baby Triskellions penetrated the glass door, ceiling and walls of the vidphone booth, swirling around her head like a miniature cyclone.

Stand still! ordered the Tisza. *They can't hurt you!*

Simultaneously the military operator, seeing the baby Triskellions swarming into the vidphone booth on her telescreen, threw her hands up to her face and screamed. At the same moment, Catherine, who had closed her eyes as she was engulfed by Triskellions, realized that they were not hurting her and exclaimed: *It works, Tisza! The null-frequency helmet works!*

Certainly it works, replied the Tisza. *As long as the null-frequency impulses are flowing through the helmet, no Triskellion can penetrate the field it generates to do you harm!*

And you're safe, too, thought Catherine. *Trabzon cannot mate with you.*

That's right!

"You're not dead!" the military operator at the spaceport exclaimed over the vidphone. "Those alien things have no effect upon you! They haven't killed you!"

"No!" Suddenly Catherine raised her hand and tried to brush aside some of the swarming Triskellions so that she

112

could see the telescreen more clearly. She wanted to explain to the woman at the spaceport about the null-frequency helmet, but before she could speak, her hand began to burn with a white-hot, agonizing pain. Instantly she gave a short scream, snatched it back, and exclaimed, "They burned me!"

I told you not to move, scolded the Tisza. *Naturally they're going to try to hurt you if you stick your hand outside the secondary null-frequency field which spills over from the primary field around your head and serves to protect your body!*

"Catherine! Catherine Rogers!" the vidphone speaker suddenly erupted with the gruff voice of General Anderson. On the telescreen, his stern face replaced that of the military operator. "What's going on——?" Suddenly, as he saw the baby Triskellions swarming around Catherine's helmeted head, his mouth fell open in astonishment.

"Sir!" Catherine leaned forward through the swarm of baby Treskellions until her nose almost touched the telescreen. "I have been trying to get in touch with you. I have a perfect defense against the Triskellions—something that will keep them from killing human beings!"

"By Triskellions, I assume that you mean those Gismos which are swarming around your head," answered General Anderson, and leaning forward, he watched with a growing sense of excitement. "It's obvious that you have something," he said, his eyes narrowing. "Otherwise you would be dead."

"Well, General Anderson—sir! I didn't plan this demonstration, but it will save me the trouble of convincing you that what I have really works."

"Suppose you tell me about it."

"Do you see the helmet I'm wearing?" General Anderson nodded. "Well, it's a device which generates a null-frequency impulse field which surrounds my head and, to a lesser extent, my body. It prevents the Gismos, as you call them, from harming me. I have some plans here——" Catherine reached into her tunic and brought out a roll of papers. "—which detail how this device can be built." Careful to keep her hand close to her body, she held up the papers. "I'd like to deliver them to you in person and give you some background information on the Gismos."

"Wait a minute!" For a moment General Anderson

113

leaned off the telescreen and spoke to someone out of sight. Then his face came back on. "No," he shook his head at Catherine, "no matter how much I'd like to, I can't risk having you come here. Those Gismos just might follow you, and no one here has any protection against them."

Catherine nodded. "I understand," she said, "but how will I get these plans to you?"

"A photographer will be here any moment. When he comes, you hold the papers up to the vidscanner lens one by one, and he'll photograph them on this end right off the telescreen."

Oh no, he won't! The small, vidphone booth was suddenly filled with Trabzon's stark cold thought projection. It could not penetrate the null-frequency impulse field to Catherine's mind, but the resonance of the projection off her null-frequency helmet allowed her to hear it as a subvocalization in her inner ear. She was so startled that she dropped the roll of papers.

General Anderson, observing her reaction, exclaimed, "Catherine—what's wrong?"

Before she could answer, a small sphere of yellow luminescence—it was Trabzon—detached itself from the swarm of baby Triskellions which swirled around her head and gyrated toward the vidphone. Instantly the vidphone console glowed with an eerie luster. Then suddenly it exploded in a burst of intense heat. Her body was lifted as if by a huge, invisible hand, slammed through the glass wall of the vidphone booth and, like a rag doll, flung several feet into the street.

Hang onto the null-frequency helmet, the Tisza fairly screamed in her mind. *It's slipping off.*

Instantly, as she flew through the air, Catherine responded, and reaching up, she grabbed her helmet. Then she hit the ground, rolling. She was unhurt, and the moment that her body came to a standstill, she scrambled back to her feet. She had just reached her knees when the cloud of angry Triskellions swarmed out of the booth and engulfed her again.

What happened, Tisza? she cried, ignoring them. *The vidphone exploded.*

Yes, Trabzon used his psi powers to disrupt the subatomic structure of the matter of which it was composed.

114

As a result, a minute amount of energy was instantaneously released, and the whole works exploded. You were caught in the backlash and thrown out of the booth. It's fortunate that you weren't hurt. And it's even more fortunate that you were able to stop the null-frequency helmet from flying off your head.

That's true, admitted Catherine, *but Trabzon was still able to stop me from letting General Anderson get photographs of the plans for building the helmet.*

She had risen to her feet, and adjusting the laser cannon strapped to her waist, walked over to the wrecked vidphone booth. She leaned over and, reaching down into the twisted metal and shattered glass, retrieved the roll of papers Patricia had given her. They were now a blackened roll of ash.

Trabzon must have set it on fire after you dropped it, came the Tisza's thought. *But, don't worry, if your General Anderson has any electronic experts on his staff, I can easily explain how the null-frequency helmet is built.*

That would be reassuring, except for one thing, complained Catherine. *Now that Trabzon knows what we're up to, he will never let us get away with it. If we head for the spaceport now, he will only follow—and you know what the result of that would be: General Anderson and everyone near him would become victims of Trabzon and the baby Triskellions. They would be killed long before you could explain anything to them.*

I have another idea, replied the Tisza. *Why not find another vidphone and call your friends at the administration building. When someone answers, try to get them to realize what the situation here is without Trabzon catching on to what you're trying to do. See if you can get the idea across to them that they must get the necessary information about the null-frequency helmet to General Anderson—while you continue to act as a decoy.*

That might work, agreed Catherine, and spinning on her toes, she turned and headed down the street which bordered on the private rocket field. The cloud of baby Triskellions followed her and continued to swirl around her head and shoulders. Fortunately the street was deserted, and hence, no one else was threatened. She reached the nearest intersection without encountering anyone whose life her approach might have endangered.

115

Why are they sticking so close to me? she asked the Tisza. *Surely they know by now that they can't penetrate the null-frequency impulse field either to reach you or to harm me.*

Yes, they know it. But Trabzon is not stupid. He also knows that as long as he and my offspring are close, I don't dare switch off the null-frequency helmet even for a moment. That means, in most instances of trouble, I would be powerless to aid you.

Then Trabzon must be planning some kind of trouble, observed Catherine as she entered the public vidphone at the intersection. She dropped the necessary coins in the toll slot and dialed the administration building.

A few moments later, Patricia's face appeared on the telescreen. "What——?" she started; then she saw the Triskellions swarming around Catherine's head and shoulders, and she stared in shock.

Immediately Catherine leaned her face close to the vidlens pickup on her end. "It's me—Catherine," she said. "Don't be alarmed! These Triskellions can't hurt me."

"T-T-The helmet works," stuttered Patricia, still staring in shock at the swarm of baby Triskellions.

Catherine nodded quickly. "Listen," she said. "I'm glad that I got you——" She paused to think of a way to put her thoughts which would keep Trabzon in the dark as to the true purpose of her call. "Do you," she emphasized her words carefully, "understand the predicament I'm in?"

For a moment Patricia stared at the telescreen blankly. Then comprehension began to fill her face, and she nodded slowly, asking guardedly: "You've accomplished your mission?"

Catherine shook her head. "Not all of it," she replied and made a face at Patricia which was intended to indicate the Triskellions who were swarming around her. "Because of——" for a moment she paused, "ah—circumstances, I can't deliver your message to—ah—my friend."

Patricia's eyes narrowed while she searched her mind for Catherine's meaning. Then when understanding came, it again showed all over her face. "Well," she spoke

116

cautiously, "in view of—circumstances—ah—what are your plans?"

"I was hoping that you could do something——"

Watch out! the Tisza suddenly screamed in Catherine's mind. In the same instant, Catherine saw a tiny sphere of luminescence leave the swirling swarm of Triskellions and gyrate toward the vidphone. She dived for the door of the booth, and as she passed through it, there came the muffled thud of an explosion.

Down! screamed the Tisza. *Get down!* And Catherine dived for the ground just in time to escape being peppered with the splinters of glass which saturated the area. Then, as she scrambled back to her feet to look with dismay at the shattered vidphone booth, the swarm of baby Triskellions came swirling around her head and shoulders again.

That was close, Catherine said to the Tisza and bent over to brush the dirt from her miniskirt and tunic. *If you hadn't warned me, I'd have been caught flatfooted again.*

I was surprised that Trabzon let you go on as long as he did! exclaimed the Tisza. *You weren't very circumspect, you know.*

Catherine shrugged. *I just wish that he had given me a moment longer before he blew up that vidphone. I don't think that I really got anything across to Patricia. . . . And that puts us right back where we started.*

You don't really know, yet, the Tisza disagreed. *You'll just have to continue acting as a decoy and hope that your friends will do some thinking on their own.*

Catherine nodded. *One thing I can be happy about,* she thought. *As long as Trabzon is preoccupied with the problem of getting into my mind so that he can mate with you, he won't be out leading large swarms of baby Triskellions into attacks upon human beings.*

The Tisza agreed, and just then Catherine chanced to look up. She saw, plunging down upon her from the top of a skyscraper which towered above her, a huge, oblong stone. It had apparently been torn loose from one of the building's ledges high above the street. Seen from beneath, as she gazed upward in shocked surprise, in an instant it swelled in size until it was suddenly so big that it blotted out the whole sky. And so close—just an instant away—

that she barely had time to realize that she was going to die, that it was going to crush her to death.

Then suddenly something happened inside her body. She experienced a sudden wrenching of her nervous system. She blinked. And then looking up, she saw that the huge stone was suddenly no longer rushing down upon her. It was floating down, its rate of descent so gradual that it could barely be seen to fall.

I've accelerated your perception of and reaction to external phenomena many thousands of times their normal rate, came the Tisza's thought. *The block of stone appears to you to be falling slowly because your own bodily functions and movements are now thousands of times faster than normal.*

Catherine nodded in astonishment and experimentally reached up and caressed the underside of the huge stone as it slowly fell toward her. Then she pressed the palms of her hands against it, trying to stop its descent.

You can't do it, advised the Tisza. *No matter how slowly the stone appears to you to be falling, its mass is the same and the laws of inertia have not changed. In fact, if you don't get out from under it while you can, it will crush you to a pulp just as it would have under normal circumstances.*

Don't worry, Tisza, I'm getting out from under it right now, Catherine assured her. Suddenly she noticed a tiny sphere of bright, yellow luminescence to the side of the large stone, following it down. *Tisza,* she cried in horror, *that's Trabzon following the stone down. He's trying to kill us!*

No, he's trying to kill you, the Tisza corrected her. *I cannot be killed by any material object in this world. But Trabzon knows that, if he kills you, I will be forced to depart from your mind. And in that event, the null-frequency helmet would be useless to me as a defense against him. So, in order to bring about your death, he must have used his psi powers to dislodge part of the stone ledge bordering the top of this building and directed it to fall on you.*

Catherine nodded and casually stepped out from under the descending stone. Then she started off down the street, but she had only moved several feet when the Tisza suddenly warned her: *Brace yourself!* And simultaneously

118

she again felt a violent wrenching of her nervous system. Instantly the huge stone, which had been moving slowly, almost imperceptibly downward, seemed to pick up speed and flash earthward faster than her eyes could follow. It smashed into the sidewalk with a loud, explosive crash.

In spite of herself, she jumped and then ducked as bits of flying stone and concrete splattered in all directions. Simultaneously, even before the noise of the stone's fall had died away, the Tisza was exclaiming: *We'd better get out of here! Trabzon has disappeared from where he was, and that means that he is up to some new mischief.*

Catherine looked where she had last seen the lone sphere of bright yellow luminescence. It was gone, but she did not take time to look around to see where it might have gone to. Immediately she turned and started to run down the sidewalk, all the time keeping a close watch overhead so that she would be instantly aware of anything which broke loose from any of the tall buildings towering above her. Her heart beat tensely. She experienced some fear; but most of all, she was very determined that Trabzon would not catch her off guard in the same manner twice.

Above and behind her, but keeping their distance, the huge cloud of baby Triskellions swarmed after her, swirling angrily like a bunch of unstable atoms around the nucleus of a runaway molecule. Still, Catherine paid them no attention because she knew that it was not they whom she had to fear. The real danger was from Trabzon, and as she ran, she kept her eyes peeled for any sign of his next attempt on her life.

She had run about half a city block when the sidewalk in front of her erupted in a series of little explosions, forming a double line of bullet holes across her path.

Down! shouted the Tisza. *Someone is firing an automatic weapon at you!*

"Oh my God!" exclaimed Catherine aloud. Skidding to a halt, she threw herself against the facade of a deserted drugstore and crouched.

"Rat-at-at-tat-tat-tat!" The bullets whizzed over her head and shattered the large plate glass window behind her. Then the firing stopped and instantly she sprinted for another position.

"Rat-at-at-tat-tat-tat!" Immediately the firing began

119

again; and this time she had to dive into the doorway of a haberdashery to escape the hail of bullets.

Try to see where it's coming from, the Tisza urged when the firing had stopped again and Catherine was able to stick her head out from behind the corner of the doorway to peer up and down the steel and glass walls of the man-made canyon of tall buildings which surrounded her.

There were no living persons in sight. From where she was crouched, the whole city seemed quiet and deserted. She knew that this was because of the fear generated by the Triskellions. On both sides of the jet-thoroughfare, most of the stores and ground-floor showcases had been wrecked and looted. Although the street itself was flooded with sunshine, the interiors of all the stores and buildings were dark.

Here and there a stalled jetmobile sat silent, turned at various crazy angles to the main jet-thoroughfare. Some of their doors hung open, and all their passengers either lay dead inside or on the street nearby, their faces shriveled. These people had had their life force sucked out of their bodies by the Triskellions, but they were not the only casualties. Catherine noticed that occasionally there was another type of corpse, lying sprawled on the sidewalk or draped half in and half out of a shattered store window. And she knew that these people had either been shot by the military as looters or by some sniper hiding in one of the dim recesses of the towering office buildings.

Like the sniper who was firing at her now. The sound of gunfire from his last burst was still echoing in her ears, but she had failed to locate his exact position. All she knew was that he was somewhere above her on the opposite side of the street. And, except for a small corner, the doorway in which she was hiding was almost directly open to his line of fire. She was, she realized suddenly, hopelessly trapped.

No, you're not, the Tisza disagreed, reading her thoughts. *Zombies are poor shots.*

I don't understand you, Tisza. Do you think that this sniper is a zombie?

With my offspring swarming around in the middle of the jet-thoroughfare, replied the Tisza, *do you think that*

120

any human being in his right mind would stick around just for the pleasure of sniping at somebody?

Catherine shook her head. *No!*

You're darn right he wouldn't. The minute any normal human being saw a Triskellion, he'd run for his life. The mere fact that this sniper is sticking around means that Trabzon has made him into a zombie and is controlling his mind—making him shoot at you.

Well, be that as it may, I still don't see how that changes the situation.

Zombies are poor shots, repeated the Tisza. *Their reactions are too slow. Do you think that you could have dodged machinegun bullets as you did had the sniper been a normal human being?*

I suppose not, Catherine admitted, *but even so, it was close.*

Well, you can't remain here! The Tisza sounded impatient. *You can't outwait a zombie. Besides, Trabzon may capture other human beings, turn them into mindless zombies and send them after you. That's why you've got to risk moving now. Keep Trabzon off balance if you can.*

Why don't you accelerate my body movements several thousands times as you did before? asked Catherine. *If you did, escaping from this sniper would be no problem.*

I would, except that your body cannot sustain such accelerated action for longer than a few seconds—and even then, not repeatedly. You would die of sheer exhaustion.

Well, then, we'll just have to try something else.

Let him fire at you again. Then at the exact moment that he stops, make a dash across the jet-thoroughfare. You should be able to reach the cover of one of those stalled jetmobiles before he can react and start firing again. Then repeat the performance.

"Rat-at-at-tat-tat-tat!" The Tisza's thoughts were interrupted by the sniper's gunfire, and Catherine ducked for cover just in time to keep the top of her head from being shot off. Her body tensed, she waited, crouching, until the hail of bullets ceased.

Now! the Tisza suddenly shouted in Catherine's mind. Instantly she rose and sprinted across the jet-thoroughfare.

She had crossed the sidewalk and was just leaving the curb when, instead of the sniper's automatic fire, she heard a jet engine cough and roar into flame. Out of the corner of her eye, she saw one of the stalled jetmobiles swing toward her. As it came, it picked up speed. In shock, her mouth fell open as she observed that it was driverless. There was no one inside, but positioned several feet above its hood and traveling along with it was a tiny sphere of luminescence. She instantly guessed who it was, and this brought her to a full stop directly in the jetmobile's path.

For Space sake, screamed the Tisza, *don't stop running! That's Trabzon controlling that jetmobile, and he's trying to run you down! Don't make it easy for him!*

I'm not! Catherine's answer was immediate. *But you can't accelerate my body, and I can't outrun or dodge this jetmobile—therefore. . . .* Suddenly the laser cannon which had been holstered at her side was in her hand, and she was firing at the right front tire of the jetmobile. *I have only one hope,* she thought at the Tisza, and simultaneously she marveled at the fact that she was facing death so calmly, without a trace of fear. Her nerves were rock steady, and her aim was good.

Suddenly the jetmobile's right front tire exploded in a blowout. Instantly the jetmobile swerved, sluing sideways and skidding toward her, then veering off at an angle to crash into the curb and careen into the front of a wrecked and looted drugstore. The tiny sphere of luminescence which had been speeding along above its hood, veered away and rose toward the upper stories of one of the office buildings towering above her. It disappeared into one of the windows, and immediately the Tisza yelled:

Trabzon is going back to his zombie sniper. You'd better find cover before he can get him to start firing at you again.

Right! answered Catherine. Holstering the laser cannon, she sprinted the rest of the way across the jet-thoroughfare to the sidewalk on the same side of the street as the sniper. Then she pressed up against the store fronts, where he could not get a clear shot at her, and edged down the street until she was beyond his range.

Above her, the swarm of baby Triskellions followed, but kept its distance.

Keep your eyes open, warned the Tisza, *and stay alert!*

My nerves won't take much more of this, replied Catherine. *They're at the breaking point now.*

Don't worry about your nerves, soothed the Tisza. *I'm helping you in that department by depressing your reactions to fear stimuli——*

The Tisza's thoughts suddenly broke off. At that moment, however, Catherine was passing the mouth of a small alleyway, and her attention was centered above and ahead of her. She did not perceive, therefore, that there was anything unusual in the Tisza's sudden silence.

A moment passed; and then: *Watch out!* the Tisza screamed. It was so sudden that Catherine froze in her tracks. At the same time, looking down the alley, she saw a huge Doberman pinscher, teeth flashing in the bright sunlight, bearing down on her at a full, loping run. She also noticed that several feet above its head and speeding along behind it was a tiny sphere of luminescence.

It's a zombie dog, came the Tisza's frantic thought. *Trabzon's controlling its mind!*

There was no time for Catherine to react to the information, however, because the Doberman was already springing into the air. And, in another instant, it would be at her throat. She was grasping at her laser cannon; but even as she clutched the handle and drew it, she realized that she would be unable to raise it in time and fire. The most she could do was throw up her free arm and shield her face just before she was struck in the chest by the full weight of the Doberman and sent flying backward as its teeth flashed toward her throat.

Chapter Twelve

ONE instant Patricia was talking to Catherine Rogers on the vidphone and watching her face on the telescreen as a cloud of baby Triskellions swarmed around her head.

The next instant she was staring in open-mouthed aston-ishment as on her telescreen she saw a tiny sphere of bright, yellow luminescence detach itself from the main cloud swarming around Catherine's head and flash toward the vidphone console. Then she saw Catherine suddenly turn and dash out of the booth. A moment later, she saw the vidphone on Catherine's end flash in the first brilliance of an explosion an instant before her own telescreen went blank.

After this happened, she stood there for a long mo-ment, staring at the blank telescreen and thinking. Then she reached down and, from the desk in front of her, picked up the device which she had intended to show to Catherine. It was a long, riflelike affair, with a series of coils protruding vertically from several points along its barrel and a short, electronic wire running from its stock.

Experimentally she sighted along its barrel. She aimed at a spot above the doorway of the office where she was standing and slowly squeezed the trigger.

"Hey! Be careful with that thing!" exclaimed Steve as he entered the office. He was carrying a null-frequency helmet and back pack for Patricia, and he placed them on the desk in front of her.

At once she lowered the riflelike device and smiled up at him. "Has everyone else been taken care of?" she asked.

"Yes," nodded Steve. "You insisted on being last, but now everyone else has one."

"Thanks for bringing mine down, then," said Patricia, and she placed the riflelike device on the desk beside her helmet. "How many extras did they manage to make from the materials we had on hand?"

"Two," answered Steve as he helped her slip into the harness of the null-frequency back pack. Then he adjusted the shoulder straps so that they fitted snugly.

Patricia reached inside the helmet and turned on the impulser by flipping a small switch. Then she slipped the helmet over her head, and when she had secured it, she picked up the riflelike affair again and, for a moment, hefted it in her hands.

"What is it?" asked Steve. "It looks like a cross between

a telescopic, high-velocity sporting rifle and a frustrated electronic radar antenna."

Making a face, Patricia handed it to him. "It's a null-frequency rifle," she explained as he fingered it. "You see this cord here?" She held up the end of the electric cord which came out of the rifle's stock. "You plug it into the null-frequency pack here——" She demonstrated by reaching behind him and plugging the cord into his pack. "That activates the rifle."

"And what do I shoot with it once it's activated?"

"Triskellions, silly," Patricia exclaimed as if it was obvious. "You point it at a Triskellion and pull the trigger. That sends an intensified null-frequency impulse charge out of the barrel here——" She tapped the tip of the solid barrel. "When the charge hits a Triskellion, it should knock him out—perhaps even kill him."

"You aren't sure which?"

"No—the entire principle of the null-frequency rifle is new to me. It involves several new unique concepts in science which I never dreamed existed. In fact, it was just an accident that I was able to figure out this much all by myself. Something the Tisza said involving null-frequency science gave me a clue. Still, I'll have to talk with the Tisza again before I can be absolutely sure that I'm right."

"You know what this means, don't you—if this rifle works?"

"Certainly! That's why I left you and the others to work on the helmets—while I worked on the rifle. I figured the risk was worth it." She reached out her hand and caressed the rifle stock. "If it works, it means that we'll not only have protection against Trabzon and the baby Triskellions by virtue of the null-frequency helmets. . . . But the rifle will allow us also to take aggressive action against the Triskellions."

Steve nodded and started to speak. Just then, the vidphone above the desk rang, and Patricia, excusing herself, reached across the desk to answer it.

"Hello!"

In answer the telescreen lit up and the face of a young woman appeared. "Rogers Group administration building?" she asked, but before Patricia could reply, her image

125

faded and the rough-hewn features of General Anderson came on.

"Who is this?" he asked gruffly.

Patricia stepped closer, smiling. "Patricia Gerhardt here, General Anderson," she said quickly. "Can I help you, sir?"

"Haven't we met before?" General Anderson peered closely at her out of the telescreen. "It seems to me——"

"We met briefly on one occasion, sir," Patricia interrupted him. "At a scientific exhibit on space——"

General Anderson nodded, remembering. "Yes—Gerhardt—you are that electronics expert who won world acclaim a few years ago."

"That's me," Patricia agreed embarrassed. "And this is Steve Hollie, sir." She reached back and pulled Steve forward. "He's my fiancé."

"What's that?" General Anderson pointed to the null-frequency rifle Steve was still holding in his hands, and immediately Steve held it up to the vidscanner lens so that he could see it better. Patricia explained what it was and what she hoped it would do.

"I already know about the null-frequency helmets you are wearing." General Anderson nodded toward the helmets on their heads. "Catherine Rogers explained that to me—but she was cut off. The vidphone on her end exploded."

"Yes, sir," said Patricia. "She called here a few minutes ago and tried to tell me about speaking with you. She suggested that I try to contact you in her stead. Then the same thing happened as with your call—her vidphone exploded."

"Have you an explanation?"

"Yes, sir, but I'll have to fill you in with a lot of background information before you will find it believable."

"Young lady——" General Anderson held up a stack of reports and then let them flutter back to his desk. "—Do you realize what is happening in the world right at this very minute?"

"I've been listening to the emergency radio stations, sir," replied Patricia. "I have a pretty good idea of what the Triskellions are doing. I know that they are indiscrimi-

126

nately killing everyone they come across—and that they have a large area of the world in virtual terror."

"Then you should also know that I'm prepared to listen to any explanation, explore any avenue of solution—no matter how fantastic—if it will lead to a means of defense or a way of fighting these Gismos."

"Well—all right," said Patricia. "I was thinking that the Gismos, as you call them, blew up the vidphone which Catherine was using to prevent her from getting information to you about the null-frequency helmet."

General Anderson nodded. "From what I could see on the telescreen," he said, "the Gismos could not harm her, so apparently the helmet which she was wearing worked. It is a defense against the Triskellions."

"Yes, sir," nodded Patricia, "it works—and it is a defense!"

"You haven't tested the null-frequency rifle, though?"

"No, sir, but I'm confident that it will work, also."

"Humm——" General Anderson scratched his chin and thought for a moment. "Do you have the plans and specifications for these null-frequency devices ready, so that, if we decide to, we can begin to put them into mass production immediately?"

"No, sir. There was only one set of blueprints. That was for the null-frequency helmet and Catherine Rogers has those. As for the null-frequency rifle, the blueprints are all in my head. I haven't had a chance to put anything down."

"Oh——" General Anderson sounded disappointed. "I was hoping that you'd have something on paper so that I could have it photographed right off the telescreen."

"No, sir, but if you'll tell us where you are, we can come there and bring the rifle and a couple of spare helmets and show your scientific people how these devices can be built."

General Anderson thought for a moment. "No," he said finally. "The way things are, anything could happen to you on your way here. These devices are too important to risk losing because adequate security wasn't provided. Therefore, I am immediately dispatching a Space Patrol jetcopter to pick you up and bring you here. In the meantime, you will remain where you are until it arrives. . . . Understood?"

"Yes, sir," answered Patricia respectfully. Ten minutes later, standing downstairs in the main hallway with the other members of the Rogers Group, she and Steve watched as a medium-sized Space Patrol jetcopter landed on the tarmac of the private rocket field outside, and General Anderson emerged and walked toward the building.

Eleanor and Dr. Fields went out to meet him and escort him into the building. "I didn't realize that you were coming yourself, sir," said Patricia when the others had all been introduced.

General Anderson rubbed his chin. "Never was much good at just sitting behind a desk," he answered. "I've always been an action man, and this may be the action that I've been waiting for. Up until now, nothing else has done any good."

"I don't think that you'll be disappointed this time," said Patricia. "I would advise, however, that you and your pilot each put on a null-frequency helmet just in case we run into a swarm of Triskellions before we get where we're going."

General Anderson agreed and immediately Dr. Fields brought forward one of the extra null-frequency back packs. When General Anderson had put it on and the shoulder straps had been adjusted, Eleanor clicked on a helmet and handed it to him to put on.

"Now you're protected against the Triskellions," she said when he had slipped it over his head. "They can't harm you as long as you're wearing that helmet."

"I'll take the other helmet and back pack out to the jetcopter," said Dr. Fields, "and have your pilot put them on."

"Just a moment and I'll clear it for you," said General Anderson, and he took a small hand communicator out of his pocket and spoke into it. Then he said, "My pilot will be waiting for you."

"If you don't mind, General Anderson, sir," said Patricia when Dr. Fields had gone, "my fiancé is coming with us."

She indicated Steve, who still held the null-frequency rifle, and General Anderson nodded. "There's room

128

enough aboard," he said. "Is there any special equipment you want to bring?"

"No special equipment is needed," answered Patricia. "The actual construction of the null-frequency helmet and the rifle is really very simple once you understand the scientific concepts involved. In fact, once I give your scientific people a rundown on construction procedures, they can broadcast them to the general public and anyone with a good home workbench can build a model."

"We'll explore the residual implications of these devices after we get them into the maximum-security environment of the spaceport," replied General Anderson. "Right now, if you're ready, I'd like to get started before anything unexpected happens."

"I'm ready," said Patricia, "and Dr. Fields should be finished fitting your pilot with the spare null-frequency helmet by now. Steve——?"

"Let's go," said Steve, cradling the null-frequency rifle in his arm. The others gathered around them, wishing them luck and bidding them good-bye. And finally they headed out of the building and walked toward the Space Patrol jetcopter.

"The pilot is taken care of," said Dr. Fields, meeting them halfway. If you run into a swarm of baby Triskellions, you'll have nothing to fear."

"I'm hoping that we do run into some," said Steve, patting the null-frequency rifle. "I'd like to get a chance to try this out before we reach the spaceport. Otherwise we can't be sure just what its effect will be on the Triskellions."

"Triskellions?" General Anderson scratched his jaw. "Catherine Rogers used the same term when referring to the Gismos." He looked around at all of them. "It's obvious that you people somehow have the benefit of special knowledge."

"We do, sir," agreed Patricia. "As soon as we're on our way, Steve and I will fill you in on everything that we know."

Grunting, General Anderson accepted this, and turning, he led them to the jetcopter. The others hung back and watched while they climbed aboard, and when the door had closed after them and the jetcopter began to rise on a horizontal flight path, they waved until the jetcopter was

129

lost among the city's tall buildings on the opposite side of the rocket field.

General Anderson and his pilot sat in the front seats, and Patricia and Steve in the rear. Over their heads and around them on both sides stretched a transparent canopy. It housed the entire front end of the jetcopter in a transparent bubble and made it possible for the passengers to have an unrestricted view of the tall buildings on both sides of the air lane through which they were traveling— and, if they wanted to lean over, to see the street below.

It also made it possible for anyone on the upper levels of any of the office buildings to have a clear view of them as they passed. They had not been in the air for more than two minutes when suddenly the canopy on General Anderson's side was peppered with bullets.

"Sniper—with automatic weapon," shouted the pilot over the whirring whisper of the jets and the rotors, and instantly he banked to give General Anderson a better view.

Meanwhile Steve, who was seated directly behind General Anderson, tried to duck. His seat belt held him firmly in place and the null-frequency rifle which was lying across his lap prevented quick movement. He cursed.

"Relax," said General Anderson, drawing his service blaster as the pilot brought the jetcopter around—hard. "The canopy is bulletproof. Those bullets can't even scratch it."

"Why are we hovering then?" asked Patricia as the pilot maneuvered in one spot. "Are you going to try to kill the sniper?"

"No," General Anderson shook his head; then nodded toward the pilot who was busy talking on the copter's radio. "We'll report the incident and pinpoint the sniper's location. Then the regular military police can——"

"Look!" shouted Steve suddenly. He was pointing down through the transparent canopy at the jet-thoroughfare below. "It's Catherine!"

Instantly both Patricia and General Anderson leaned forward to see, and the pilot noting their interest stood the copter almost on its head, elevating its tail about sixty degrees. This allowed them to look directly down on the jet-thoroughfare where, from the mouth of an alleyway leading from between two tall buildings, a huge Doberman pinscher was leaping at Catherine Rogers' throat.

Even as they watched, the dog's forepaws struck her in the chest. And as the impact sent her flying backward, its teeth viciously sought her throat. The only thing which saved her was that the dog's zombielike coordination reacted too slowly to her backward momentum. Its teeth closed on empty air. The dog and Catherine went rolling into the center of the jet-thoroughfare. A moment later, the huge Doberman recovered its footing and crouched for another leap. This time, Catherine was defenseless, her arms spread-eagled as she tried to struggle up from where she lay.

Again the Doberman sprang for her throat. In the same instant, General Anderson leaned out of the jetcopter and blasted the Doberman from existence. He did it with the speed, precision and nonchalance of the professional spaceman who is accustomed to dealing with split-second situations. It all happened so fast that, for several moments afterward, the others did not quite realize the dog was dead.

Catherine herself, propped up on her elbows and lying in the middle of the jet-thoroughfare, stared in frozen amazement at the fireball that just an instant before had been a huge Doberman pinscher about to tear out her throat. Above her in the jetcopter, Patricia and Steve were marveling at the speed and accuracy with which General Anderson had fired and killed the beast. Only General Anderson and his pilot were alert enough to observe the large cloud of baby Triskellions which suddenly swarmed at the jetcopter and engulfed it.

They penetrated the jetcopter's transparent canopy as if it did not exist and entered the passenger compartment from all sides. Then they swarmed around General Anderson, Patricia, Steve, and the pilot like angry wasps, and for several moments the four of them sat frozen in their seats with a wild panic mounting in their hearts. Then all at once, the tension in their bodies dissolved as, simultaneously, they realized that they were not being hurt, that the null-frequency helmets they were wearing were successfully protecting them from the Triskellions.

"It really works," muttered General Anderson as if he

131

had been in doubt all the time. "The null-frequency helmet really works!"

"Naturally it works," said Patricia, but it was obvious that she too was relieved and reassured.

Steve was looking down at the null-frequency rifle lying across his lap. "If you'll have your pilot take her down, General Anderson," he said after a moment, "we can pick up Catherine Rogers, and at the same time, I can get some legroom in which to try out this rifle on the Triskellions."

"I was thinking the very same thing," General Anderson replied, nodding to the pilot to take her down. "Under the circumstances, this is an excellent opportunity to test the null-frequency rifle."

Below, Catherine Rogers was on her feet and waving as the jetcopter descended and then landed near her on the jet-thoroughfare. The moment its wheels touched the ground, the door flew open, and Patricia jumped to the tarmac and ran to embrace her exclaiming, "Oh, thank God, you're all right!"

"Thank God you got here when you did," replied Catherine, returning her hug. "That dog almost had my throat." Suddenly she pushed Patricia from her and held her at arm's length. "Whom," she asked, "do I have to thank for the expert shooting?"

"General Anderson." Patricia smiled. "He saved you while the rest of us were just sitting there gawking at your predicament."

"Well, I'm great——" The words died in Catherine's throat as, over Patricia's shoulder, she saw Steve and General Anderson climb from the jetcopter and stand for a moment conferring. Every now and then one of them would point to one of the baby Triskellions swarming around them and the jetcopter or gesture to the strange, riflelike device Steve held in his hands. It was this device which caught Catherine's attention. "What on Earth," she asked Patricia, pointing, "is that?"

"That," said Patricia, "is a model of the null-frequency rifle I constructed, using the principles of the null-frequency helmet which the Tisza taught me." As she spoke, she turned so that she was facing Steve and General Anderson. "Watch," she said, "in a moment Steve is going to try it out."

No! the Tisza exclaimed within Catherine's mind. *You must not let them use that weapon on my offspring!*

Tisza, how can I . . . Catherine began. At that moment, Steve raised the rifle to his shoulder and fired at one of the baby Triskellions gyrating near his head.

Instantly, resonating off each of their null-frequency helmets and registering on their inner ears as a subvocalization, came a short, high-pitched wail that sounded like a scream. Then the tiny sphere of yellow luminescence imploded in a winking flare of bright yellow which, in a moment, was gone.

No! the Tisza sounded another frantic plea within Catherine's mind. She moaned and wept as Steve fired again and destroyed another Triskellion.

Its life had barely winked out before he was firing again and again, while Patricia jumped up and down and shouted, "It works! The null-frequency rifle works! Now we can fight the Triskellions. If we mass-produce enough rifles, we can destroy them all!"

General Anderson, who was standing a little distance away, smiled, nodding. "Yes," he said. "Within thirty-six hours every able-bodied man within the affected areas will have one of these rifles."

No! the Tisza cried within Catherine's mind, but before Catherine could converse with her, Patricia suddenly shouted:

"Look!" And then she pointed upward as the swarm of baby Triskellions converged about one of their number— Catherine guessed that it was Trabzon—and then in a spearhead formation, they all shot off between the tall buildings and disappeared from sight.

"By God, they're retreating!" exclaimed General Anderson, a large smile covering his broad face.

Steve agreed with him, but he was regretful. "Well," he lamented, "I destroyed about five of them anyway." Fondly he patted the null-frequency rifle. "From now on," he declared, "this baby is going to change things for human beings."

No! again came the Tisza's anguished thought in Catherine's mind. *You must not let them use this weapon on my offspring.*

Tisza, Catherine frowned the thought, *what can I do? Human beings have to defend themselves.*

133

No! shouted the Tisza. *Those are my offspring and I love each one of them, just as any human mother would love her children. And when I see them threatened, I feel the same way a human mother would feel.*

But your offspring have killed thousands of human beings!

That doesn't change my feelings about them. I'm their queen mother! Besides, they act the way they do only because they've been misguided by Trabzon. It is not their fault. They have never had a chance to learn what proper conduct for a Triskellion is.

I understand that, and I sympathize with you, Tisza. But other human beings don't know the whole story. They see their kind being killed—horribly—by the baby Triskellions, and all they can think of is finding some way to protect themselves.

I've given you that! exclaimed the Tisza. *I have given human beings the null-frequency helmet.*

Yes, but you can't blame human beings for also seeking some way to fight back—to kill the Triskellions who have killed their kind.

I'm sorry, I understand your position and I sympathize with you. But nevertheless I can't sit idly by and allow your people to use that weapon on my offspring. Do you know what will happen if human beings generally get their hands on the null-frequency rifle? They would begin destroying Triskellions, and they would never stop until there were no more Triskellions left alive on Earth!

Yes, but it's too late to stop things now, Tisza. The null-frequency rifle is a fact. Both General Anderson and his pilot know of its existence. General Anderson has seen it work, and you can bet he won't rest until his men have all been equipped with it.

Maybe it's not too late, the Tisza whispered. *Not if you will help me.*

I can't do anything against my own people, Tisza.

No, but you expect me to work against my own people . . . is that it?

No, that's not it. I understand how you feel, Tisza. Catherine sighed wearily and tried to think. *We've come this far together, Tisza,* she finally formed the thought. *Let's not let something like this break us up. There must be some compromise that we can reach.*

134

Sure there is. We can keep working together like we have in the past to find some way to contact my people. . . . And in the meantime, let your people mass-produce the null-frequency helmet for their protection and self-defense—but not the null-frequency rifle! I won't have my offspring hunted and destroyed as if they just so much vermin!

Catherine shook her head. *But don't you see, Tisza,* she exclaimed, *Patricia is not the only brilliant electronics expert on Earth. The minute that the principles of the null-frequency helmet become generally understood, some other scientist—somewhere—is going to think along the same lines that she did and eventually arrive at the same scientific conclusions. When that happens, the null-frequency rifle will be reinvented!*

Time! thought the Tisza. *That's all I ask for before you start killing my offspring en masse. Time to contact my people!*

Catherine grimaced, thinking hard. *Tisza,* she thought finally, *you're asking me to make a choice between Triskellions and human beings.*

No! the Tisza disagreed violently. *I'm asking you not to force me to make such a choice. I'm saying let's work together to keep things from getting to the point where either of us has to make that choice.*

Catherine suddenly made up her mind. *I'll help you suppress the null-frequency rifle, but God help us both if we don't succeed in stopping Trabzon some other way.*

This exchange lasted only several seconds and was over before Steve had finished marveling over his success with the rifle. In fact, he was still smiling broadly over the fact that he had destroyed five baby Triskellions when Catherine walked over to him.

"Let me see that rifle," she said. When he had placed it in her hands, she asked, "Do you have any idea how this rifle works? I mean, do you understand the null-frequency science involved in its construction?"

Steve shook his head. "Patricia said something about the rifle's being built according to an extension of the principles used in the null-frequency helmet, but it's all Greek to me. Matter of fact, she said it was a pure accident that she was able to figure out how to build one herself—something the Tisza said about the science of

135

null-frequency impulses started her to thinking in unique directions——"

"Where——" Catherine turned to Patricia. "—are the blueprints to this rifle?"

"I didn't have time to put anything on paper," Patricia replied. "I was going to let General Anderson's scientific people do that while I showed them its principles—and how they could be applied."

"I see," Catherine nodded; and while she was doing so, she flashed a secret message, simultaneously, to both Patricia and Steve: D-o-n-t m-e-n-t-i-o-n T-i-s-z-a t-o A-n-d-e-r-s-o-n. She used the rapid eye-wink code which the Rogers Group had used successfully on other occasions against the Five Company secret police. It was done so rapidly that an outsider observing it would think only that Catherine had gotten a speck of dust in her eye and that her eyelid was fluttering because of it. Patricia and Steve read her without any trouble, however, and both nodded imperceptibly.

Then Catherine continued. Turning her face away from Steve, she flashed a message specifically to Patricia: S-u-p-p-r-e-s-s k-n-o-w-l-e-d-g-e n-u-l-l f-r-e-q-u-e-n-c-y r-i-f-l-e.

A confused expression passed over Patricia's face; but before she could question the message, Catherine turned back to Steve. "Mind if I disconnect the null-frequency rifle from your impulser back pack for a moment?" she asked. "I want to check something."

"Sure," said Steve. Reaching behind him to the plug on his null-frequency back pack, he pulled out the wire connected to the stock of the rifle. "The Triskellions have all fled, and there won't be any need to fire the rifle again—not right away, anyway."

"Just what do you have in mind, Catherine?" General Anderson asked, pressing in close. He seemed aware that something had transpired between them but could not place his finger on it. Hence, he could not make up his mind on what to do about it. "I'd like to get started for the spaceport," he said, glancing at them curiously. "I want to get these devices into mass production immediately."

"I'm sorry, General Anderson," Catherine replied immediately, "but I can't allow you to use this weapon on the Triskellions!"

136

As she spoke, the Tisza, from inside of her mind, switched off her null-frequency helmet and re-established psi contact with the outside world. Before General Anderson could react to what she had said, Catherine tossed the null-frequency rifle straight up into the air.

"Get down!" she yelled, and instinctively everyone ducked.

At once the Tisza reached out with her psi power and caused the null-frequency rifle to explode into a small fireball of energy. It blazed and then dissipated, leaving a fine powdery debris. As this drifted back to Earth, General Anderson straightened and glared at Catherine. He was confused and almost beside himself with rage. Yet, when he spoke, it was with a deadly calm.

"Why did you do that?" he demanded. "Why did you sabotage the null-frequency rifle?"

"I can't explain now," answered Catherine, looking him straight in the eye, "because you would not understand. I can only tell you that I had to do what I did for the good of everybody concerned."

"For the good of everybody concerned?" General Anderson took a deep breath and made a superhuman effort to control his temper. "Do you realize," he managed to get out through his gritted teeth, "how many people have been killed so far by these—these Triskellion monsters?" He did not wait for an answer. "Thousands of people have been killed—and you destroy the one weapon that we've come across so far that can be used to combat them!"

He spoke as if such a thing was unbelievable. Suddenly he lashed out and struck her hard across the face, knocking her to the ground.

"You're a traitor to the human race!" he exclaimed, his eyes blazing. "Your father, if he were living, would disown you!"

"Aren't you going off half-cocked?" Steve shouted suddenly, angrily. He was ready to fight, and he clutched and unclutched his fists at his side. "If you take a moment to think," he spat out the words, "you'll realize that there's a lot more here than meets the eye. Catherine wouldn't have destroyed that rifle without good reason!"

"No reason she could give would satisfy me," snapped General Anderson. Then he turned to Patricia. "How long

137

will it take you to prepare a set of blueprints on the null-frequency rifle and build another model?"

"I'm afraid, sir," Patricia shook her head and spoke with sudden frigidness—almost open hostility, "that I won't be able to give you any blueprints on the null-frequency rifle—or build you another model!"

"She will, however," Catherine spoke up as she rose from the ground and wiped the trickle of blood which flowed from her mouth, "give you all of the help which you need to mass-produce the null-frequency helmet and the impulser back pack."

"That's very kind of her," said General Anderson acidly. He stepped back and drew his service blaster. "Now!" he said, covering them, "you will all raise your hands and get into the jetcopter. I'm taking you to the spaceport and placing you under arrest until I can get the bottom of this obvious conspiracy!"

Chapter Thirteen

UNLIKE the Rogers Group private rocket field, the spaceport was a giant complex of squat buildings, spiraling radar transmission towers and gleaming launch cradles. It was big. It was spread out. And it was awe-inspiring. There was one of its kind in every large city in the world. Spaceports were a common thing, and practically every grownup had spent hours with his or her nose stuck in the cracks of the rambling fences which skirted their perimeters—and his or her heart hanging on the tail of every big, little or medium-sized spaceship that departed from Earth.

From a window of the quarantine detention center where she had been imprisoned by General Anderson, Catherine Rogers could look out upon the vast concrete apron where the big, interplanetary ships set down. The apron could easily accommodate a score of ships, but at the moment there was only one large cargo freighter on the flight line. Catherine knew that this was because, to keep the Triskellion menace from spreading to other planets, the World Government had grounded all ships already in port and warned all others away. The order had caught the large cargo freighter before it could unload its cargo and depart. Now it sat empty, and the flight line was deserted. From her barred window on the second floor of the quarantine detention center, Catherine could see no one.

Suddenly she turned from the window and began to pace back and forth within the small room. *I don't see any flaws in the plan,* she spoke to the Tisza. *Except for the obvious one.*

I don't see any obvious flaw.

Then you're not reading my mind very closely. Catherine paused, faced the window again and looked out. *If you can get me to that spaceship*—she indicated the solitary atomic freighter on the flight line—*I can fly it all right. But just because I have a captain's ticket that doesn't mean that I'm an expert space pilot. Command is my function, not piloting! Jerry is our pilot.*

I see all that in your mind, replied the Tisza. *But all you have to do is get that ship into the air, land it again at the Rogers Group private rocket field just long enough for us to pick up your friends . . . and then take off again.*

Catherine sighed inwardly. *Do you realize, Tisza,* she argued, *the skill required to lift a spaceship of that size off planet, take it up several miles and then drop it to another landing point about four and a half miles away? No,* she shook her head violently, *Jerry could do it, but I don't think that I could.*

But you've got to. We agreed that it was our only hope of escaping from this place before General Anderson gets around to questioning you.

Catherine grimaced. Then she asked: *Are General Anderson's technicians still setting up the brain probe?*

After asking the question, she quickly blanked her mind so that it would be easier for the Tisza to concentrate, to reach out with her psi powers and reconnoiter the situation just as she had been doing repeatedly since General Anderson had first locked them in the detention room.

General Anderson's technicians have finished setting up the brain probe, the Tisza projected after several minutes. *However, at the moment, General Anderson himself is conferring with a group of engineers in one of those machine shops you see across the field just to the right of the flight line.*

Looking at the row of machine shops in the distance, Catherine nodded. *Even though it might give us more time,* she thought, *I don't want to wish him bad luck where the mass production of the null-frequency helmet is concerned.*

He's not having bad luck, returned the Tisza. *Patricia has supplied his engineers with a complete and comprehensive blueprint for the null-frequency helmet and impulser back pack. They know the production specifications, and they're going ahead with production as fast as they can get set up. The trouble is General Anderson now wants to know about the null-frequency rifle. I've peeped into his mind, and, I tell you, he's determined to get the information. He fully intends to use the brain probe on Patricia to make her talk. He's hesitating only because he's not sure if he can pull all the information about the rifle from her before it destroys her mind.*

We've got to move immediately!

I agree. Shall we follow the plan which we have agreed upon?

I guess we'll have to. Catherine sighed and went to the door. *What's he doing now?*

The Tisza knew that Catherine meant the guard stationed just outside of the door, the guard who, when he locked her in the detention room, had taken her null-frequency helmet and impulser back pack and put them on himself. *He's smoking a cigarette,* she answered.

Nodding, Catherine turned and looked around the small detention room. Except for a single chair in one corner, it was bare. There was nothing she could use as a weapon, except perhaps the chair. But both she and the Tisza had realized earlier that to use the chair would smash the very thing which they were trying to recover, the null-frequency helmet, so they had decided upon another plan.

I have quietly unlocked the door, came the Tisza's thought. *Now, hold out your hand. I will teleport the guard's service blaster from the holster at his waist into the curl of your fingers.*

Catherine obeyed, setting herself with her hand outstretched. *Okay, Tisza,* she replied, *I'm ready.*

Remember, the Tisza cautioned, *the instant that I teleport the blaster into your hand—you move! Open the door and cover him before he feels the sudden absence of the weight of the blaster at his belt and has a chance to react.*

Right, Catherine acknowledged, and a moment later, a Space Patrol service blaster appeared from nowhere into her hand. Instantly she tightened her fingers around its handle, and with her thumb flicked off the safety. Then she touched the door's "open" panel and promptly the door slid silently into the wall. She stepped forward and thrust the barrel of the blaster into the back of the guard who was, at the moment, looking down at his empty holster with a stunned look upon his face.

"Don't worry about your blaster," said Catherine. "I've got it right here."

The guard froze.

"That's right," Catherine said, and she pressed the barrel a little harder into his back to emphasize her words. "Now just keep your mouth shut and back into the room—quietly, like a good little boy!"

The guard obeyed, but his muscles tensed for action.

"Don't try any tricks with me!" Catherine warned him suddenly. "I've had all the courses in hand-to-hand combat there are. Just stand where you are for a moment."

Quickly she moved away from him and touched the "close" panel beside the door. *Lock it, Tisza,* she ordered as it slid shut.

Right!

"Now turn around," Catherine ordered the guard. She moved to the side of him, making sure that she kept the blaster centered on him from a position well out of range of a sudden lunge. He glared at her as he turned, but she ignored him, saying: "On your knees, quick!" She motioned with the blaster, and he obeyed. "Hands clasped together over your stomach! That's it!"

As he obeyed, she stepped around in back of him and without warning lifted the null-frequency helmet off his head. "No!" he shouted and grasped at it, but she side-

141

stepped him and put the barrel of the blaster to his temple.

"As you were!" she ordered. When he hesitated, she snapped: "Quickly!"

"The Gismos will kill me!" he exclaimed with real terror. "If they come here and I don't have the helmet, I'll have no way to defend myself!"

"In the first place," said Catherine, slipping the helmet over her own head, "this helmet belongs to me. General Anderson only gave it to you because I wouldn't cooperate with him—and because you were supposed to be guarding me."

"You're a traitor to the human race!" The guard spit out the words. "General Anderson should have had you shot right off!"

"I can't stop you from thinking that," replied Catherine as she quickly removed the null-frequency impulser from his back and slipped it on her own. "But you're dead wrong about me—and if it will make you feel any better, General Anderson is going to have this helmet produced in quantity. You'll be able to get another one—probably the minute that you wake up!"

Tisza! Catherine finished adjusting the null-frequency impulser back pack, careful to leave it off so that the Tisza could maintain contact with the outside world. Then she put the Space Patrolman's service blaster into the vacant laser cannon holster at her waist. Simultaneously the Tisza reached out and struck the guard's mind a stunning blow. Instantly he toppled over onto the floor, his big body sprawling unconscious.

Looks like my psi abilities are getting stronger, observed the Tisza. *A few days ago I could not have done any more than stun him.*

You're getting a lot of practice, replied Catherine drily. *How long will he be out?*

Long enough for us to accomplish what we've planned. Are you ready to go?

Yes! Catherine moved to the center of the room, but the Tisza was not quite ready.

Just a moment! She reached out with her psi powers and probed the detention room on the floor above them where Steve was being held. *Okay,* she projected finally.

Catherine nodded. An instant later her own room disappeared, and simultaneously she found herself standing in the same detention room with Steve. He was standing at the barred window, looking out. When he heard her behind him, he turned but showed no surprise because he had been in telepathic contact with the Tisza and he knew that she was coming.

"Our friends have just arrived," he said and indicated the window.

"What——?" Catherine rushed over and looked down. From Steve's window she could see the front entrance to the building. Below her a bus had pulled up and, under heavy guard, was discharging the members of the Rogers Group who had been left behind at the group's private rocket field.

As they entered the building, she whirled toward Steve. "General Anderson must have sent a military patrol to arrest them and bring them here for questioning."

Steve nodded grimly. "This changes things," he said. "We could never get away with what we're planning now."

"I don't know——" answered Catherine thoughtfully. "This might make things easier if we move fast enough— take them by surprise. It means that all our friends are here. So, if we can capture that atomic freighter on the flight line and take off, we won't have to land again at our private rocket field to pick them up. We can go straight to our other destination."

"Okay," Steve agreed after a moment's thought. "Is the plan still the same as the Tisza outlined it to me?"

"Yes!"

"Does Patricia know?"

"Yes, the Tisza has been in telepathic contact with her. She's ready, but General Anderson's brain-probe technicians might come and get her at any minute. That's another reason we have to hurry. Tisza?"

Catherine spoke aloud for Steve's benefit, but he as well as she could hear the Tisza's telepathic response. *Here!*

"Where is the guard?"

He's sitting just outside the door.

"Is his back to us?" asked Steve.

The Tisza hesitated. Then: *No! . . . And he's alert!* she cautioned *He's one of those humans who takes his duty very seriously.*

Steve turned to Catherine. "Give me your blaster."

"What are you planning to do?" she asked as she handed it over. Steve smiled.

"Don't worry," he said. "I realize as well as you do that we must not kill anybody while we're doing this. I just want to get the drop on him."

Reassured, Catherine nodded and went to the door.

You don't have to ask, came the Tisza's sudden thought. *I've already unlocked it, and also reduced the friction surfaces on its sliding mechanism. It should open without any noise.*

"Are you ready?" Catherine turned to Steve, her hand poised over the "open" panel. When he nodded, covering the door with the blaster, she let her hand fall and stepped aside. At once the door opened soundlessly, and immediately Steve stepped into the hall.

"Hold it right there, sonny!" He leveled the blaster on the young, wide-eyed Space Patrolman guarding the door. "Come up out of that chair slowly, and keep your hands away from your blaster!"

"You'll never make it!" the Space Patrolman said calmly. But he stood up with his hands raised high in the air, and Steve stepped backward back into the detention room, motioning with his blaster.

"Come on in here," he said, "and we'll see!"

When the Space Patrolman entered the room and saw Catherine, a baffled look crossed his face. He could not figure out how she had gotten there.

"Don't let it trouble you!" said Steve, seeing his expression. Then he nodded at Catherine, and at once she moved forward and relieved the Space Patrolman of his service belt with its holstered blaster. This she tossed to Steve, who caught it with his free hand, and then she proceeded to remove the guard's null-frequency helmet and back pack. When she had finished, she stepped back from the Space Patrolman, who was looking at them questioningly.

"What are you going to do?" he asked bravely. "Kill me?"

"No!" Steve shook his head. "Tisza!" He nodded toward the guard, and instantly she reached and struck his mind a jarring mental blow which sent his body collapsing to the floor.

144

"Come on!" said Catherine as she jumped over the spaceman's sprawled body toward the barred window. Below, the bus which had arrived with the other members of the Rogers Group was standing alone and empty. "In another few minutes," Catherine observed, "those other guards will be up here with our friends!"

"I'm ready," grunted Steve. He had put on the null-frequency helmet and slipped on the back pack which the guard had been wearing. He tossed Catherine her Space Patrol service blaster and headed out the door, strapping on the service belt and blaster she had taken from the guard.

She followed quickly, and together they ran down the hall toward the elevator. "Let's take the stairway," called Catherine. "We'll have a better chance of surprising them."

"Right!" Immediately Steve veered off from the main corridor and pushed through a door marked "STAIRS." Together, blasters in hand, they raced down to the first floor. "Hold it!" Steve said when they reached the last landing, and cautiously he pushed the main floor door partially open and peered through the crack.

Looking over his shoulder, Catherine saw that the Space Patrol guards had the other members of the Rogers Group lined up in two columns and were making them march down the main corridor toward the elevators. "We're just in time," she whispered.

Those guards are not wearing null-frequency helmets, came the Tisza's thought. *Do you want me to go to work on them?*

Yes, Catherine nodded, and immediately one of the guards who was walking along beside the column slumped to the floor. Then another one followed the first—and then another—and another. The last two, before they were struck down, drew their service blasters and frantically began to look around for the invisible enemy. They found nothing to shoot at, and when the Tisza struck out at their minds, they slumped to the floor unconscious with an incredulous look upon their faces.

Meanwhile the members of the Rogers Group had stopped before the elevators, and some of them were kneeling to help the stricken Space Patrolmen.

"Don't bother with them!" Catherine shouted as she

145

and Steve broke from cover and ran down the corridor toward them.

Immediately pandemonium broke loose as, all at once, everyone started yelling and shouting in surprise. Valerie and Linda rushed into Catherine's arms, and Steve was swamped with a barrage of questions.

"Calm down!" he shouted. "There isn't time to answer all your questions!" Quickly he turned to Catherine. "What are we going to do now?"

"I'll tell you if everybody will give me their attention!" Catherine released Valerie and Linda and held up her hands for quiet.

General Anderson's technicians have taken Patricia to the brain probe, suddenly came Tisza's urgent warning. *General Anderson is going to question her himself!*

Instantly Catherine's face turned pale white, and Steve exclaimed, "I heard that!"

"Quickly!" Catherine cried. "Listen to me—everyone! There's no time to waste!"

Immediately everyone was silent but Steve. He exclaimed, "What about Patricia? If they turn on that brain probe——"

Urgently Catherine waved him down. "Dr. Fields," she said, pointing, "Sid, Jerry, you—Steve, Phil, Johnny—strip those Space Patrolmen and put on their uniforms. Then escort the rest of our friends out to the bus—try to act like real Space Patrolmen under orders! Herd them into the bus and drive out to that atomic freighter on the field. The flight line is deserted so no one should stop you." Hurriedly she looked around to make sure that everyone understood. Then she continued: "When you reach the spaceship, get on board and stand by to take off the minute I get there!"

"Aren't you coming with us?"

Catherine shook her head and looked at Steve. "No," she said, "I've got to go and see about Patricia."

"You'd better hurry," he answered in a tone of urgency. "Once they turn on that brain probe——"

"Don't worry," Catherine interrupted him. "I'll hurry—but you hurry, too!"

Steve nodded and squeezed her hand, gratefully. "Take care of yourself," he said. Then turning, he motioned to the others: "Let's go, folks!"

For several moments Catherine watched them as they busily changed clothes. Then, within her mind, she spoke to the Tisza. *Let's go,* she formed the thought, and immediately her surroundings, the main corridor, her friends disappeared to be simultaneously replaced by a small interrogation room. She found herself standing in a corner directly behind Patricia, who was strapped into a brain-probe chair, and General Anderson and his technicians, who were clustered around her.

During the first instant after the Tisza had teleported her there, she watched silently as one of the white-tunicked technicians turned on a tape recorder. Then, responding to General Anderson's motion, he moved toward the switch which would turn on the brain probe, a hideous machine which surrounded the brain-probe chair on three sides and enclosed Patricia's head in a viselike, transparent bubble of thought-process plates. Within the apparatus, Patricia strained at the straps holding her and whimpered in a desperate voice: "No! No!" over and over.

"You can prevent this!" General Anderson spoke to her, restraining his technician for a moment. "You can save your mind—and us the necessity of using this barbaric method!"

"No!" replied Patricia, squirming. "I can't tell you."

"In that case," General Anderson said as he sighed inwardly, "I can't waste any more time arguing with you about it. You obviously have some scheme of your own in the making which you think justifies your withholding vital information from us. But, since you refuse to take me into your confidence—or even offer a reasonable explanation, I have no other course but to force the information from you!"

Reluctantly, for he was weary, he nodded to his technician. Immediately the man reached for a switch on the brain-probe panel. Simultaneously Catherine raised her service blaster and fired, disintegrating the panel in a flash of heat. The technician withdrew his scorched hand and, with a shrieking howl, whirled toward her. The others turned also, surprise and shock on their faces. Catherine swung the service blaster to cover them.

"Don't move," she ordered. Within her mind, she spoke to the Tisza: *General Anderson's wearing a null-frequency helmet. You won't be able to get him, but the others——*

I've got you, interrupted the Tisza, reading her thoughts even before they reached conscious level. Instantly she reached out with her psi power and began hammering the four technicians with a series of stunning blows to their minds. Immediately three of them pitched forward, unconscious by the time they hit the floor. The fourth collapsed backward, sprawling over Patricia in her brain-probe chair.

General Anderson, with his hands half-raised in the air, glared at her incredulously. "How," he blurted, "did you manage that?"

"I'll explain later!" Catherine gestured with her service blaster. "Right now, you unbuckle your service blaster—slowly—and let it fall to the floor!"

"And if I don't?"

"Then I'll blast you!"

General Anderson shook his head. "I don't think so," he said, scrutinizing her carefully. Then he began to advance on her. "You forget, I was an old friend of your father. I've known you since you were a little girl. I know your background. I know what motivates you. You're too high principled! You'd never press that firing stud!"

"You think not!" exclaimed Catherine. "Well, I thought I knew you, too! I thought you were a wonderful man, but you—you were going to use that brain probe on Patricia! You would have destroyed her mind!"

"I had no choice!" barked General Anderson, and his face was suddenly sternly cold. "I am responsible for the lives of millions of people! People whom the Triskellions are threatening!"

"If you come any closer, I'll kill you!"

"I don't believe you!"

Catherine backed away, and General Anderson kept coming.

"I warn you!" said Catherine desperately. "If you don't stop, I'll blast you!"

"No, you won't!" General Anderson's hands were still raised; but there was conviction in his voice, and he never stopped his advance. "You're not a murderess," he pointed out. "Somehow, I think that you're just misguided!" As he spoke he looked her dead in the eyes, and slowly he reached for her blaster.

Tisza, Catherine formed the desperate thought, *I can't blast him, and he knows it. He's calling my bluff!*

Let me handle him, came the Tisza's immediate answer. *I'll give him plenty to think about. Let go of the blaster!*

You mustn't blast him, Tisza! Catherine opened her fingers. *You would destroy the good will of human beings forever!*

Oh, don't worry! The Tisza reached out with her psi power and snatched the blaster as Catherine's fingers let it go an instant before General Anderson's fingers could close over the barrel. The Tisza snatched it out of his reach, and it went flying through the air as if it had volition of its own. General Anderson's mouth flew open as he turned to watch it. Ten feet away, it stopped its flight and turned in mid-air, the barrel swinging around to cover him.

Get your hands back up in the air where they belong! the Tisza resonated a subvocalization off the wire meshwork of the null-frequency helmet he was wearing. He heard it with his inner ear, and turning a deathly white, he glanced unbelievingly from Catherine to the blaster suspended in mid-air—and back again.

"Better do as you're told," Catherine advised, fighting to suppress a smile. "It's out of my hands now!"

Remove his service belt! The Tisza's command, deadly cold in quality, filled the room, and the blaster, suspended in mid-air, gestured menacingly.

General Anderson, his hands still half-raised in the air, swallowed hard. Catherine moved immediately to unbuckle his service belt with its holster and blaster attached.

Now go and unstrap Patricia, the Tisza ordered when she had finished. *I'll watch him. If he tries anything ...* she did not finish the thought, but all by itself the blaster motioned, its barrel wobbling in a circle which covered the general area of General Anderson's chest and abdomen. He got the message and remained unmoving; yet the expression on his face suggested that he was deep in thought.

Meanwhile, Catherine released Patricia from the brain-probe chair. "Where's your null-frequency helmet?" she asked as she finished freeing Patricia's hands and pushed

149

aside the thought-process plates which enveloped her head. "I'll get it for you while you put this on!" She handed Patricia General Anderson's service belt and stepped back to allow her room.

Patricia smiled gratefully as she slipped out of the chair and took the belt from Catherine. "My helmet and back pack are lying on a desk in the next room," she said as she quickly adjusted the belt to fit her small waist. "I'll get them while you——" She nodded toward General Anderson. "—watch him!"

Catherine nodded, and Patricia left the room.

"You'll never get away with this!" General Anderson spoke up suddenly, looking at Catherine curiously. "I haven't figured out just how you manage these magician's tricks——" He nodded at the blaster still suspended in mid-air and covering him. "—but don't think that they will do you any good! At this moment, this spaceport is the most well guarded spot on this Earth. A mouse could not enter or leave the premises without a special pass from me!"

Before Catherine could reply, Patricia came back into the room wearing her null-frequency helmet. "He's right, you know," she advised Catherine. "I heard them talking. There are patrols and spotters all over this place."

"Makes no difference," said Catherine. "The way that we're going out, nobody will be able to stop us.... And we're taking General Anderson with us!"

Chapter Fourteen

MINUTES later, a sleek Space Patrol jetcar left the building where General Anderson had attempted to question Patricia with the brain probe and sped onto the rocket field toward the atomic space freighter in the distance. In the front seat, driving, sat Catherine Rogers. Beside her, with a blaster suspended in the air directly

150

behind his head and the barrel pointing at the nape of his neck, sat General Anderson. And in the rear, sat Patricia, keeping her eyes glued on the buildings behind them, alert for any sign of pursuit.

"The bus I told Steve and the rest of our friends to use to get out to the ship," said Catherine over the muffled whine of the jet, "is already there." She pointed for Patricia's benefit. "See it—parked about a hundred feet from the base of the freighter. It's empty, so that must mean that they made it." Suddenly she looked down at her watch. "Jerry should have the reactor going by now and be ready for takeoff as soon as we get there."

Patricia absorbed this information, nodded and went back to watching their rear without any comment. Catherine suddenly slued the jetcar roughly over onto the concrete apron of the flight line, causing the tires to squeal as they sideslipped on the rough surface. "Any pursuit?" she asked Patricia, glancing backward.

Patricia shook her head. "Not yet," she answered, "but we're attracting a little attention. Some spotters on the roofs of the buildings around the flight line have their binoculars trained on us."

"That's all right," replied Catherine, returning to her driving. "We'll be there before they catch on to what is happening."

"I think we should have left him behind." Patricia indicated General Anderson. "He'll be a drag on us. Someone will always have to be standing guard over him."

"If we can win him over to our point of view," said Catherine, "it will be worth the trouble."

"Better save yourself the effort!" General Anderson spoke for the first time since they had forced him into the jet car. "Nothing can ever persuade me to betray my fellow human beings as you people are doing now!"

"We don't consider ourselves traitors," replied Catherine. "And I don't think that you will either once you know the whole story."

A minute later she pulled the jetcar to a skidding stop beside one of the giant fins of the atomic freighter. "Out!" she cried. "We're got to move fast. Those spotters will know something is up the minute that they see us enter the spaceship with General Anderson."

Almost before she had finished speaking, she was out of the jetcar and moving around to General Anderson's side to hold the door open and watch him as he emerged. The service blaster, still suspended in mid-air, moved along with him, remaining at a point directly behind his head and occasionally letting him know that it was still there by nudging the nape of his neck with its barrel. Patricia, her own blaster in her hand, emerged behind them. And at the same time, Steve, who had been watching their approach from the air lock of the atomic freighter, pressed the button which hydraulically lowered the ship's inboard access ladder.

"Walk toward the ladder!" Catherine gave General Anderson the command. "Keep your hands down—at your side—and act naturally."

Reluctantly General Anderson obeyed. They were all well within the shadow of the giant spaceship when suddenly the air was rent by a series of high, wailing alarms, rapidly rising and falling up and down the chromatic scale.

"Hurry up!" Steve yelled from the air lock high above their heads. "Two armored jetcars are heading this way—fast!"

"Up you go, General Anderson!" They had reached the ship's inboard access ladder, leading up to the air-lock, and Catherine stood back, indicating that he should go first.

To enforce this command and prevent him from balking, the Tisza projected: *If you delay or try anything funny, General Anderson, I will blast you from existence!* To emphasize her words, she caused the service blaster which she was keeping suspended in mid-air with her psi power to press threateningly against the back of his head.

For an instant, he glared at Catherine; then he started slowly up the ladder. Next came Catherine, and then Patricia brought up the rear. When General Anderson reached the top, Steve yanked him into the air lock and then ducked just in time as a bolt from a heavy-caliber laser cannon flashed over his head and filled the air lock with searing heat.

"Quick!" he shouted, crawling to the edge of the air lock and looking over the side at Catherine and Patricia, who were scrambling up the access ladder with bolts of

152

laser lightning striking the hull of the spaceship all around them. "Give me your hand!"

He reached down and hauled Catherine in. Then he reached for Patricia, and just as the ladder below her feet turned red-hot, then white and then disintegrated in a blaze of energy, he caught her by the hand. To keep her from being burned, he had to swing her sideways away from the ladder. Then he hauled her in on the backswing. The moment that she cleared the portal, Catherine hit the lever to close the outer air-lock door. Before it could swing shut, however, two lightning bolts from a heavy-duty laser cannon flashed into the air lock, forcing them all to hit the deck as the shots ricocheted against the bulkheads before dissipating.

An instant later, as the outer air-lock door sealed shut, Steve jumped to his feet, shouting: "It's okay now!" and pressed a communicator switch beside a red light which had suddenly begun flashing. "Steve here," he said into a mike which was inset into the bulkhead.

At once the speaker above the light came to life: "THERE ARE A COUPLE OF ARMORED JETCARS OUTSIDE," it crackled. "AND THEY'VE GOT LASER CANNONS—HEAVY-CALIBER STUFF."

"Are you telling me?" exclaimed Steve. "They almost got us!"

"WHAT'S THE SITUATION DOWN THERE?"

"All aboard——" Steve glanced around quickly. "No one hurt! Give us three minutes to clear the air lock and reach acceleration couches—then take off!"

"I'LL GIVE YOU A MINUTE AND A HALF," the speaker crackled. "ONE OF THE ARMORED JETCARS HAS RADIOED FOR A PORTABLE DESTRUCT BEAMER!"

Steve whistled. "That means they must intend to disable the ship and burn their way in to us!"

"RIGHT—SO WE'LL HAVE TO CLEAR OUT OF HERE BEFORE IT COMES! A MINUTE AND A HALF IS ALL I CAN GIVE YOU!"

"Okay," said Steve. "A minute and a half it is." Flipping the switch, he spun around to find that Catherine, Patricia and General Anderson had picked themselves up from the deck of the air lock and were watching him. Looking at Catherine, he said, "You heard?"

She nodded. "You and Patricia take General Anderson —couch him for takeoff and keep him under guard. I'm going to the control room!"

"Right!" Steve reached for the lever that opened the inner air-lock door.

At the same time, Patricia went over to General Anderson and reached for the blaster still suspended in mid-air behind his head. "We won't need this anymore," she said as her fingers closed over the handle and the Tisza released it from the influence of her psi power. Then she stepped back and covered him with it herself. "Let's go!" She motioned. "Steve, you lead the way. I'll bring up the rear."

By this time Catherine was already through the inner air-lock door and heading—fast—down a corridor toward the control room. At the end of the corridor, she scaled a ladder and, in a moment, was out of sight.

Jerry, sitting in the pilot's chair, smiled at her when she reached the control room. "Takeoff in thirty seconds, Captain!" he said and nodded at the vidscreens above his head. They showed the exterior surroundings of the spaceship. Catherine instantly saw that a large weapons carrier was racing onto the flight line toward the ship.

"Instrument check complete!" Phyllis spoke up from a readout console to the right and rear of the pilot where she was busy crosschecking the readings on Jerry's console. "Everything is ready to go!"

Immediately Catherine walked over to the astrogator's chair and leaned over Eleanor, who was plotting a trajectory with the aid of a small inboard computer. "Did Steve tell you our destination?"

Eleanor nodded quickly and pointed to a spot on a map of the city and surrounding countryside which she had in front of her. "This will be the shortest space hop on record," she said. "In fact, we won't even touch space!" For an illustration she touched two points on the map. "The apogee of our flight path will be about eight miles high. Then Jerry will drop back to earth in a U-bolt trajectory and land us here——"

Catherine nodded, as Steve called, "Takeoff minute ten seconds. . . . Mark!" Simultaneously his finger flicked a takeoff alarm which sounded inside and outside the ship, alerting everyone. "—eight . . . seven . . . six——!" he

154

counted. On some of the vidscreens he could see the Space Patrolmen from the armored jetcars, who had been scurrying around the base of the giant ship, scatter and begin to pull back.

Meanwhile Eleanor gathered up her maps and some computer data and passed them to Catherine. "These are for Jerry," she said. "I have duplicates."

Nodding, Catherine quickly took the papers and fitted them into the clipboard above the pilot's console. Then she slipped into the captain's chair behind the pilot and in front of the auxiliary control console. Quickly she strapped on her safety belt.

Simultaneously, about two seconds before Jerry was scheduled to fire the four huge atomic rockets in the landing fins, the captain's intercom crackled, "STEVE REPORTING HERE. . . . I HAVE GENERAL ANDERSON STRAPPED DOWN IN THE FIRST OFFICER'S CABIN. . . . ALSO, PATRICIA AND I ARE GO!"

Just as he finished, the countdown reached "Takeoff." Jerry's finger stabbed down on the firing stud. Outside, at four points around the ship, the huge booster atomic rockets purred with the start of a sudden, minutely controlled fission, and four giant electron clouds billowed downward. Then the big ship began to rise upward, gently, as if it weighed no more than a few ounces.

The acceleration couches were hardly needed. They were an ancient holdover from the early days of space travel when man had only very limited power at his disposal and, therefore, had to blast his way into space before it was all used up. With the unlimited power of the giant atomic rockets, a spaceship could take its time and accelerate so gradually that its crew and passengers experienced virtually no increase in weight. The acceleration couch was retained only as an added safety factor in the event of accident occurring during takeoff or landing—acceleration or deceleration.

As the ship rose, Jerry was busy over the pilot's console, reading his instruments and simultaneously playing his fingers over the buttons before him, dampening out the yaw, pitch and roll which the aligning gyroscopes could not handle. In response to his commands, steam vented from the steering jets in the side of the ship, stabilizing its attitude and interlocking with the stabilizing fins and the aft atomic thrusters as they swiveled slightly on their gimbals to make minute course adjustments.

Several feet from the pilot, in the astrogator's chair, Eleanor concentrated over a bank of instruments even more complex than those before the pilot. Her inboard computer monitored every action the pilot made and translated it against all the ship's telemeter summaries and any manual information the astrogator could feed to it. As the flight progressed, it evaluated the pilot's every action, and stood by to upstage him, to kill any signal, to shut down any sequence of events in which its monitor functions detected too much deviation from preprogramed specification.

On the other side of the pilot, opposite the astrogator's chair, sat Phyllis, who served as the flight dynamics officer, constantly updating the readouts and checking for any instrument discrepancies. "Our track looks good!" She was the first one to speak after takeoff. "So far the instruments indicate that our performance is right on the mark!"

"Considering the age of this ship and how long it has been since I've sat in a pilot's chair, I'm certainly glad to hear that," said Jerry. "I was pretty worried there for a while."

"My instruments show," Louise suddenly spoke up from the communications console, "that the spaceport has a radar lock on us!"

"Let them track us if they want to!" Catherine turned in the captain's chair. "It won't do them any good. When we land again in a few minutes, we'll fall below their tracking horizons, and they'll never be able to figure out where we've gone in time to prevent us from taking off again."

"They could send a peek-a-boo atomic missile looking for us!"

"Not with General Anderson aboard. This ship is not that important to them. General Anderson is. Besides, their real problem is not us but the Triskellions."

"Well," sighed Louise, "since takeoff, they've been on the radio demanding that we return to the spaceport. But, since I knew that you wouldn't consider it, I've kept it off the intercom."

"We're approaching apogee," reported Eleanor, and Jerry, who had been resting for a moment, got busy.

"Vent all pressures!" he snapped as he yawed the ship slightly to its previous bank angle and then brought it around about four degrees to aim its tail at their landing point. This maneuver practically pointed the ship sideways to its line of flight; and the gyroscopes labored to keep it from pulling in an added velocity increment which might send it hurling off course to a fiery crash somewhere below on the surface of the Earth.

"All airborne pressure valves are open!" Phyllis reported as they reached the height of their apogee. "All tanks are venting."

"Astrogator!" Jerry turned toward Eleanor. "Give me a readout on our present trajectory!"

"You don't need one," Eleanor answered quickly. "You're right on the money! Just cut back on your thrust power and fly her on in."

In reply, Jerry gave her a big grin. "Roger!" he said. As the giant ship topped out its trajectory, he reached up to his overhead instrument panel, lifted a guard and switched on his Doppler computer-controller unit. This would give him a reading on any deviation North, East, South or West of his course as the giant ship fell back toward Earth. It used the same principle that police radar on Earth used in its radar checks of speeding jetcars. The Doppler antenna aboard the spacecraft radiated four separate radar signals toward Earth and received reflected signals. The frequency or pitch of the signals received shifted in proportion to the horizontal speed of the spacecraft in its diagonal descent toward its landing point. The difference between the radiated frequency and the reflected, shifted frequency was routed through the inboard computer and converted directly to an eight-ball before Jerry's eyes. The eight-ball displayed distances and rates of descent in three dimensions. By keeping his eyes on it, Jerry could witness an actual simulation of his landing and manipulate his control console accordingly.

Catherine, as captain of the ship, had nothing to do but watch the whole operation on the vidscreens above her head. As the ship maneuvered toward a landing, she brought her vidscreens up to high-intensity ground magnification. After several minutes, she could begin to make

157

out the abandoned farmhouse on the outskirts of the city that was their destination.

Then Jerry was saying, "We are no longer supersonic! We have one hundred and twenty-five seconds to zero velocity and touchdown!"

"The spaceport no longer has us on their radar!" reported Louise.

Catherine leaned toward Jerry and pointed to a spot on his vidscreens. "Do you see that dilapidated barn?" she asked and waited while he squinted at the screen. "The one that looks like it's falling down———" When he finally nodded, she asked, "Can you set the ship down in that meadow to the right of it?"

"Yes—it'll take some yaw steering. But if that's where the secret cavern is located———"

"That's where the secret cavern is located!" As she finished speaking Catherine settled back and let him concentrate on the controls as the giant ship sideslipped back to Earth on four small pinpoints of flame. Inside the control room the four big atomic engines made no more noise than a deep-throated purr, and the power required from each of them to bring the ship down to a feather-soft landing was minute. Jerry's maneuvering sequences were so fine that, to stay within fixed vectors, he had to tap his accelerator levers back and forth with his forefinger.

"We're going to burn up a lot of grass," he called over his shoulder as he came in over the meadow.

Then, as they fell lower and their rate of closure with the Earth became so gradual that, on her vidscreens, Catherine could barely tell that they were descending, she called: "Just get us as close to that barn as you can . . . with the main cargo hatch pointing that way!" She motioned as she spoke, and Jerry nodded at her in his rear-view mirror. A couple of moments later, he gently set the ship down on all fours and cut the power.

From around the control room there were sighs of relief, and Catherine immediately slipped out of her acceleration couch. "Good job," she complimented Jerry; then turning to the others, she said: "We'd better get started right away. We've got a lot of work to do!"

Chapter Fifteen

AN hour later, both the cargo freighter's gigantic hatches were open, the hole leading down into the secret cavern of The Inventors had been greatly enlarged, and a large elevator crane had been constructed over it. Down in the secret cavern, Catherine and the Tisza, aided by Dr. Fields, supervised some of the servomechanisms as they loaded the contents of the cavern, its fantastic machines, instruments and tools, onto the crane elevator which then hoisted them up out of the hole and swiveled on its frame to swing its load into one or the other of the cargo freighter's gigantic hatches.

The task was almost completed. Down in the secret cavern, standing over the remains of the matter and psyche teleportation machine which Trabzon had wrecked, Dr. Fields turned to Catherine and said, "I think if we gather up all these bits and pieces and store them on board the ship, later, with the Tisza's help, I might be able to reconstruct this machine."

Before answering, Catherine considered the matter gravely. "If you think that you can do it," she said finally, "go ahead. Take a couple of servomechanisms and crate up the pieces. But remember, we want to get a space platform and beacon built before anyone goes off on any private projects."

"Of course," replied Dr. Fields. "I realize that our main problem is still to contact the Tisza's people."

"Yes, but there's no reason why we can't kill two birds with one stone!" said Eleanor, who had overheard Dr. Fields' statement as she walked up. In her hand she held two formulas: one for an alloy of plastic and metal, Plasti-Metal, which had one thousand times the tensile strength of the strongest steel yet developed by man; and the other for a combination of plastic and glass, Plasti-Glas, which was transparent and absolutely unbreakable. She also held an operations manual for a machine which she had just helped to load onto the crane elevator. It was a machine, so said the manual, which could produce these two alloys in unlimited quantity.

The prospect excited her, and as Catherine and Dr. Fields gave her their attention, she exclaimed: "Why should we do things by half measures! I say, if we are going to build a space platform, let's build a space platform which will do more than just house a space beacon to contact the Tisza's people. Here!" She slapped the formulas and the manual she held in her hand. "Here is the answer to the problem of obtaining basic construction materials to build a real space platform! I mean a satellite big enough to accommodate hundreds of scientific people!"

"Granted," replied Catherine, "using those formulas——" she nodded at the papers in Eleanor's hand, "the basic construction materials would be available. But still, we haven't got time to go off on a tangent, building a larger space platform than we need."

Building a larger space platform would not necessarily take more time, the Tisza suddenly projected. *We have a lot of servomechanisms to do the work. They have been designed to operate in space and to build a space beacon and platform. The size and architectural dynamics of that platform make no difference. Whatever these factors are, they can be programed into the servomechanism's master brain. The space beacon will, naturally, be built first. Then, however, there is no reason why the servomechanisms can't continue on and build as large a space platform as you want, since such a platform would not interfere with the operation of the space beacon.*

"Looks like I'm overruled." Catherine smiled at Eleanor. "Okay. After we get the space beacon built and in operation, we'll go on and build your satellite city!"

At this, Eleanor fairly glowed with excitement. Before she could answer, Steve, in company with General Anderson, came up behind them and called, "Everything has been loaded on board the ship, Captain. Is there anything else you want done before takeoff?"

Turning, Catherine checked that except for the bits and pieces of the wrecked teleportation machine, lying at their feet, the secret cavern was empty. All the marvelously

160

advanced machines and fantastic instruments and tools had been moved out and stowed in the holds of the atomic freighter. The bodies of Dr. Griskell and Inspector Becket had been taken to the surface and buried. Now the crane elevator waited on the floor of the cavern to take them up to the surface.

There was only one thing left to clear up, and immediately her eyes went to General Anderson. "Have Steve and Patricia filled you in?"

He nodded, the beginnings of a smile touching the corner of his mouth. "They have," he said, "and they have let me use the ship's radio to contact my people."

"Then what's your verdict?" Catherine glanced at Steve for some clue.

He shook his head. "I'll let him tell you."

"Oh, we'll support you," said General Anderson. "That is, if you build a space platform, no one will get excited and blow it out of the sky. Also, on my recommendation, the World Government will consider allowing a rescue party of Triskellion spaceships to enter our solar system without touching off an interstellar war—but only on the condition that I am allowed free access to every part of this operation as an observer."

"Condition accepted," said Catherine, and she held out her hand. "I'm glad to have you with us."

"Don't be too glad!" General Anderson took her hand and shook it. "This whole thing is very difficult to believe, and I'm not entirely convinced myself, yet."

In what areas do you still remain in doubt? the Tisza suddenly inquired, projecting the question so that they could all hear it.

General Anderson's face changed color, but he did not flinch at direct telepathic contact with the Tisza. "For one thing," he replied almost immediately, "you're asking me, a military man, to believe that when you contact your people, they will come here and kill this monster, Trabzon—then pick up all the baby Triskellions who are loose on Earth—and then go away and leave us with all these wonderful machines which I've seen as compensation for the loss of human life and the damage which has been done to our world. You're asking me to believe this. You're asking me to believe that your people have no designs on Earth—will develop no designs on Earth!"

The only thing which I am asking you to do, the Tisza projected without hesitation, *is not to attribute the same motivations to Triskellions that are characteristic of your fellow human beings.*

You human beings place a very high value on material things. But tell me, of what value would material things be to someone who can change the form of matter at will? For instance, with my psi powers, I can transform lead into gold. I can turn the waters of your oceans into wine or any other liquid or substance I desire. Therefore, I submit to you, General Anderson, that it is not possible for a human being and a Triskellion to place the same value on material things.

But it is possible for two totally different, intelligent life forms, such as we, to have the same moral values, to make the same ethical judgments when dealing with one another. The Golden Rule of your Christian religion, "Do unto others as you would have others do unto you," was not invented just on Earth. There are many life forms out there in that big universe you see when you look toward the stars who have been practicing it for millennia before this solar system was ever formed!

General Anderson nodded thoughtfully. "You're saying," he answered, "that Triskellions would never think of enslaving human beings."

No, I'm asking you: What would our motive be for doing such a thing? And I'm telling you that, if you must suspect us, suspect us for motives which are applicable to Triskellions. Don't suspect that we will do something merely because this is what some power-hungry human beings would do under similar circumstances.

"I admit," said General Anderson, "that I can't think of any reason why Triskellions would want to take over Earth. But then, I don't know all the facts—what you are like—what it's like where you come from!"

In that case I would invite you and other human beings to come to our home world, Triskellia. Meet us and learn about us. You would be welcome!

"Before that can happen," broke in Catherine, "we still have to build the space beacon and platform!"

"I agree," said Dr. Fields. "Do you mind if I get a few servomechanisms to help me get the parts of this machine

162

—" He indicated the teleportation machine, "gathered up, crated and put on board the ship."

"Go ahead," said Catherine, "but hurry. I want to take off the minute you get squared away."

"Right!" At once Dr. Fields headed for the crane elevator; but before he had taken more than three steps, Steve called after him:

"Wait! We'll ride up with you. There's no reason that we should remain here."

Catherine and General Anderson concurred and immediately fell in behind Steve and Dr. Fields. They all stepped onto the elevator platform, and a few moments later, they were on the surface, shielding their eyes from the late evening sun. Immediately Dr. Fields went off to round up some servomechanisms, and Catherine, Steve and General Anderson strolled toward the air lock of the giant cargo freighter. Jerry saw them coming and came over to meet them.

"I'd like to get off the ground before the sun sets," he said to Catherine. "The ship will have a full load in her cargo holds, and she'll be sluggish. For a safe liftoff, I'll need all the light I can get!"

"You can prime the engines now," replied Catherine. "Except for Dr. Fields, we're ready to go! And he'll be ready just as soon as he gets the teleportation machine aboard."

"Can you install another acceleration chair in the control room?" General Anderson asked. "I'd like to be where the action is."

Jerry looked at Catherine for approval, and when she nodded, he said, "Will do!" and turning, left them.

Fifteen minutes later, they watched as the last of the teleportation machine was crated into the hold of the ship, and the servomechanisms began to dismantle the crane elevator. When this was stowed in the ship's hold, the last of the servomechanisms was deactivated. Then the giant cargo hatches began to close. When they were sealed, Catherine heaved a sigh of relief. "We made it," she said. "Now let's report to the control room so that Jerry can lift off——"

Look! the Tisza suddenly projected. *Behind you— coming across the meadow!*

Catherine whirled, and the others followed suit. "It's a

163

swarm of baby Triskellions!" exclaimed Steve. "And they're heading this way—fast!"

"Of all the times," Catherine moaned, "for a swarm of baby Triskellions to show up!"

It's no accident, the Tisza projected. *Trabzon is leading them!*

"But how did he find us?"

Your null-frequency helmet has been turned off for some time now. Probably Trabzon has taken advantage of the fact to get my offspring to home in on me.

"Of course!" exclaimed Catherine. "All our helmets have been turned off! Quick! Everybody switch on your null-frequency helmets and run for the ship!"

No one argued. Everyone except Catherine, whose helmet was controlled by the Tisza, reached a finger up inside of their null-frequency helmets and switched them on. Then they made a dash for the ship's inboard access ladder and began climbing toward the air lock as fast as they could.

Bringing up the rear, Catherine called upward to Steve when she reached the ladder: "When you get inside," she yelled, "tell the others to switch on their helmets, too! If the Triskellions reach us before we become space-borne, they will probably penetrate the hull of the spaceship!"

Steve nodded as he disappeared through the air lock's outer door, and then General Anderson was scrambling after him. Before Catherine followed, however, she looked back to see how close Trabzon and the swarm of baby Triskellions had gotten. She gasped when she saw that they were almost halfway across the meadow, that the whole cloud of them was spreading out to engulf the giant spaceship, and that a spearhead of glowing luminescences was streaking straight for the air lock.

"Come on, lady!" Suddenly General Anderson reached down, and grabbing her by both wrists, was hauling her through the air-lock door. "This is no time to spend gawking!"

In the next few minutes, the Tisza suddenly projected, *you'd better get this ship off the ground. If you don't, you'll never have another chance—because when Trabzon realizes that we've got the contents of the secret cavern in this ship, he'll do everything within his power to keep it from taking off. He knows that once we build a space beacon and contact my people, he will be finished!*

Immediately Steve, who had been shouting instructions over the air lock's intercom, ordering everyone to turn on their null-frequency helmets, turned to Catherine as General Anderson pulled her through the outer door. "I heard what the Tisza just said," he shouted. "Do you want me to give Jerry a takeoff order?"

Catherine nodded, breathing too hard to speak, and General Anderson rushed over to the lever which would close the outer door of the air lock. Simultaneously Steve turned, shouting into the intercom: "Air lock to pilot! Air lock to pilot! Come in, Jerry!"

"HERE!" Jerry's answer crackled from the speaker. "WHAT IS IT?"

"Take off!"

"WHAT——?"

"I said, 'Take off!' Everyone is on board! The air lock is secured! And the Triskellions are almost upon us! The captain wants you to take off!"

"Roger!" replied Jerry. Instantly through the hull of the spaceship they heard the deep-throated rumble of the ship's four giant atomic engines. Then they felt the ship begin to rise, but the liftoff was too slow for the Tisza.

At this rate of acceleration, came her sudden thought, *we'll never escape Trabzon.*

At once Catherine pushed Steve away from the intercom and shouted, "Air lock to pilot! Jerry, come in!"

"I'M HERE, CAPTAIN! WHAT'S WRONG?"

"You're taking too much time to get away from Earth! I don't want you to be leisurely! I want you upstairs right now!"

"BUT YOU'RE NOT ACCELERATION-COUCHED! THE G-FORCES——"

"Damn the G-forces! If Trabzon catches us, we'll have more than G-forces to worry about! Get this ship upstairs, now!"

"I read you," Jerry sighed regretfully. "You'd better hit the deck before it comes up and hits you!"

In the control room, his hand pulled back on the atomic thrust accelerator levers in front of him. All at once there was a tremendous roar, the sound of four huge volcanoes all erupting simultaneously.

165

In the air lock, Catherine, Steve and General Anderson dived for the deck and began to hug it as suddenly a gigantic weight struck their bodies and began to crush them.

Below, a huge cloud of baby Triskellions streaked across the meadow to where the ship had been but a moment before. There they whirled about in circles of infantile confusion. Only Trabzon understood what had happened.

Chapter Sixteen

I've done everything I can for her, projected the Tisza to the people who were standing around Catherine's bunk, gazing down at her still form. *She'll be weak for a little while longer, but she's all right!*

"I think she's coming around now!" exclaimed Valerie, and a moment later, Catherine opened her eyes.

"Where am I?" Looking up at them from her pillow, she asked the classical question. Phil, the Rogers Group doctor and expert on internal space medicine, pushed forward. Immediately he leaned over her and made a rapid physical examination. Finally he straightened with a smile and said:

"You've done a good job, Tisza. I can't find any trace of the injuries she suffered in the air lock!"

"The air lock?" Catherine muttered and brought her hand up to her forehead. "Oh, I remember now. I was in the air lock with Steve and General Anderson——" She looked up at them for confirmation and received their nods. "Trabzon was racing across the meadow with a huge cloud of baby Triskellions. He would have destroyed the ship. There wasn't time to leave the air lock, to reach the acceleration couches. I had to order Jerry to take off immediately, to blast his way into orbit. There wasn't time to——"

"Don't think about it now!" interrupted Phil. "Wait until you get more of your strength back."

"No!" said Catherine. "There isn't time to wait!" Suddenly she tried to sit up in bed. "We've got to get started on the construction of the space beacon to contact the Tisza's people."

"No! No, you don't!" Phil was firm as he and Valerie pushed Catherine back to a reclining position. "There is no urgency there. We've had over one thousand servomechanisms working around the clock for three days now on the space beacon!"

"The space beacon is already built and in operation," said Eleanor, who was standing behind Valerie. "While you were unconscious, the Tisza left your mind and supervised the whole operation. Right now, most of the servomechanisms are working to enlarge the space platform. We have a real city in space—a satellite city under construction!"

Catherine listened as if she could not believe what she was hearing. "You said that the servomechanisms have been working around the clock for three days!" she blurted. "Do you mean that I've been unconscious for that long?"

Everyone nodded, but it was the Tisza, from within Catherine's mind, who spoke. *The tremendous G-forces to which you were subjected on takeoff injured you pretty seriously. It took all of my psi power to keep you from being crushed to death against the deck of the air lock.*

There was a sudden, tense silence while Catherine digested this information, and for a moment it seemed to her that no one would look her in the eye. "How about Steve and General Anderson?" she finally asked the question. "Did they make it?"

"No!" Phil's answer was accompanied with a sigh. "I wanted to spare you the details."

Their null-frequency helmets were turned on, projected the Tisza, interrupting Phil. *I could not reach them with my psi power to prevent them from being crushed to death as I did you.*

"We gave them a hero's burial in space!" Eleanor blurted, but Catherine had already turned her face away from them. Tears slipped from under her closed eyelids, and pain etched deep lines in her expression.

167

"Oh, how she must hate me!"

"Who?"

"Patricia! She and Steve were in love. I was the one who gave the order for Jerry to blast off into space like that."

"Patricia understands," comforted Eleanor. "She's taking it hard, but she doesn't blame you."

You did the only thing you could under the circumstances, projected the Tisza. *I know. I left your null-frequency helmet turned off so that I could maintain contact with the external world. I know how close Trabzon was. If you had not ordered Jerry to blast off into space as you did, and if he had not instantly obeyed that order as he did, Trabzon would have overtaken the ship. And have no doubt, he would have wrecked it long before we could have achieved orbit!*

"You had no choice," Phil spoke up. "Everyone understands that!"

"General Anderson was an old friend of my father," said Catherine, the pain still in her face. "He had no family of his own, and he used to say that he wanted me to be his little girl!"

Suddenly she sobbed, and Johnny leaned forward. "We've contacted the World Government," he said quietly. "They know the situation, and they're sending another observer to take General Anderson's place."

"Sure—send another observer," sobbed Catherine. "That's all they care about a man of General Anderson's caliber. He's dedicated his whole life to conquering space for human beings, yet when he dies, all they can say is: 'We'll send another observer!'"

Suddenly all her restraint seemed to leave her, and she broke down and cried uncontrollably. At once Phil opened his medical bag and started to give her a tranquilizer, but the Tisza forestalled him.

Let her get it all out of her system, she projected. *We are not out of danger yet, and I don't want to take the chance of fogging up her mind.*

Phil nodded, and Valerie sat down on the bunk next to her older sister and wiped her tears with her handkerchief. After a few moments of silence, Eleanor spoke softly:

"Catherine," she said, "you've got to pull yourself together now. Earth is being gutted by Trabzon and the baby Triskellions. Even the areas which they have not yet reached are in chaos. People are hysterical. They are in fear. They are looting, burning, rioting and committing suicide——"

"Then——" Catherine's sobbing subsided, and she sniffled, "——the null-frequency helmet has not lived up to our expectations."

"Certainly it has. It's being mass-produced and distributed all over Earth, and it has greatly reduced the ability of Trabzon and the baby Triskellions to kill human beings. People are beginning to realize that as long as they keep the helmets on, they are safe."

"Then what is the problem?"

"The human race still feels threatened! That's why people are rioting, burning, looting and some of them committing suicide. They are reacting to a loss of their sense of security. And they will continue to feel insecure as long as the Triskellions remain on Earth."

"Yes," conceded Catherine, "but if the space beacon is in operation as you say, then it will only be a matter of time before the Tisza's people spot the signal it is putting out and come running to rescue her and clear Earth of all the Triskellions, including Trabzon."

That's true, admitted the Tisza. *But we've still got to keep the beacon in operation until my people detect it and arrive here.*

"What's to prevent us from doing so?"

"The Tisza seems to fear that Trabzon will try to destroy the space beacon."

You don't think for a minute, do you, the Tisza asked Catherine, *that he will just give up and wait for my people to come and capture him?*

Before answering, Catherine sat up on her bunk, and this time no one tried to stop her. "What precautions," she asked when she had assumed a comfortable position, "have been taken?"

"The usual!" It was Johnny who answered. "Claudia is in charge of security, and you know that she knows her business. The real trouble is we don't know enough about the capabilities of Trabzon!"

What specifically do you want to know? asked the Tisza. *I'll answer any question that I can.*

"Well." Johnny scratched his head. "For one thing, can

Triskellions exist in space without artificial protection—a spaceship or some type of space suit?"

Yes, we can exist in space without artificial protection. Any life form which has the ability to make themselves immaterial, as we do, can do it.

"Does that mean then——?" Johnny screwed up his face, thoughtfully, "that Trabzon does not need a spaceship to reach us? That he could use his own locomotive power to reach us in our present orbit?"

You could say that, but the tremendous amount of energy he would be required to expend to escape the Earth's gravitational pull would make it impractical for him to try it. He would be exhausted nearly to the point where his light was ready to expire.

"Wouldn't it be much easier," Catherine spoke up, "for him to teleport himself here?"

Yes, answered the Tisza. *Theoretically speaking. But in practice, no! Just as there is a limit to the area of matter which psi power can affect at any given moment, so too is there a limit to the distance over which psi power can affect matter, teleport it, and so on, relative to the amount of psychic energy which the mind can handle at any given moment.*

"You're saying that Trabzon doesn't have the mental energy to teleport himself from Earth to here?"

I'm saying that Trabzon's psi powers are not sufficiently developed to be equal to the task. Besides, where is here? We are about one thousand miles out and moving in a circular, equatorial orbit around the Earth at a velocity in excess of eighteen thousand miles an hour. At the same time, the Earth is spinning on its axis at the center of our orbit. It would take a computer to figure out where we will be in space in relation to any given point on Earth five seconds from now. Trabzon, for all his psi powers, couldn't do it all by himself.

"Yes——" Johnny stroked his chin wisely, "—but Trabzon has never had any trouble getting help in the past!"

I'm not saying that Trabzon won't be able to get help. I'm just indicating in what direction your efforts to establish security should lie.

"In other words," said Catherine, "look for Trabzon to

170

take over the mind of a human being who can help him find out where we are."

"Like the director of a radar installation," Eleanor suggested. "And radar installations also have computers——"

The idea of his taking over the mind of a director of a radar station is impractical! projected the Tisza. *Merely knowing where we are would not do him any good. He would not only have to know where we are at any given moment, but he would have to have immediate access to a spaceship which would enable him to get here.*

"He could take over the mind of either the pilot or captain of a spaceship!"

"That alone wouldn't do him much good either," said Catherine. "He would be reduced to searching for us with the spaceship's radar. And because of its limited range, he might never find us."

"That narrows it down to two possibilities," Johnny spoke up. "One, our radioing our position to Earth—or two, our putting out a signal to guide a spaceship here to us."

"If we don't want Trabzon to find us, we must not do either," said Catherine. "At least, not until the Tisza's people have been contacted and have arrived here."

To this there were several nods of agreement, but before anyone could speak, Louise entered the compartment. "I've been on the radio, speaking to Earth," she said. "General Anderson's replacement took off about a half hour ago."

"You haven't broadcast our position?" There was a sudden, tense silence as everyone looked at Louise and waited for an answer.

"Why, yes——" she began. Not having heard their previous conversation, their tenseness confused her. "I've been broadcasting a position signal for ten minutes now, and General Anderson's replacement should be approaching our orbit." She looked at her watch. "In fact, he should be starting his co-planer maneuvers just about now."

If Trabzon is on the ball, projected the Tisza with a sudden grimness, *he'll be aboard that spaceship!*

"What are you saying?" exclaimed Louise. "The Space

Patrol would never let Trabzon sneak aboard one of their ships!"

"I hope that you're right," said Catherine, as she slipped off the bunk and weakly climbed to her feet. "But we've got to make absolutely sure before we allow that ship to rendezvous with us!"

"Get back to the radio and cut that signal," snapped Johnny to Louise. Then he asked Catherine: "Are you strong enough to take command?"

"I think so," she nodded, reaching out to Valerie and Eleanor for support. "Is there some sort of control room built into this space platform?"

"Yes—two levels up!"

"Let's get there then! I want to observe that spaceship!"

Johnny nodded and led the way out of the compartment. The others followed. Catherine saw, for the first time, how the space platform was being constructed.

At first glance, as they headed down the corridor leading from the compartment where she had lain unconscious for three days, it was impossible for her to tell that they were in space at all. She could not see outside because the corridor was windowless. Made of the fantastically strong alloy Plasti-Metal, it glowed with a soft luminescence of its own—a radiance whose tone was designed to give the people aboard the platform a sense of calm tranquility. In addition to this the platform's artificial gravity was maintained at slightly under Earth normal so that movement from one place to another was not hindered by lack of traction, and there was no sense of being in the free-fall environment of space.

At the end of the corridor, they crowded into an elevator and were transported to another level. Here, they hurried down a causeway of futuristic design. Spaced at intervals along the wall and ceiling were large, transparent Plasti-Glas panels through which Catherine could catch glimpses of space and other sections of the space platform. Towering high above their causeway, which seemed to be on a main level, were the towers of a whole complex of modernly designed structures still under construction. These gave the space platform the appearance of a fantastically modern, miniature city in space.

Noticing Catherine's interest, Eleanor paused and pointed through one of the transparent panels. "When the

172

servomechanisms finish the tops of those buildings——"
Her finger traced the skyline of the city against a breathtaking background of a multitude of brilliant stars. "—
we're going to turn on the force-field generators which we
have spaced around the circumference of the platform.
This will enclose the top of the city in a transparent
bubble dome of energy which we will fill with air so that
the people who will someday populate the city will not
need space suits when they go outside from one building
to another. I've even managed to design in a couple of
parks between the buildings. There will be broad walks,
green grass and maybe even some real trees if we can
bring them up from Earth."

Catherine nodded, impressed in spite of herself.
"What's the diameter of the space platform going to be
when its complete?" she asked, taking a last glance at the
breathtaking vista of the miniature city in space.

When she turned and walked on, Eleanor moved along
at her side. "The space platform presently has a diameter
of one mile," she said. "But theoretically, because of the
weightless environment of space, there is no restriction as
to size. Therefore, I figure that we will be able to add to
it, as needed, indefinitely."

Catherine nodded. "I think you're the only one of us,"
she said, "who is looking beyond the time when we will
have defeated Trabzon."

"Well, you know that this is what I've always dreamed
of." Eleanor smiled happily. "A space platform—a city in
space where hundreds of Earth scientists can carry on
significant space research projects without fear of retaliation from the Five Company secret police."

"I've almost forgotten about our troubles with them."
Catherine laughed. "It seems like it was a hundred years
ago that all we had to worry about was being terrorized by
the Five Company secret police."

"It's actually been less than a week!"

"We turn here!" Johnny suddenly called back to them
over his shoulders, and immediately he disappeared
through a doorway off the main causeway.

They followed and found themselves in a domed compartment with a transparent ceiling which looked out upon
the stars. A half-moon silhouette of Earth filled one
corner of their view, and beyond it they could see the

brilliant corona of a section of the sun. Catherine gasped at the beauty of the sight, then turned her eyes to the inside of the dome. The base of the inner walls was spanned by a complex of computers, telemetering equipment, radar, radio and astrogation instruments. A number of chairs took up the space before the manually operated consoles, and a command and observation deck dominated the central section.

The whole layout gave Catherine the fleeting impression that she was standing in an enlarged control room of one of the big interplanetary spaceships, and immediately she climbed to the command deck and got down to business. "Have you got a radar track on General Anderson's replacement?" she asked.

At once Louise turned in her chair before the radar console and called, "Yes, but his spaceship is near enough for a visual sighting."

"Where?"

"Southeast quadrant!" Louise pointed upward to the transparent dome. "He's still at the extreme limit of visual range, but the sun's light is reflecting off his hull. See that tiny, moving light?"

Catherine studied the area of space which Louise had indicated. It took her a moment, but finally she made out a tiny speck of light. It was moving beyond the space platform's busiest construction area. Scattered through space near the platform's perimeter were a variety of machines, servomechanisms of all sizes and types, busy performing the particular construction functions for which each had been designed. Strung out into space along the rim of the space platform on tether lines were various tools, instruments and packing boxes full of materials and supplies. And among all this, Catherine noticed several space-suited figures.

"Who?" she asked suddenly, "is working out in that area of space?"

"Sid and Dr. Fields," answered Johnny, standing beside her. "We've been rotating the space-suit duties, and it's their shift." As he answered her question, he pointed at the huge atomic freighter which had originally brought them into orbit and which was now parked beside the space platform, hanging motionless in space about a mile away and traveling along in orbit behind them. "Jerry's on duty in the atomic freighter," he finished.

Catherine nodded; but before she could reply, Eleanor, who had walked over to the radar console and was leaning over Louise's shoulder, called out: "General Anderson's replacement is closing with us pretty fast, Captain. Hadn't we better re-establish radio contact?"

"Is he trying to contact us?"

"No," Louise answered. "I've had nothing from him since he began his co-planer maneuvers."

"His radar track indicates," Eleanor reported, "that he has completed co-planer maneuvers and is now approaching the space platform on a collision course!"

"See if you can raise him on the radio then," said Catherine. "Tell him to decelerate and stand off until we can clear an area for him to park!"

It won't do any good, came the Tisza's thought. *The fact that he's on a collision course with the space platform should indicate to you that Trabzon is on board and in control of that spaceship!*

"I'm afraid, we'll have to accept the Tisza's estimate of the situation," warned Eleanor. "Unless General Anderson's replacement begins deceleration maneuvers within the next ten seconds, it'll be pretty obvious that he intends to ram us."

At once everyone glanced from the tiny speck of light, moving toward them through deep space, to their watches. For the next few seconds there was silence.

"Looks like he's going to ram us all right!" Johnny finally delivered the verdict. "The ten seconds are up, and he's near enough for us to see his retrorockets if he were going to use them!"

"We'd better abandon the platform then," said Catherine grimly. Her suggestion was met with silence. She looked around at all of them, then shrugged her beautiful shoulders. "I'm sorry!" she exclaimed suddenly. "There's nothing else that we can do! We can't move the platform out of his way!"

"There's no time to abandon the platform, either!" exclaimed Eleanor. "Half our group is sleeping. We'd have to wake them up—get them into space suits! There just isn't time before that ship comes smashing into us!"

For a long moment they all looked at each other help-lessly; then suddenly the radio crackled into life:

"WHAT'S THAT GUY TRYING TO DO?" It was Jerry speaking from the control room of the atomic freighter parked in orbit behind the space platform.

Instantly Louise pushed the push-to-speak button on the radio panel beside her. "We're going to be rammed!" she said into the console's microphone.

"I CAN SEE THAT FOR MYSELF! I'VE BEEN TRACKING HIM ON MY SHIP'S RADAR, AND THE INBOARD COMPUTER SAYS THAT HE'S ON A COLLISION COURSE."

"The Tisza thinks," Louise interrupted him, "that Trabzon is on board."

"COULD BE. RAMMING IS AN EXCELLENT WAY TO DESTROY THE SPACE BEACON AND THE PLATFORM. THAT SHIP'S ATOMIC ENGINES WOULD GO OFF ON IMPACT AND THERE WOULD BE ONE HELL OF AN EXPLOSION. IT WOULD ENGULF THE WHOLE PLATFORM AND EVERYTHING AROUND IT. HAVE YOU TRIED TO RAISE THE PILOT BY RADIO?"

"No response!"

"THERE'S NO TIME TO EVACUATE THE PLAT-FORM!" Jerry seemed to be muttering to himself. "HOLD EVERYTHING WHILE I GET HIS EXACT TRAJECTORY FROM THE COMPUTER."

"Ask him what he's got in mind," Catherine said to Louise.

Louise asked and Jerry was evasive. "JUST AN IDEA!" he said, but a moment later the four atomic engines of the huge freighter blowtorched four great clouds of electron flame, and it slowly began to move out.

"No!" Louise yelled into the mike. "Jerry, no!"

"IT'S OUR ONLY CHANCE!" Jerry called back. "SO DON'T BOTHER ME FOR A FEW MOMENTS. I HAVE TO PUT THIS SHIP RIGHT ON COURSE!"

Silently they watched through the transparent dome as the giant ship pulled away from the space platform and slowly increased its rate of separation. In moments it dwindled and soon became just four pinpoints of sapphire flame—then one.

"MY TRANSLATIONAL MANEUVERS ARE COMPLETE!" Jerry's voice sounded over the speaker.

Immediately Catherine climbed from the command deck and hurried to the radio console. "Jerry!" she snatched up the console's microphone. "What does your computer say?"

"I'M ON AN INTERCEPT TRAJECTORY WITH GENERAL ANDERSON'S REPLACMENT," he answered. "ALL I NEED TO DO NOW IS TRIM OUT OUR RELATIVE TRAJECTORY DISCREPANCIES!"

"Jerry, listen——" Catherine started upward through the dome as she spoke over the mike. "You've got an automatic situation on your hands. Let your inboard computer handle the mid-course corrections. You take the lifeboat and get out of that ship before it's too late!"

"THAT'S WHAT I INTEND TO DO!" said Jerry, "JUST AS SOON AS I CAN GET THE COMPUTER PROGRAMED PROPERLY!"

"Hurry!"

"He'll never make it," muttered Louise as the two tiny specks of light, burning brightly against the star-filled blackness of deep space, moved toward each other.

"I'M ON MY WAY!" Jerry shouted. A minute later, the two tiny specks of light merged, and suddenly there was a brilliant nova.

It lasted for a few seconds, and then when it finally faded in brilliance, Louise broke the tense silence. "He didn't have time to make it to the lifeboats!"

The others in the dome were grim-faced, and no one displayed any pleasure at the fact that the space beacon and platform had been saved.

"Phyllis will have to be told," said Catherine after a long silence. "Where is she?"

"Sleeping," answered Johnny. "Do you want me to wake her?"

"No, I'd better——"

"SPACE PLATFORM, COME IN!" the speaker in front of Louise suddenly crackled. "CATHERINE— LOUISE—ARE YOU THERE?"

Catherine whirled toward the microphone, and simultaneously Louise slapped the push-to-speak button. "Here!" she shouted. "Jerry, is that you?"

"I THINK SO!" Jerry managed to laugh. "I THINK THAT I'M STILL IN ONE PIECE!"

"How on Earth did you get out of the ship before the collision?" asked Louise, leaning forward. "You didn't have time to reach the lifeboat!"

As she spoke the tension seemed to go out of everybody, and there was a lighter, less grim atmosphere in the dome.

"I DIDN'T TRY FOR THE LIFEBOAT," Jerry was saying. "I ALREADY HAD ON MY SPACE SUIT, AND I ESCAPED THROUGH THE AIR LOCK. I REMEMBER PUSHING OFF FROM THE SHIP. I HAD GONE SOME DISTANCE WHEN I FELT A SUDDEN, INTENSE HEAT. IT WAS FROM THE EXPLOSION OF THE TWO SHIPS WHEN THEY COLLIDED. I GUESS THE AIR-CONDITIONING UNIT IN MY SUIT COULDN'T HANDLE THE LOAD. THE RADIATION FROM THE EXPLOSION WAS CONVERTED INTO HEAT WHEN IT HIT MY SUIT, AND IT GOT SO INTENSE THAT I PASSED OUT."

"Jerry, listen to me!" Johnny left the command deck and walked over to take the microphone from Catherine's hand. "Can you see the space platform from where you are?"

"YES, I'M VECTORING IN ON YOU NOW. I CAN SEE THE SUN GLINTING OFF THE SIDES OF THE TOWERS ABOVE THE PLATFORM. FROM HERE THE SATELLITE LOOKS JUST LIKE ONE OF THOSE ULTRAMODERN CITIES YOU ALWAYS SEE PICTURED IN THE SCIENCE FICTION MAGAZINES."

"Give me a pressure reading on your space suit's translation motors."

"MY SUIT ROCKETS PUT OUT SIXTY POUNDS OF THRUST—AS YOU KNOW. BUT I'VE ONLY GOT ABOUT TEN POUNDS OF FUEL IN MY TANKS."

"Not enough for him to make it back," said Eleanor, doing a fast calculation in her head.

Johnny nodded. "What," he asked, "is your out-of-plane deviation?"

"NEAR AS I CAN TELL, IT'S NEGLIGIBLE. THE PROBLEM IS I CAN'T CATCH UP WITH YOU."

"I think that I've got him on radar," Louise spoke up, pointing to a particular blip on her screen, "and he's right, he'll never catch up. In fact, we're leaving him behind. Our separation distance is increasing at the rate of——" She quickly checked the instruments and made the calculation in her mind. "Let's see——" she went on, her face screwed up in concentration, "—seven feet per second!"

"Jerry!"

"YES!"

"HEY! HAVE YOU FORGOTTEN ABOUT US?" The speaker suddenly crackled with Dr. Fields' deep voice. "SID AND I HAVE BEEN LISTENING IN, AND WE KNOW THE SITUATION. DO YOU WANT ONE OF US TO TAKE A SERVOMECHANISM AND GO BACK AND PICK UP JERRY?"

"Dr. Fields!" Catherine said as she took over the microphone, "we haven't forgotten you. It's just that you've been working out there in space for such a long time now. How much air time have you got left?"

"ENOUGH TO MAKE THE RESCUE. SID CAN STAND BY TO ASSIST IF NEEDED!"

"POSITIVE!" came Sid's agreement. "BUT DR. FIELDS SHOULDN'T HAVE ANY TROUBLE. SOME OF THESE SERVOMECHANISMS ARE SO DESIGNED THAT THEY MOVE ABOUT IN SPACE AS IF THEY OWNED IT. ALL DR. FIELDS HAS TO DO IS SWITCH ONE OF THEM OFF THE MASTER BRAIN'S MAIN CHANNEL AND THEN MANUALLY COMMAND IT TO PERFORM THE RESCUE OPERATION."

"I CAN GUIDE IT MANUALLY AND RIDE IT IN PIGGYBACK," came Dr. Fields' voice over the speaker. "THEN, WHEN I REACH JERRY, ALL HE HAS TO DO IS GRAB HOLD AND HANG ON."

"HEY——!" It was Jerry speaking. "THERE'S SOMEONE ELSE IN A SPACE SUIT OUT HERE!"

"What——?" Though Catherine was doing the speaking, everyone else in the dome was now crowded around the radarscope and in front of the radio panel. Once again, there was a grim tenseness in the air.

"THERE'S SOMEONE IN A SPACE SUIT, UP

AHEAD OF ME, WHO'S CROSSING MY TRAJECTO-
RY!" Jerry's excited voice came again. "I'M GOING TO
CHANGE COURSE—SEE IF I CAN'T GET CLOSER
TO HIM!"

No! the Tisza suddenly projected from within Catherine's mind. *Tell him, no! He's not to go near that other
space-suited figure!*

"But why, Tisza?" Catherine asked aloud. "If there's
someone else in this vicinity of space, we should know
about it."

No! the Tisza was adamant. *It is obvious that, whoever
he is, he comes from the spaceship which was carrying
General Anderson's replacement! That means that
Trabzon may be occupying his mind!*

"THE FIGURE IS CARTWHEELING ALONG
AND SPINNING SLOWLY!" suddenly came Jerry's
voice. "IN A MOMENT HIS FACE PLATE WILL BE
VISIBLE——WAIT! GREAT GALAXIES!"

"What is it, Jerry?"

"THE MAN IN THE SPACE SUIT IS DEAD!
WHEN HIS SPIN BROUGHT HIM AROUND TO
FACE ME, I COULD SEE HIS FACE THROUGH HIS
HELMET VISOR. IT WAS ALL SHRIVELED LIKE
A MUMMY'S!"

"Listen, Jerry," Catherine called, "you're not to get any
closer to that corpse!"

It doesn't matter now, the Tisza projected. *If Trabzon
has killed the man—fed on his life force—then he's no
longer within the body.*

"But where could he go?"

*If Trabzon was able to see the space platform from
where he was, he could teleport here. Obviously he teleported the man and himself out of the spaceship which
was going to ram us. He must have done it just before it
collided with the atomic freighter Jerry was piloting.
Then, when he saw how close he was to the space platform, he must have decided that he didn't need the man
anymore. So he killed him by feeding on his life force,
and then he must have teleported here, leaving the man's
body to drift endlessly in space.*

"If you're right," said Johnny, "then Trabzon is somewhere aboard the space platform right now."

180

"We've got to find him!" exclaimed Louise suddenly as they all stared at each other in fear.

"HEY! THE SERVOMECHANISMS!" Dr. Fields' voice came in excitedly over the speaker. "THEY'RE OUT OF CONTROL! THEY'RE ATTACKING US!"

The compartment housing the servomechanisms' master brain! the Tisza exclaimed. *That must be where Trabzon is. He's taken over the servomechanisms' master brain and is turning them against us!*

"Look!" Louise called, suddenly pointing through the transparent dome to where they could see some of the servomechanisms—automatic arc welders, hammer machines, free-fall screwdrivers and bolt tighteners, saws, planers and drills—chasing Sid and Dr. Fields around the rim of the space platform. At the same time, others were tearing into the completed parts of the structure and ripping large sections out of it.

"Sid—Dr. Fields!" Catherine called into the mike. "Can you hear me?"

"YES!"

"We think that Trabzon has teleported himself aboard the space platform—that he's in the compartment with the servomechanisms' master brain—and that he's manipulating it to cause them to attack us and destroy the space platform."

"WE CAN TAKE CARE OF OURSELVES OUT HERE!" exclaimed Sid. "WE'RE SMALLER AND MORE AGILE THAN THE SERVOMECHANISMS. AS LONG AS WE HAVE PLENTY OF ROOM, WE CAN OUTMANEUVER THEM. BUT HOW ABOUT YOU?"

"We don't know yet how tough the situation will be," answered Catherine; then she froze. Through the doorway of the domed compartment came a servomechanism, one of the big energy slicers, moving fast on a pair of caterpillar treads with its electromagnetic eyes swiveling on two gleaming pivots above its sleek front housing. Held forward, ominously swinging from side to side, was its operating tool, a massive terminator which could deliver a lance of energy that could cut through solid steel as if it were butter.

Without preliminary, it ran straight toward them. Johnny yelled: "Scatter!"

181

Instantly Catherine dropped the mike, and Louise scrambled out of the chair in which she was sitting before the radar console. As the big servomechanism bore down on them, they ran in opposite directions. Simultaneously Johnny vaulted to the command deck and Eleanor, Valerie and Phil, petrified with fear, pressed back against the radio panel.

Grab hold of something solid—quickly! came the Tisza's urgent projection in their minds. A moment later the artificial gravity within the space platform was switched off. *There! Now you should be able to maneuver better!*

Suddenly Catherine found herself floating in a condition of weightlessness, while the others, who had reacted more quickly to the Tisza's command, remained grounded as they held onto something solid. The big servomechanism, its caterpillar treads suddenly losing their traction, left the deck and shot off into the air out of control. But only for a moment. Almost instantly the tiny air jets at its base fired, slowing its lunge and bringing it around until its energy slicer centered on Eleanor.

Quickly, before the servomechanism's energy lance could flick out like the tongue of a snake and cut her in half, she released her hold on the radio panel and shot upward into the air. Valerie and Phil followed.

"Keep moving," Catherine yelled to them. "As long as it can't find a stationary target, it won't fire its cutting lance."

Don't be too sure of that, the Tisza projected. *You don't know in what way Trabzon has reprogramed the servomechanism's master brain.*

"Watch out, it's coming after you!" Johnny warned suddenly. Catherine rebounded off one of the control panels to expertly twist in the air and face the oncoming monster. Before she could move, however, the servomechanism's forward air jets suddenly hissed into life, and it slowed to a standstill.

Quick! projected the Tisza. *I've switched it off the master brain's main channel! Get around behind it and take over the manual controls.*

"Right!" exclaimed Catherine, and immediately launched herself straight at the motionless servomechanism. Simultaneously Johnny launched himself upward from the command deck in an effort to help her.

"We've got to do something," he said, "before any more of these things come jetting in here!"

"This one caught us by surprise," replied Catherine, taking over the controls of the big energy slicer and guiding it to a gentle landing on the main deck. "If any others show up, the Tisza can switch them off the master brain's main channel as fast as they come!"

"HELLO, SPACE PLATFORM, COME IN!" Dr. Fields' voice broke in excitedly over the speaker. "SOMEBODY COME IN!"

At once Louise launched herself through the air to the radio panel. Clutching the back of the radio console chair, she pulled herself up short. "We're here!" She pressed the push-to-speak button and yelled into the mike. "What is it?"

"THE SERVOMECHANISMS ARE HEADING TOWARD THE SPACE BEACON!" yelled Dr. Fields. "IT LOOKS LIKE THEY'RE GOING TO DESTROY IT!"

"There!" Eleanor pointed upward where, through the transparent dome, they could see most of the servomechanisms. They had formed a vast frontal wave and were surging through space toward the top of a tall spire at the center of the space platform.

"Is that where the space beacon is located?" asked Catherine, looking where Eleanor was pointing.

Johnny nodded. "On the top of the central spire. But you can't see it from here."

We've got to go up to the compartment which houses the control console of the master brain, came the Tisza's sudden thought. *And we've got to find some way to take control of it away from Trabzon before he is able to destroy the space beacon with the servomechanisms.*

"But how?" asked Catherine. "Tisza, you yourself claimed that there is no way that a human being can destroy a Triskellion." Catherine was exasperated. "Of course, this was not true, but after we found that out with the null-frequency rifle, you insisted that I help you destroy it, the one weapon we had which we could have used to fight Trabzon. Also, you asked that Patricia not use her

183

knowledge to build another one. She didn't, and now we have nothing which we can use against Trabzon!"

I know that you're angry, the Tisza replied. *But regardless of what has happened in the past, we still have to stop Trabzon now. If the space beacon is destroyed before my people have been contacted, our cause is lost. . . . And the human race is lost, too!*

"Tisza," said Johnny, drifting in the air near Catherine, "I am willing to do anything—even give my life—if it will save the situation!"

Catherine, do you feel the same?

"I think that I've demonstrated that all along."

Okay, then let's get up to the compartment which houses the master brain for the servomechanisms as fast as we can!

"I'm ready," said Catherine eagerly. "But what do you have in mind?"

The only thing possible, replied the Tisza. *I'm going to fight Trabzon myself.*

"But, Tisza——" Catherine was horrified. "—you know you're no match for Trabzon. Why, your fighting him would be like a young girl of our race fighting a grown man. He would only hurt you as he did before!"

He may, agreed the Tisza. *He may even kill me! But I've got to try. If I can stop him from destroying the space beacon for even a few minutes longer—maybe that will make the difference between success and failure.*

"Okay," sighed Catherine. Looking upward through the transparent dome, she saw that the wave of servomechanisms was nearing the top of the central spire. "We'd better hurry!"

"Wait for me!" exclaimed Johnny as Catherine launched herself toward the doorway of the dome.

As he shot after her, Eleanor exclaimed for the rest of them: "Hold it! We're coming, too!"

"You're darn right we are!" Louise concurred. She punched the push-to-speak button on the radio panel and spoke into the mike: "Sid—Dr. Fields, come in!"

"HERE!"

"We're going to see what we can do on this end to stop the servomechanisms," she yelled. "We'll be out of radio contact for a while. Do you think that you can take care of yourselves?"

"ROGER! BETTER HURRY AND GOOD LUCK!"

"Thanks!" Louise dropped the mike and propelled herself after the last of the group following Catherine and Johnny.

I would advise, came the Tisza's terse thought as they headed down the causeway, *that the rest of you not come all the way with us. You must know that, if I don't succeed, Trabzon will surely kill Catherine, perhaps both of us. There is no point in your being close by where he can kill you, also.*

Johnny, who was following close behind Catherine, shrugged his shoulders. "I can't see that it will matter, Tisza. If Trabzon kills you and Catherine, we won't have much chance of staying alive afterward—even with our null-frequency helmets on!"

That is true, admitted the Tisza. *And since you realize it yourself, there is no point in my denying the truth of it.*

"We turn here," Eleanor, who had moved up beside Johnny, called ahead to Catherine, who had come opposite a side corridor leading away from the main causeway.

Catherine took it, and the others followed. At its end, the Tisza directed them upward inside a tall shaft which ended on a level high above the main deck of a space platform. They moved along it in single file by catapulting themselves from one handhold to another. When they came out of it, they glided down another corridor which led them directly to the compartment housing the servomechanism master brain.

Okay, now! the Tisza projected. *Everyone switch on your null-frequency helmets!*

When they had obeyed, the Tisza followed suit, switching on Catherine's helmet and then saying within her mind: *This is the only reason that I asked you to accompany me and risk your life like this—to give me protection against Trabzon, inside your null-frequency helmet, until the very moment I am ready to attack him!*

Catherine nodded absently, only vaguely hearing the Tisza. They had come to the doorway of the compartment which housed the control console of the master brain; and her attention was held by the sight that met their eyes. At the end of the compartment, through a massive, transpar-

185

ent panel which spanned the entire wall, she could see a huge, spotlightlike machine that revolved around and around on a tripod mounted on top of the space platform's tallest and most central spire. She knew instantly that she was looking at the space beacon, a machine that, even as she watched, was sending forth a beam of some unknown energy which somehow had the power to traverse interstellar distances and sweep the stars with its signal just as a searchlight on Earth could reach out and sweep the sky.

This magnificent machine was about to be destroyed because surrounding it and closing in was a solid wave of servomechanisms. Some of them were being destroyed in flashes of bright incandescence as the beam of the space beacon swept over them in its unceasing sweep of the heavens; but others moved in for the kill through areas of space which the beam did not cross.

Catherine, came the Tisza's jarring thought, *tell the others to remain here in the doorway. Only you and I will enter the compartment.*

"Stay here." Catherine turned to the others and relayed the Tisza's command. Then she released her grip on the doorframe and began to drift slowly forward.

The control panel of the servomechanisms' master brain was a large, complex piece of electronic equipment which spanned two of the compartment's walls. As Catherine drifted forward, she saw that the console's instruct lights were blinking and flashing frantically in an intense, pulsating rhythm. Suspended in the air weirdly gyrating before the master brain's programer was a tiny sphere of golden luminescence. It was Trabzon.

Trabzon's using his psi power to direct the servomechanisms' master brain in the destruction of the space beacon, came the Tisza's thought as Catherine stared in both fascination and fear at Trabzon. *He's not very familiar with the forces he is trying to control, however, and he doesn't know how to program the master brain so that he can achieve an automatic and coordinated sequence of events in the activities of the servomechanisms. Hence he has to respond to each feedback impulse from each of the hundreds of servomechanisms out in space, and this task is employing all his psi faculties.*

Is that why he hasn't noticed us?

186

Yes, he's concentrating very deeply. The Tisza's thoughts paused for a moment, then she suddenly projected: *I'm going to switch off your null-frequency helmet now and try to take him by surprise before he becomes aware of us. Try to set your mind against the backlash which will follow when I attack him.*

Drifting near the center of the compartment, Catherine held her body almost motionless and responded to the Tisza with only a slight nod. *I'm ready,* she subvocalized, and instantly tried to steel her mind as she felt the null-frequency helmet switched off and the Tisza lash out at Trabzon.

The first blow, with the full force of the Tisza's psi power behind it, sent Trabzon reeling drunkenly into the master brain's control console. His glowing sphere of a body penetrated halfway into the instrument panel and instantly caused an electrokinetic disturbance in some of the circuits. Wires fused white-hot. Outside in space, some of the servomechanisms, out of control, spun away from the space platform. Others came to a standstill. Simultaneously, the Tisza, not pausing for an instant, struck at Trabzon again before he could recover and throw up a mind shield. Like a vicious wildcat, she lashed out at him, striking into the exposed areas of his mind, ripping and tearing and pounding until her own psi powers were blunted and numbed with the effort.

Somehow Trabzon managed to weather the attack. Snarling like a wounded tiger, he drew inward and coiled like a snake. Suddenly he lashed back, and the blow struck with such force that, within Catherine's mind, the Tisza buckled. The strength went out of her attack upon Trabzon like the air leaving a punctured balloon, and he instantly pressed home his advantage. Viciously he reached out and struck her again, and this time the blow was so violent that Catherine as well as the Tisza felt the effect. The shock of it seemed to knock her mind off its foundation of sanity, and she went spinning into a depthless void of blackness. Everything dissolved in darkness. Everything was forgotten; but from somewhere deep inside of her mind, a mighty anger surged upward and filled her whole consciousness with a violent and unreasoning hatred of Trabzon and everything which he represented.

187

Suddenly she opened her eyes, but she did not see the surging wave of servomechanisms which, outside in space, still converged on the huge, whirling space beacon. She was no longer aware of the flashing lights on the control console of the master brain. Even the Tisza, whimpering in agony from the merciless lashing which Trabzon was giving her, was forgotten as Catherine's mind was suddenly consumed with a vibrant and bursting anger. The anger pulsed and swelled into a thing uncontrollable. And then it exploded, and the incredible happened.

Something in Catherine's mind lashed out at Trabzon. It struck the mental barrier he had erected against the Tisza's assault and shattered it as if it were no more than tissue paper. Then, with a soundless cry of violent anger, it pounced upon him. With a thousand, rapid, hammerlike blows, it battered his mental substance into a formless, thoughtless mass of screaming agony.

Under Catherine's mental onslaught, Trabzon retreated, drawing inward, his mental fiber thrashing and convulsing. Instinctively he tried to escape by teleporting away, but the Tisza, half-recovered, reached out and smashed his effort before his instinctive processes could will it into being. Then, as Catherine held him in a mental grip of pure anger, the Tisza weakly bludgeoned him again and again until his light grew pale and his mental fiber disintegrated into mists of incoherent thought.

"Watch out!" Johnny suddenly shouted from behind Catherine. He had drifted halfway into the room and was frantically pointing through the transparent panel at the wave of servomechanisms which had topped the space platform's central spire. One of them, a big energy slicer, had jetted ahead of the others and was lancing out at the space beacon's tripod with its cutting beam.

"Tisza!" Catherine shouted, instantly realizing the situation, and in her excitement, releasing Trabzon from her mental grip. "You've got to get to the control panel quickly! You've got to stop that machine!"

Yes, answered the Tisza weakly. But even as she responded, pulling away from Trabzon's shattered mental hulk and sending her psi power probing into the master brain's programer, the big energy slicer struck out at the space beacon's tripod and severed it from its mooring with one pass of its slicer beam.

188

Instantly as the huge beacon swung around, it tore loose from the top of the central spire and went spinning off into space.

Duck! projected the Tisza urgently. *The space beacon is spinning off out of control, and its beam is sweeping this way! It looks as if it will sweep across this section of the space platform. If it does, from this range, it will burn everything it touches!*

Barely had the Tisza finished speaking when the invisible beam of the space beacon hit the space platform and a wide swath of brilliant, scorching incandescence swept over the Plasti-Metal and Plasti-Glas surface.

"Back down the corridor—quick!" Johnny shouted and launched himself back to the doorway. "The beam is sweeping upward from the main deck, and it's going to pass over this compartment! If we don't want to be burned to death, we've got to get out of here!"

"What about Catherine?" Eleanor yelled as the others launched themselves away from the open doorway and back down the corridor. No one answered. She hesitated at the doorway, considering the advisability of attempting to go into the compartment and aid Catherine. Before she could make up her mind, however, Catherine decided the issue for her.

"Get out of here!" she yelled, motioning her away from the doorway. "Don't worry about me! There's no time!"

Eleanor heeded her warning and immediately pushed herself back along the corridor. At the same time, Catherine frantically tried to make her body move toward the one place in the compartment where she could secure cover, but she had no anchor, nothing solid to push against. Her frantic efforts only caused her body to pivot uselessly in mid-air at the center of the compartment.

Hold still! the Tisza projected, as the invisible beam of the space beacon penetrated the transparent panel at the end of the compartment and, with a blinding flash of brilliance, began to sweep toward them. An instant before it reached them, the Tisza teleported Catherine to a position against the one bulkhead in the compartment where the beam could not touch her as it swept by.

Suddenly the compartment was filled with a long, high-pitched scream.

189

Trabzon! the Tisza exclaimed. *The space beacon's beam has got Trabzon!*

Catherine, clutching the wall, turned her head just in time to see the small sphere of yellow luminescence that was Trabzon flare in a bright nova of light and then wink out into nonexistence. Without pausing, the beam swept on, sending the control panel of the servomechanisms' master brain up in a flare of bright incandescence.

Twice more it revolved and swept the compartment before the space beacon, spinning off into space, was no longer in line with the space platform. Then and only then was Catherine able to relax her grip on the bulkhead and float freely within the wrecked compartment.

If you'll warn the others so that they won't be caught by surprise, came the Tisza's immediate thought, *I'll switch the artificial gravity back on. Then we can begin the job of cleaning things up!*

You mean, Catherine asked in surprise, *that you aren't discouraged by all of this destruction? The space beacon is gone, and——*Her hand made a sweeping gesture of the wrecked compartment—*just look at the control console of the master brain!*

We can rebuild the control console. The Tisza laughed happily within Catherine's mind for the first time since she had known her. *And once we get the servomechanisms going again, we can rebuild the space beacon to contact my people. The important thing now is that Trabzon is dead. Now I can return to Earth without fear and assume lawful sovereignty and the duties of motherhood over my offspring. I have a lot of straightening out to do. There's no telling what kind of ideals Trabzon has put into their minds. But I can assure you of one thing: the killing of human beings by Triskellions will stop immediately!*

Catherine smiled in happy response. *I'd almost forgotten that Trabzon is dead,* she thought. *I almost can't believe it!*

We had him defeated anyway, replied the Tisza. *Or, I should say, you did! Apparently the human mind has a psi ability even though you don't seem to be aware of it and don't seem to be able to use it at will.*

I don't know how it happened! exclaimed Catherine. *I was just so angry at Trabzon, I couldn't control myself—*

190

and then, before I knew what I was doing, I was reaching out for him with something in my mind.

Yes, the Tisza replied, *I think what happened was that your anger released some hidden mechanism within your mind, which in turn triggered your hitherto dormant psi faculty.* Catherine nodded, and the Tisza sighed. *The thing which scares me about it the most, however,* she continued, *is the fact that, by comparison, the psi faculty of human beings, though dormant, would seem to make that of the average Triskellion look puny!*

I can't see why that should scare you, Tisza.

Well, it does! exclaimed the Tisza. *This incident would seem to indicate that the human mind is like an iceberg—that there is more to it than appears on the surface. And that means that you human beings don't know what you really are . . . who you really are! It means that you are only partially awake, that you are only partially aware of yourselves!*

Is that bad, Tisza? Catherine asked as she pushed her way out of the wrecked compartment and started down the corridor in search of her friends.

Perhaps not! the Tisza replied thoughtfully. *Perhaps it merely indicates that the human race is very young and still growing.*

THE END
THE END
THE END